PRAISE FOR *TRAJECTORY*

'Thoughtful, soulful . . . It will abruptly break your heart. That's what Richard Russo does, without pretension or fuss, time and time again.' *New York Times*

'Another of the author's peerless depictions of small-town life.' *Wall Street Journal*

'[*Trajectory* is] so rich and flavoursome that the temptation is to devour it all at once. I can't in good conscience advise otherwise.' *Boston Globe*

'Thoughtful and warmhearted, [Russo's] fiction has the engaging quality of tales told by a friend, over drinks, about a person we know in common. And so we lean forward, eager to hear what happened next.' *New York Times Book Review*

'Russo's [characters] are sharply in view, and like opera singers performing quintets or sestets, they are all vital contributors. Equally significantly, their problems spring from their personalities, and the resolutions are heart-warming because they do indeed feel like real possibilities...All four stories are challenging because they raise questions about why we live our lives the way we do, and if that's all right.' *Washington Times*

'Russo has fashioned tales compact enough to make an immediate impression (and to read in a single sitting), but rich [in] believable characters, graceful plotting and pointed dialogue.' *Columbus Dispatch*

'Entertaining and compellingly provocative . . . vibrant narratives with distinctive characters.' *New York Journal of Books*

ALSO BY RICHARD RUSSO

Mohawk

The Risk Pool

Nobody's Fool

Straight Man

Empire Falls

The Whore's Child

Bridge of Sighs

That Old Cape Magic

Interventions

On Helwig Street

Everybody's Fool

Trajectory

Trajectory

RICHARD RUSSO

This is a work of fiction. Names, characters, places and incidents are products of the author's imagination and are used fictitiously. Any resemblance to actual events, locales, or persons, living or dead, is entirely coincidental.

First published in the United States of America in 2017 by Alfred A. Knopf, a division of Penguin Random House LLC, New York

First published in Great Britain in 2018 by Allen & Unwin

'Horseman' originally appeared in *Atlantic Monthly* (2006); 'Voice' was originally published as a novella, *Nate in Venice* (Byliner, 2013); and *Intervention* originally appeared as a novella, in *Intervention: A Novella & Three Stories* (Down East Books, 2012).

Allen & Unwin
c/o Atlantic Books
Ormond House
26–27 Boswell Street
London WC1N 3JZ

Phone: 020 7269 1610
Fax: 020 7430 0916
Email: UK@allenandunwin.com
Web: www.allenandunwin.com/uk

A CIP catalogue record of this book is available from the British Library.

Hardback ISBN 978 1 76029 720 6
E-book ISBN 978 1 92557 650 4

Printed in Great Britain

10 9 8 7 6 5 4 3 2 1

For Steve Murtagh and Tom Butler

Contents

Trajectory

Horseman

Whenever the moon and stars are set,
Whenever the wind is high,
All night long in the dark and wet,
A man goes riding by.

Though only four in the afternoon, it was already dusk outside and the wind was blowing hard enough to set the quad's trees in motion, the nearest branches scratching insistently on the window of Janet Moore's office. Was it the turbulence outside that had invited the horseman to gallop into her consciousness, or the silence of the sullen boy sitting across from her? The lines were from a children's poem, the one Robbie read to Marcus, their son, every night before he went to sleep, and they haunted her with the force of a childhood memory, even though she'd never heard the poem until just over a decade ago, as a grad student. Now it kept her up long after Robbie had come in and fallen asleep beside her—*All night long in the dark and wet*—and sometimes she'd wake in the middle of the night with the verses still echoing. Had they been some sort of dream, repeating on an endless loop? Lately, the horseman had appeared in her daylight thoughts as well. When jogging in the woods behind the college, she'd realize she was running to that unwelcome, unforgiving iambic cadence—*Whenever the moon and stars are set*—as if she were a horse herself. And then, when it suddenly seemed like she was clomping not through the woods but an endless cemetery, there came an even-more-familiar heartsickness.

A moment before, she had been feeling both angry and self-righteous—easy, unambiguous emotions that in these circumstances she was entitled to. It angered her, and rightly so, that students were more likely to cheat in her classes than in those of her male colleagues, or to be tardier, to openly question her authority, to give her mediocre evaluations at the end of the term. Worse still, that they held her to a higher standard was actually unwitting. Had anyone asked if they were prejudiced against female professors, not one would answer yes. Hook them up to a lie detector, and every last one would pass.

This probably included James Cox, seated before her now, sockless boat shoe balanced on khakied knee, still smug, even though the fact that she had him dead to rights was beginning to dawn on him. He was studying, or pretending to, the two typed pages she'd given him—one with his own name in the upper-right-hand corner, and another that had been handed in to her four years earlier—with feigned astonishment, as if the similarities between them were just the damnedest thing, amazing, really, like frogs, thousands of them, falling out of a cloudless sky.

Next door she heard Tony Hope, her best friend in the department, bang his office door shut behind him. Earlier, she'd told him about this plagiarism case she had to deal with, and he'd offered to loiter outside, just in case. These days, all teachers were vulnerable. Cornered, female students would sometimes accuse male professors of making sexual advances, while similarly cornered males could act belligerently with female teachers. But James Cox had arrived late, no surprise, and Tony had already agreed to meet a couple of his seniors at the Hub Pub. When he paused, eyebrows arched, in her half-open doorway, she gestured that everything was fine and it was okay for him to leave. Probably it was.

Tony shrugged and then, before she could look away, did the jockey thing that always gave her a shiver. At the beginning of the term she'd made the mistake of telling him about the horseman, how Marcus refused to go to sleep until Robbie had read him the poem, and that afterward Robbie, unaware how deeply those lines weirded her out, would appear in their bedroom looking forlorn and hoping for sex. At times he even pretended to *be* the horseman of the poem, straddling her on the bed, reciting melodramatically—*Whenever the moon and stars are set*. That was about as far as he'd get before she hissed, "Stop it!"—not wanting him to wake Marcus up, but also genuinely furious that he couldn't see how creepy this scenario was as foreplay.

As good as it had felt to tell someone, Tony Hope had been the wrong person to confide in. She might have predicted he'd turn it into a joke, and the very next afternoon, emerging into the quad after class, she heard her name shouted, and there was Tony bestride the library steps in a jockey stance, bent knees together, hands out in front, gripping invisible reins, his butt lowering and rising rhythmically. Over the course of the semester, this act had become a flexible metaphor—that it was time to saddle up and teach another class, or to grab some lunch at the union, or, as it did now, to lock up and head on out, *See ya in the mornin', sweetheart*.

When she heard the double doors at the end of the corridor

clang shut, Janet turned back to her student, whose demeanor had changed dramatically. The feigned astonishment had evaporated. He slumped in his chair now, like a beaten fighter in the late rounds, with barely enough cognition left to recognize futility when he saw it up close. He met her eye for a split second, and if he'd held it a beat longer Janet herself would have been the one to turn away, but the branch rustling against the windowpane caught his attention and he stared outside at the tiny cyclones of the dead leaves whistling over the windy quad.

Had he cheated before? she wondered. Was cheating the habit of his short lifetime? Even if it wasn't, that didn't matter; he'd cheated now, in her class, and she'd caught him, only after ransacking four years' worth of files to find the essay he'd stolen. That had taken hours, time she couldn't afford to waste, not two days before Thanksgiving. Knowing what she was in for, she'd almost let it go. After all, she hadn't been certain. Cox's essay felt familiar, but it was possible she was just recalling one with a similar topic and thesis. And even if she was right, what would her reward be? Proof that she had a good memory for ideas? She already knew that. Justification for not liking this particular student? By now, she had plenty of reasons. Hadn't he vacillated, all semester, between sullen inattention and stubborn obstruction in class, then, out in the hall, plied her with half apologies and assurances that he didn't mean to be a pain in the ass? *But you are a pain in the ass.* This had been on the tip of her tongue since September. Tony Hope would've just gone ahead and said it.

Of course he would have handled the entire thing differently. When suspicious of academic dishonesty, Tony was fearless—even, in Janet's opinion, foolhardy. She would never have dreamed of confronting a student without proof, whereas Tony—by his own admission too lazy to gather any evidence—simply put on his poker face and forged ahead as if he held the winning hand. He recommended asking the suspect two straightforward questions: *Is this your own work?* and *Would you be able to reproduce this effort under my supervision?* The second, he maintained, rarely needed to be asked because the offender usually folded his tent at the first. And to answer yes to the second required the kind of "brass balls" that most undergraduates lacked. Only the most hardened, adept cheaters slipped through his net. Tony was also different in that he never took dishonesty personally, which had aroused her own suspicions, so one day she'd asked on impulse if he himself had ever cheated.

"Mostly in high school," he replied, with surprising candor. "A couple times in college. How about you?"

"No." Not that Janet would have admitted it if she had.

"Never?"

"You don't believe me?"

"I do, actually."

"You needn't make it sound like a failure of imagination."

"Quite the opposite, in fact. At least in my case. I couldn't imagine ever succeeding if I *didn't* cheat."

"Do you feel guilty about it now?"

"Not particularly. Should I?"

"I don't know. Should you?"

"A little judgment, just a tad, in that question, sweetie, but I forgive you. For the record, I don't cheat anymore."

"You don't take tests anymore," she pointed out.

"An altogether superior arrangement, don't you think? To be the test *giver* as opposed to the *taker*?"

What she couldn't reconcile herself to was that the few who escaped Tony's net were the very ones she was most determined to snare—the habitual liars who could look you in the eye and tell a whopper, having coldly calculated the system and how much you could reasonably expect to exploit it, how the first suggestion of a lawsuit would spook you and your dean. Such students were cancers, and she figured James Cox might well be one of them, which was why she'd spent so much time making the case against him airtight.

But maybe she'd been wrong, because now that he realized he'd been busted, he dropped the customary bravado. In fact, he looked like someone who'd been waiting so long in the doctor's office that when the feared diagnosis was finally delivered, it came as a relief. "So," he said, handing the identical pages back to her.

She waited until it became clear he didn't intend to elaborate. "Meaning what?"

"You got me, right?" He made a pistol of his thumb and forefinger, put the barrel to his temple and pulled the trigger, his head then jerking as if struck by an invisible bullet. Sure, the gesture was a cliché, but she was still startled by the boy's willingness to metaphorically off himself.

Finally she said, "Do you want to tell me why?"

"It was easy. My fraternity keeps files."

"So do professors."

Again he made her wait for him to say, "So, what do you want?"

The question, so simple and direct, took her off guard. "What do I want?"

He shrugged. "Well, this is where I get what's coming to me, no?"

"And what do you think that might be?"

"Not up to me, is it?" he said, getting to his feet.

How brash men are, she told herself. How controlled, even in defeat. "Whatever you decide." At the door he paused, his back to her and his head tipped at an odd angle, as if he were listening for something. What he said then surprised her. "My advice? Don't hold back." Then he simply walked out.

Moving pretty well, she thought, for someone with massive head trauma. And in the ensuing silence:

By at the gallop he goes, and then
By he comes back at the gallop again.

What did he want of her, this horseman? That was the mystery. She knew, of course, and had known from the beginning, who he *was*.

A decade earlier, on the other the side of the country, the day of her first conference with the great Marcus Bellamy, Janet parked in the dusty, unpaved X-lot on the farthest reaches of the university, the only place graduate students could afford a permit, and trekked across campus in the sweltering desert heat to Modern and Romance Languages. The faculty lot, which cost more to park in than she made as a teaching assistant, was right across the street, and Bellamy was just then arriving in his vintage roadster, which he parked, and then strode off, leaving the convertible's top down, a breathtakingly confident move. After checking to make sure no one was watching, she walked over for a closer look. Amazingly, the front passenger seat was littered with cassette tapes, mostly jazz, and the corner of a box that likely contained others was visible beneath the seat. Did he have some reason to believe his music wouldn't be stolen? Everyone knew Marcus Bellamy, of course, the department's one true academic superstar, so maybe he felt protected by his reputation. Or perhaps the F-lots were guarded by cameras. She'd never noticed any, though it was possible. But afternoon thunderstorms were in the forecast. Did Bellamy believe his privilege warded off both petty thieves and the elements themselves?

She had a full day before her, a comp class to teach, a Henry James seminar to attend and a stack of essays she'd have to get started on if the whole weekend wouldn't be ruined, yet in truth she wasn't able to think of anything besides the conference with Bellamy. At lunch Robbie remarked on how distracted she seemed, and as the afternoon wore on she felt increasingly light-headed, at times almost ill. Robbie was also meeting with him that afternoon, and Janet was glad the conferences weren't back-to-back. No doubt Bellamy had already noticed they were a couple, but she preferred him to think of her simply as a young scholar. For their first session she saw no need for any context beyond the essay they would be discussing, she hoped, at length. She'd spent a long time on it, and there was a good deal to talk about. She'd signed up for the last slot of the afternoon so that, if needs be, they could run long.

Bellamy's office was the largest on the corridor, its most ostentatious feature a large fireplace. Seeing it, Janet thought that if things went well this semester, maybe by the holidays she'd be invited in for what—brandy and eggnog in front of a roaring fire? Probably it would never get cold enough in the desert to justify that, but it was a pleasant fantasy. The rest of the office was crammed with books and periodicals on floor-to-ceiling built-in shelves. In the unlikely event she ever managed to snag an office like this herself, she thought, she'd stay put. What possessed a man with such a cushy life to pack up all those books and move every couple of years? Bellamy had no sooner arrived on campus than the speculation began about how long he'd stay, where he'd go next and what salary and perks would be required to lure him away. It was a bull market for brilliant black English professors, as Bellamy was well aware, and it was whispered he was already receiving and weighing offers for the year after next. That was why she'd wanted so desperately to study with him now, this term. His class in proletarian fiction was wildly oversubscribed, since even students in linguistics and creative writing wanted in. And thus far, the course had been electrifying.

Bellamy's smile was warm when he greeted her at the door, but she'd barely sat down when he said, rather ominously, "Ms. Moore, in conference I always like to be forthright."

To which she murmured something silly, pretty close to the exact opposite of the truth, like she assumed he would be, or hoped he would be or, worse still, that she was always grateful for honest, rigorous appraisal.

"Excellent," he said, handing back her essay, "because though there's much to recommend here, I have serious misgivings about your work."

Apparently it was true, then. Yesterday she'd overheard a classmate claim that Bellamy was reading not only the papers they'd just turned in but also previous efforts from other courses, everything he could get his hands on. She hadn't believed it—only a madman would take on so much extra work—but there it was on the desk between them, a big blue Graduate Office folder with her name on it that probably held a dozen essays from past semesters. These misgivings about her work—did he actually mean all of it? Work that had already established her as perhaps the most promising scholar in the program?

She examined the essay he'd just handed her. There was no letter grade on the cover page, and Janet had marked enough freshman compositions to know what this could portend. She herself always put a poor grade on the last page, along with her reasons for giving it, to keep that safe from prying eyes. Though it was probably the wrong thing to do, she quickly turned to the end of the essay to see if Bellamy graded in the same fashion, only to discover that page was blank as well. As were all the others. If there was "much to recommend," weren't those things worth mentioning?

"Misgivings?" she said finally, her voice sounding strange, distant, whiny and frightened.

Bellamy, who'd stood up and was scanning his bookshelves, didn't answer immediately. Turning his back on her like this had the effect of compounding her fears. "I'll try to explain, but it's going to be easier to show you."

"Actually, I thought this essay was good," she ventured. "I spent a long time on it." She couldn't believe she'd said that. She was always telling her own students that this was completely immaterial.

"I'm sure you did, Janet. It's meticulous. Flawless." He stepped back for a better angle at the books and periodicals on the top shelf. "It's just not really yours."

"I don't know what you mean," she replied, swallowing hard. "Are you saying it's plagiarized?"

"Good heavens, no. Relax."

As if any such thing were possible.

"Actually," he went on, still without turning around, "theft would've been more revealing. Then at least I'd have known what you admired, whereas in what you wrote I can't locate you anywhere. It's the same with your previous essays. It's as if you don't exist . . . ah, here we are!" He'd found the volume he was looking for on the top shelf. Bellamy was tall—a skilled basketball player, according to Robbie, who'd reported this fact almost apologetically, perhaps fearful of perpetuating a stereotype—but he still had to use a footstool to reach it. Stepping down again, he set the journal, a twenty-year-old issue of *American Literature,* on the desk between them, then sat back down.

"But . . . I *do* exist," she offered, suddenly unsure if she was entitled to this opinion. Would he attempt to reason her out of it?

"Indeed," he said, "here you are. In the flesh."

The word *flesh,* spoken in such an intimate setting, in a room with a leather sofa in front of the fireplace, made her apprehensive. Earlier that morning, stepping out of the shower, she'd looked forward to this meeting with pleasure. Nothing sexual, of course, or even terribly intimate. Ignorant of the sofa and fireplace, she'd assumed their conversation, the first of many, would go well, that Bellamy would be as fond of her as she was of him. He'd certainly seemed so in class, though no fonder than he was of her classmates. He obviously knew better than to display overt signs of favoritism. It was in conference where you let your guard down a bit, showed your real enthusiasm for good work. She'd felt confident this was exactly what would happen today. Maybe after they were done talking he'd suggest a beer at the Salty Dog, where grad students hung out and Robbie's band played on Saturday nights. Or perhaps he'd want to go someplace else, a bar that played jazz, not rock and roll, and wasn't crawling with university types. Would that have been so wrong? Wasn't it the equivalent of the intimate access to Bellamy that Robbie and the other guys had in their Sunday-afternoon basketball games?

"I thought," she said carefully, rubbing her moist palms against the cushion of her chair, "that was the whole idea of literary criticism. Isn't the *I* supposed to disappear? Isn't the argument itself what matters?"

"That's what we teach," he conceded. He'd taken his glasses off and was cleaning them with a handkerchief, unnecessarily, it occurred to her, an affectation. "It's what I was taught, and I used to believe it. Now I'm not so sure. The first-person pronoun can be dispensed with, it's true. But not the writer behind the pronoun."

"I guess I don't know what you mean, then," she said, aware this was the second time she'd made that observation. Also, she *guessed* she didn't understand? If one of her freshmen had written that, she'd have scratched *Can't you be certain?* in the margin.

"It's true the writer shouldn't intrude upon the argument," Bellamy admitted, "but that's not the same as saying he should disappear, is it?"

She caught herself, luckily. A third "guess" would've been disastrous. "Isn't it?"

"Okay, let's back up. Why did you write about Dos Passos?"

"Because I was interested in—"

"But why were you interested?"

Now she was squirming, angry. Because he hadn't given her a chance to explain? Or was it the challenge implied in his question?

"Did you choose a topic you had a real connection to? Or just one you knew I was interested in?"

Well, sure, Bellamy's admiration of Dos Passos had been the main reason, but she'd considered that a good starting point for their ongoing dialogue. Isn't that what the study of literature was supposed to yield—a series of dialogues between writer and reader, reader and teacher? And why was he challenging a conversation so recently begun unless he'd already decided it wouldn't lead anywhere? What evidence could there possibly be for such a conclusion? She tried to focus on what he was saying, to neither personalize nor be overwhelmed by disappointment, but with each new question (What are you risking in this essay? From what passion in your life does it derive? Where did you grow up? What did your parents do? Did you attend private school or public?) she could feel herself flushing. What did her *life* have to do with anything? She'd come prepared to argue her essay's nuances, to accept his suggestions for bolstering its thesis, even for him to question its validity, but instead it was as if what she'd produced didn't matter. This was almost like asking her to take off her clothes.

"Look, Janet," he said, perhaps intuiting her distress. "The truth is, I can teach you very little. You have a lively intellect and genuine curiosity, and you work hard. You read carefully, synthesize well and know how to marshal evidence. If a scholar's life is what you want, you're well on your way. That's the good news. But there's one last piece of the puzzle. Unfortunately, it's a big one, and for some people it can be elusive."

A big existential something she hadn't even noticed? She didn't want to believe that. Her other professors all agreed she was probably ready to start submitting her work to academic periodicals. (Bellamy knew the editors of these journals personally, and a word from him . . .) And if what she'd overlooked was so big, how could it be elusive? That didn't make sense at all.

Then again, what if what he was saying was true? Hadn't she sometimes worried, in the aftermath of extravagant praise, that something was missing? Or had the distinct impression that what she'd really succeeded in doing was fooling her professors yet again? Is that what Bellamy was getting at? Had he seen something in her work, or just noted the absence of something? He was arguing for some kind of passionate, personal connection—she understood this much—but what if that connection wasn't there? What if what she possessed—and what her other professors admired—was merely a facility? If she was just doing what she was good at, and it didn't go any deeper than that?

"This elusive thing," she heard herself saying, in a frightened, childlike voice, "I won't succeed until I find it?"

"Oh, you'll succeed just fine," he told her, waving that concern aside. "You'll just never be any good."

But the circumstances were hardly analogous, she told herself as she emerged into the windy quad. James Cox, the little prick, was a cheat, a plagiarist. True, when Bellamy had said that the essay wasn't really hers, she'd thought at first that was what he meant, but no. His "misgivings" about her work had been vague, abstract, spectral, whereas her own objections to Cox's criminal essay were concrete and clear-cut. There was no parallel whatsoever, so forget it. Go home.

She was halfway to her car, passing the student union, when a Frisbee whistled so close overhead that she ducked. Normally, it would've run out of air and skimmed through the brown grass before coming to rest, but this Frisbee was riding a gust of wind that tunneled down the quad—*Whenever the wind is high,* the words were suddenly there—and it flew on and on, actually gaining altitude.

Her first thought was that it must have been thrown at her intentionally, perhaps by James Cox, but she turned around and saw that the Frisbee could have been tossed only by one of the students standing on the lighted library steps over a hundred yards up the hill. Apparently they'd found the thing there, and somebody was curious to see how far it would travel on such an impressive tailwind. "Whoa!" she heard him shout as the Frisbee flew on down the terraced lawn, all the way to the macadam road, where it struck a passing pickup truck right in the windshield with a loud *whump*. The truck immediately skidded to a halt, and the driver, either a townie or someone from Grounds and Maintenance, jumped out, glared at her and yelled, “Hey!”

“Yeah, right,” she called to him sarcastically, though she couldn’t really blame the guy for jumping to the wrong conclusion. Except for the kids on the library steps, an impossible distance away, she was the only person in the deserted quad.

“The hell’s wrong with you, anyway?” the man wanted to know, his voice all but lost in the wind.

“Search me,” she called back, and when he looked like he might want to make something of it she made a sharp right and headed down the steps of the union into the Hub Pub, which she normally avoided, having no desire to run into students or, worse yet, grousing department colleagues. So it was a relief to discover that late on the Tuesday afternoon before Thanksgiving the place was almost as deserted as the quad. A large circular table was occupied by a group of students involved in a drinking game that involved bouncing quarters off the tabletop. Tony Hope occupied a booth in the far corner, where his seniors were cramming papers into overstuffed backpacks, their meeting concluded.

“Remember,” he was telling them. “In effaced, you can’t have it both ways. If you’re dunna dit in, dit in. If you’re dunna dit out, dit out.”

The students, apparently understanding this advice, nodded their agreement, slid out of the booth and wished him a happy Thanksgiving.

Sliding into the booth, she said, “Well, that sounded truly bizarre. ‘Effaced’?”

Tony chuckled, clearly pleased by her mystification. Pushing what she hoped was an unused glass in her direction, he poured the last of the pitcher's beer into it. "Effaced point of view," he explained. "Sort of like a camera eye. The writer disappears, just reports what the characters do and say without revealing their thoughts and motivations. No judgments. Totally objective."

"'If you're dunna dit in, dit in'?"

"My father had a speech impediment. When we went to the drive-in for burgers, all us kids would get out and run around, always slamming doors and making a ruckus. When he couldn't stand it anymore, he'd yell, 'If you're dunna dit in, dit in. If your dunna dit out, dit out. No more doddamn dittin' din, dittin' out.'"

"And your students understand such references?"

"They've heard the story, yeah."

"Teaching creative writing really is a scam, isn't it? How do I join that club?"

"Did your father have a speech impediment?"

"No."

"Well, there you go. Sorry. Don't you ever tell your students any stories about yourself?"

"No, I teach literature, remember? We have actual texts to occupy our attention. Things would have to go terribly, terribly wrong before I'd resort to personal anecdote." Such reticence, she knew all too well, ran counter to the entire culture, but she hadn't the slightest interest in the confessional mode, nor did she intend to reduce the study of literature to issues, or ratchet up the interest by means of irrelevant autobiography. Besides, what would she tell them? *Did you know I have a damaged son?* (I do!) *Guess how long it's been since my husband and I had sex?* (Here's a hint: a long time!)

"Yeah, but don't you people believe everything's a text these days?" Tony said. "Tolstoy? *Us Weekly?* A tattooed buttock?"

"Oh, stop."

"And speaking of living texts, there's one of your favorites."

In the entryway, Tom Newhouse, professor emeritus, was just then hanging his tweed hat on a peg. Forced into retirement at seventy, Newhouse continued to teach his Joyce seminar, famous among students for his bonhomie and infamous among colleagues for his critical misreadings. Turning, he planted his feet wide apart and surveyed the disappointing scene before him, his white hair crazily wild.

"Looks like he's got his usual load on," Tony observed.

"Don't," she pleaded, when he started to wave. "Maybe he won't notice us."

"He's just lonely, Janet," Tony said.

"It's not your ass he'll grab when he comes over here," she reminded him.

"There was nothing to that at all, in case you're interested," he replied. Earlier that semester a young woman accused Newhouse of so-called inappropriate touching. *"Inappropriate,"* Tony had remarked at the time. "Now, there's a word I wouldn't mind never hearing again." The charge was dropped when the committee learned the victim had overheard a professor of women's studies suggest that someone ought to put a stop to the old fool's groping. "Besides," Tony went on, "you're *sitting* on your ass. Don't stand up, and your dignity will remain intact."

"*That's* your solution?"

"No, it's yours. I don't require one myself."

The bartender was drawing Newhouse a pitcher of beer. Not a good sign, though it was possible he intended to send it over to the coin-flipping students. His wife having died a decade earlier, his house and car paid off, Newhouse was also famous for his largesse, especially with his seniors, the only students on campus old enough to drink legally.

Janet leaned forward on her elbows, hoping that if Newhouse saw the two of them having a possibly intimate conversation he wouldn't intrude. "Are you going anywhere over the break?"

Usually, Tony fled for New York or Boston after his last class. When they first met, Janet assumed he was gay, but evidently not. In fact, he'd dated most of the college's eligible female faculty, as well as a few of the administrative staff, and recently she'd heard a rumor about a custodian. Which made Janet wonder why he'd never shown any interest in her. True, she was married, but he'd never even flirted with her, at least not seriously.

"No, I'm staying put," Tony said, surprising her. "My brother and his wife are visiting from Utah, if you can believe it."

Janet risked a glance and saw the bartender was now drawing a second pitcher. "I didn't know you had a brother."

"We don't see that much of each other," Tony said. "He and the little woman are both strict Mormons, which means I won't even be able to anesthetize myself. They're determined to experience a genuine New England Thanksgiving and don't seem to understand that these celebrations can't be done sober. What are you and yours up to?"

She'd been dreading the holiday all week, and it now occurred to her this probably accounted for her willingness to squander all those hours hunting evidence of Cox's plagiarism. Anything was better than contemplating such an awful, endless day. Robbie would cook a huge meal for just the three of them. Two, really. Marcus would eat only what he did every day, a grilled cheese sandwich—and then only if Robbie cut off any cheese that had turned brown on the bottom of the pan. It was possible he'd eat nothing at all if he was out of sorts, which he was likely to be. When his regular TV programs weren't on, he often became agitated, inconsolable. Last year, the balloons of the Macy's parade had upset him terribly, and it had taken forever to calm him down. Then there was the matter of her own presence. Marcus did best when his routine wasn't compromised, and her being home on a weekday—Thanksgiving or any other—could make him restless, as if he was waiting patiently for her to go away and for things to return to normal. Robbie claimed this wasn't true and swore that Marcus loved her, but it certainly seemed true to Janet. The doctors had warned that it wasn't unusual for children like Marcus to prefer one parent over the other. Usually the mother, though not in their case. It was nothing personal, they'd told her, but what could possibly *be* more personal?

"*Moooooore!*" Tom Newhouse bellowed as he approached, beer slopping over the lip of the pitcher he was holding, having dropped the other off at the undergraduate table. Now he slid gracefully into their booth, on Janet's side, naturally. She'd have bet the farm on that one. She slid as far away from him as she could, until her right shoulder was flush against the brick wall.

"You *know* what I like about you, Moore?"

Newhouse called everyone, whether students or colleagues, by their last names only. His other irritating habit was dramatically emphasizing, at deafening volume, a single word in nearly every sentence, not always the one you might expect.

Yes, Janet thought, you like my boobs. At least they were what he was always ogling, as he appeared to be now.

"Do you know what I *like* about Moore?" he asked Tony, when she declined to speculate.

"Sure," Tony said. "The same thing we all like."

Newhouse blinked at him drunkenly, then fixed Janet with a rheumy gaze. "*He* has a dirty mind."

"You arrived at that conclusion how?" Janet said, causing him to scroll back, then break into a big grin.

"I see what you mean," he said. "It's *my* mind that's dirty, isn't it?" He returned to Tony. "What I was *going* to say was, what I like about this lady is that she's a good dancer."

"It's what we *all* like about her," Tony repeated.

"You've never seen me dance, Professor Newhouse." She was sure she hadn't danced in public since joining the faculty here, seven years before. Longer, probably.

"I've heard *stories,*" he said, again presenting his argument to Tony. "Besides, you can tell by how a woman walks if she's got the music in her. And *this* lady's got the music."

"Nice tits, too," Tony added.

Newhouse absorbed this comment thoughtfully, then turned back to her. "Now that time it *was* him. You can't blame me for *that* one."

"I guess you're right," she said. "Just this once, I'll let you skate."

He topped off their glasses. "*Thank* you," he said, fixing Tony again. "That's the problem these days. Nobody lets anybody *skate* on anything." He still hadn't forgiven Tony for serving on the committee that required him to take a sensitivity seminar as a condition of his inappropriate-touching acquittal.

"That's *one* of the problems," Tony agreed cheerfully.

"We have a student in *common,* you and I," Newhouse said, leaning toward her as if about to impart a secret that must be kept from their companion at all costs, his elbow brushing against her left breast. Tony noticed and grinned, her predicament highly entertaining to his apparent way of thinking. "*That* one." He was now offering his index finger for her to sight along, not that she needed to. Though his back was to them, she now recognized one of the students at the round table.

"*Cox,*" Newhouse thundered. "James Cox. Wrote the best paper on *Dubliners* I ever read."

"Who do you think wrote it?" she said.

"He could *publish* the damn thing," Newhouse went on, an alcoholic beat behind. Then, finally, "What do you mean who wrote it? Cox *wrote* it."

"Well, okay, if you say so."

Now it was Newhouse's turn to lean away. "Why would you suspect *Cox*?"

"If you aren't suspicious, fine," she said, lowering her voice in the vain hope that he might as well.

"I'm *not* suspicious. Why would *you* be suspicious?"

"Do you get a lot of publishable work from undergraduates?" Tony, bless him, asked innocently.

"*You,*" Newhouse said. "You stay out of this. I want this lady to tell me why I should suspect *Cox*."

"Maybe I'm wrong," she told him.

"You *are* wrong," he said, pushing out of the booth and taking the mostly empty pitcher with him. His face had gone beet red. "You *are* wrong. You're *worse* than wrong." Then he turned to Tony. "And *you*."

"Yes, Tom?"

"*You* aren't even a good dancer. There's no *excuse* for you." And with that he pivoted and returned to the bar to drink alone.

"What's 'worse than wrong,' do you suppose?" Janet said when he was out of earshot.

"Might it include being naïve? Intellectually lazy? Failing to comprehend that you've become a figure of fun?"

She was studying the students at the coin table, seemingly oblivious to what had just occurred across the room. All except James Cox, something about the cant of his head suggesting he'd heard Newhouse say his name. Had he noticed her come in?

"So, was he right?" Tony Hope wanted to know. "*Are* you a good dancer?"

By the time she emerged from Modern and Romance Languages, the sky had grown menacingly dark and a hot desert wind, full of electricity, was auguring rain. Good, Janet thought. In the air-conditioning of Bellamy's office she hadn't sensed the gathering storm, which probably meant that he hadn't, either. Otherwise, he'd be headed for his top-down convertible at a dead run. By the time his office windows started rattling, it would be too late.

She was holding that old issue of *American Literature,* in which he'd turned down the opening pages of the articles he wanted her to read. One, he'd explained, was his first published essay, written when he was still a grad student, a careless effort containing, by his count, no fewer than six errors, all pointed out to him over the years by fastidious would-be fact-checkers who seemed to consider any mistakes, no matter how innocent or inconsequential, unforgivable. He hoped she'd see why, despite its flaws, this semi-embarrassing essay had been worth publishing. Though he hadn't actually said so, her assignment was presumably to look for signs of the passion that led Bellamy inevitably to greatness, with the best office on campus and the vintage roadster right across the street. The other essay he recommended was by someone called Patricia Anastacio, suggesting—again, rather than stating—that its admirable if somewhat-minor and feminine virtues—industriousness, organizational skills, attention to detail—were predictive of a workmanlike but uninspired career. ("You read carefully, synthesize well and know how to marshal evidence.") Really, the man's arrogance was breathtaking. He'd cast himself as Tennyson's Ulysses, fearlessly sailing uncharted waters, while she (like this Anastacio) would remain behind like Telemachus, blamelessly tending the household gods. Okay, Telemachus wasn't a girl, but the gender prejudices at the core of Bellamy's assumptions bordered on infuriating.

At the bottom of the steps was a metal trash can, and it was all Janet could do to not deposit the periodical there. What prevented her was an even-better idea—to drop it on the driver's seat of the roadster, where it would swell like the man's bloated ego once the skies opened. If Bellamy said anything later, she could claim she'd xeroxed the essays immediately and wanted him to have his copy back.

She was still so worked up when she arrived at the F-lot that she was flummoxed by what she saw there: standing next to Bellamy's roadster was a young man dressed in brightly mismatched clothes. His large head was shaved bald, and he was flailing his arms wildly, as if battling invisible demons, and as she drew near he let out a startling howl. Had his eyes not been clamped shut he would've been looking right at her, which was why she briefly entertained the irrational notion that by walking up she'd caused this fit. What he looked like was some sort of demented, idiot genie summoned by her proximity for the express purpose of protecting Bellamy's car and dignity.

These were, of course, the impressions of an instant. Later, guiltily, she would try to reconstruct exactly what had happened and why. The young man was a frightening apparition, come upon so suddenly, his arms flailing about his head, as if he'd received an electrical charge from the approaching storm that set him dancing and windmilling. (Did he mean to share that electric jolt if she came within reach?) But by the time she took her first, instinctive step around him she realized that he was blind and the hot wind, gusting fiercely and carrying all manner of grit, had frightened and disoriented him. His white cane lay under the convertible's wheel. Why, then, once she'd registered this truth, was it so hard to banish the original, clearly false impression of the young man as someone to be feared?

And then, like a switch had been thrown, his howling and gyrations stopped and he cocked his head, as if to listen. Did he sense someone close by? Did he mean to cast a spell? Grant her a wish she'd later regret? Slowly, he turned toward her, and—if his eyes weren't blind and still clamped shut, he again would've been looking right at her. The two of them stood there frozen, a couple feet apart, until he finally reared back his head and bellowed, "Pleeeeeease!"

As if in answer, the rains came, the first fat drop hitting Janet on an eyebrow, releasing her, and she ran. She looked back just once, to make sure it was only his terrible howls pursuing her.

Robbie looked up and smiled when she came in through the garage and hung her shoulder bag on the hallway hook. Marcus was sitting next to him on the sofa, where they were watching cartoons that Robbie, at least, seemed to be enjoying. Marcus's face was blank, as usual, but he was caressing his father's earlobe between his thumb and forefinger, as was his habit in calm moments. The significance of that gesture was one of many things they couldn't agree about. Robbie thought it was sweet that their son found his earlobe comforting. Until recently, Marcus had strictly forbidden any touching whatsoever, so Janet supposed that, yes, this might be an encouraging sign, but it troubled her that he still didn't like to be touched himself, and also that rubbing Robbie's earlobe was the only sort of touching he seemed comforted by. When she'd pointed this out, her husband reminded her of their doctors' repeated admonitions. "And besides, have you noticed it's just the right ear? I've tried switching places on the sofa, hoping he'd reach for my left lobe, but no dice. It's the right side or nothing."

"He doesn't want either of mine."

"Hey, I'm the one who's around. If you were here all day long, it'd be you." When she replied that she didn't think so, he added, "Well, I guess we'll never know." He said this without sarcasm, just a simple fact, one of many simple facts that made up Robbie's life, none of which he seemed to resent.

In graduate school, he'd been a year behind Janet. Though universally well liked, he was generally conceded to be the least gifted student in the Ph.D. program. The others had all done their master's work elsewhere, whereas Robbie was a holdover, admitted at the last minute after a more highly regarded Ivy Leaguer backed out. At least once every term he needed to be convinced not to just drop out. Once Janet accepted her tenure-track position, Robbie started writing grants for local nonprofits, a job he could do at home and still mind their son. The year before, when she was up for tenure and working long hours on the book she hoped would guarantee it, they appeared to be drifting toward divorce, but now that her job was secure, everything seemed a little better. They'd found a morning program for Marcus, which meant Robbie could finally finish his dissertation, though he hadn't yet shown any such inclination. His rationale was that the college already had a professor in his specialty, so what difference did it make? Even if a better job at a research university came along for Janet, he'd still be considered baggage. She couldn't fault his logic, but the idea of not finishing something you'd worked toward for so long was beyond baffling. Still, that was Robbie for you.

"The grant came through," he told her, turning down the TV's volume and nudging Marcus gently. "Move over, sport. Let's make room for Mom. She looks like she's had a rough day."

And she's late, was what he didn't say. Late coming home on a day when she might have been expected to return early.

"That's okay," she told him. "I need to change clothes. But which grant? And how much?"

"The Contemporary Art Institute. Seventy-five K. They're over the moon."

"They should be. Congratulations." And how much did *you* get? Why do you let these people take advantage of you, making them look good and working for peanuts?

In their bedroom she shed her teaching outfit and pulled on a pair of jeans. Outside it had begun to rain. The bedroom blinds were drawn shut, but she could hear rain lashing the window in wind-driven gusts. *Why does he gallop and gallop about?*

Why had she circled back to the F-lot? She remembered telling herself that she just wanted to make sure the young man was all right. If he was still in distress she could call the campus police, who after all were paid to handle situations like this. But even then she'd known she was more curious than concerned. Had he tried to cross the street and gotten run over? (Would that be her fault?) Or in his literally blind rage had he assaulted the next passerby? (Proving how wise she'd been to steer clear?)

At least ten minutes had elapsed, so she wasn't surprised to see that someone had taken him in hand, though she hadn't expected it to be Bellamy. He was holding the boy—who looked younger now, for some reason—by the elbow, about to help him cross the suddenly flooded street. She considered just driving by, but what if Bellamy saw her? Was it possible he'd recognize her car? She knew his, after all.

"Janet," he said, when she pulled up next to them, "you're a lifesaver." He led the boy around to the other side of her car and opened the passenger door, which seemed almost like an accusation. *See how harmless he is?*

"God bless you," the boy kept muttering as Bellamy, still out in the rain, got him situated, fastening his seat belt. "God bless you." Was she included in this blessing? Facing straight forward, the young man might well have been completely unaware of her. Did he imagine the car drove itself? Or had he caught a whiff of her in the lot before she darted off and now remembered her scent? Another possibility also occurred to her. What if the boy was only partially blind? Maybe that's why he was refusing to look in her direction.

"Here," Bellamy said, taking him by the wrist and slipping his cane in his hand.

"God bless you."

"William here needs a lift to the Newman Center," Bellamy said as he slid into the backseat, dripping wet. He already knew the kid's name?

"Where's that?"

"Turn right on Glenn. Two blocks, on the left," Bellamy told her. Was he Catholic? Why else would he know where the Newman Center was? She tried to picture the Great Man on his knees, praying.

It was raining even harder, straight down now, even though the wind had abated some. "Don't you want to put your top up?" she asked, pointing at the roadster.

Bellamy regarded her curiously, perhaps surprised she knew which car was his, then burst into laughter. "That's hilarious," he said.

"Everything okay?" Robbie wanted to know. He was standing in the doorway, regarding her wistfully as she sat on the edge of the bed in her bra, and she felt a wave of something like nausea pass over her as past and present merged. "You looked like you were about to cry."

She went over to the dresser, took out a sweatshirt and pulled it over her head. "I'm fine. But I just had to deal with a plagiarist."

"Those are always fun," Robbie said. "Did he come clean?"

She nodded. "Then, just to make matters worse, I ran into Tom Newhouse."

She wouldn't mention where this had happened. One of Robbie's complaints, back in their days of estrangement, was that except for the rare dinner party, they never went out anymore. He loved live music, even garage bands playing loud, junky blues in the mill-town dives that ringed the campus, the kind he'd played in himself back in their university days.

"Turns out my plagiarist is also taking a class with him, and Tom starts raving about this Joyce paper the kid wrote. Then he gets mad at me for suggesting he might want to look into it."

Robbie frowned. "Why'd you do that?"

"Do what?"

He just shrugged.

"No, what are you saying?"

"Don't get angry. I was just remembering how in high school I always hated it when the nuns compared notes. If I got into trouble in one class on Monday afternoon, by Tuesday morning they were all pissed off at me. It didn't seem fair."

"The solution to that problem, I suppose, would've been not to fuck up with the first nun."

He shrugged again, unwilling, as usual, to take the bait. "You want me to cook something, or just go out for pizza?"

"Whichever."

"Pizza, then. Marcus can come with me. He loves Pizzoli's."

Really? How can you tell? Not saying this, of course. Because that probably wasn't the real reason he wanted to take Marcus. It was better than leaving him alone with her.

"It's the greatest of mysteries, I think," Bellamy said later.

She'd waited in the car while he walked the boy into the Newman Center, then gave him a lift back to his waterlogged convertible. Though she'd run all the way to the X-lot, she was soaked to the skin by the time she got there, and she was aware now that her shirt was semi-transparent. But if Bellamy noticed, he gave no sign.

"What it's like to be another person, to be William," he continued. "What it feels like, I mean. Literature. Life. They give us little glimpses, leaving us hungry for more." When she said nothing, he finally glanced over at her, then away again. "I'm sorry I pushed you so hard today," he said. "I like to know who people are, but I sometimes forget it's none of my business."

Go away, she remembered thinking. *Please stop talking and go away.* His kindness to the blind boy had stolen her righteous anger, leaving her hollow, in need of another emotion, though she couldn't think of one she was entitled to, unless it was despair.

She was sobbing now, her body shaking so violently it frightened her, and for a long time she couldn't stop. Only when she quit trying did she feel herself begin to come out the other end. How long did the jag last? She wasn't sure, but probably no more than half an hour, or else Robbie and Marcus would've gotten back with the pizza. The face that stared back at her from the bedroom mirror was barely recognizable as her own—pale, swollen, naked. Not one she wanted Robbie to see, or Marcus, either, for that matter. Other than anger and frustration, their son seemed to have no emotions of his own, but when others showed any, it often upset him. She definitely did not want to be here, looking like this, when they returned.

Backing out of the driveway, she had no idea where she was going. Didn't know, in fact, until she got to the end of the street and turned left onto College Avenue. Was she losing her mind? What could she possibly hope to gain by going to campus? James Cox and his friends were probably long gone, the pub locked up. But she knew now what she wanted to say to him, what she should have said earlier. And suddenly the idea of postponing that until after the break was insupportable. The resumption of classes was simply too far in the future. She couldn't bear forgetting, or risk the return of her sanity and equilibrium. Given time and opportunity, she'd reason herself out of saying the words. For her own sake more than his she needed to tell him what she believed, this very moment, to be true: that his dishonesty wasn't a condition. It was nothing but a habit, and habits could be broken. Just because you cheated doesn't make you a cheater. Not if you stopped. He could begin his new life by writing a new essay. Something by James Cox, not some long-forgotten fraternity brother. Maybe this time he'd discover a James Cox who wasn't lazy, incompetent, sullen and belligerent. Possibly there was a better self he could be. Don't hold back, he'd advised her, and she didn't plan to. She *would* make him understand.

But by the time she arrived back at the Hub Pub, Cox and his friends were indeed gone, and her disappointment was crushing out of all proportion. To make matters worse, Tom Newhouse was still sitting there at the bar. He hadn't seen her come in, though. She could turn right back around and he'd never know. You could do that in life. Just slip away before you were noticed, no one the wiser. What was the term Tony had used? Effaced. You could become effaced.

"*Moore,*" Newhouse said when she slid onto the stool next to him. "You're *back*." His smile suggested he'd either forgotten she'd recently pissed him off or had already forgiven her.

"Would you like to join us for Thanksgiving dinner, Tom?" she heard herself say.

He blinked at her and paused before answering. "What are you serving?"

She laughed out loud. "What do you mean?"

"Sommelier!" he called over to the bartender. "A glass for the lady. A *clean* one. This is Professor Moore. You *know* Professor Moore, our rising star?"

The boy behind the bar put a glass in front of her, which Newhouse proceeded to fill to the brim and then a bit over.

"What I *mean* is, I'm *weighing* several options. I assume you're serving a roast *fowl* of some sort?"

"Turkey, yes."

"Will it be a *stuffed* turkey?"

She said yes, she thought it probably would be.

"Will there be *cran*berries? *Yams?*"

"Why not?"

He regarded her seriously with bleary-eyed benevolence. "Well, then. It all comes down to *pie,* doesn't it?"

"What kind of pie do you like, Tom? Is there one that would seal the deal?"

"*Mince*meat."

"You're shitting me."

"*Pumpkin* would be okay. What *time?*"

"Midafternoon?"

"And I can bring *what?*"

"A mincemeat pie, if you really want mincemeat."

When she stood up, he said, "You're leaving? You just *got* here."

"Robbie and Marcus went out for a pizza. I forgot to leave them a note, so . . ." She shrugged.

"I'll see you *Thursday.*"

"I should warn you," she told him, feeling her throat constrict, "my son has good days and bad. If he's having a bad one, you may wish you hadn't come."

He lumbered down from his own stool then and took her in his arms and she didn't resist. "You're okay, Moore."

It didn't escape her that her professional life at this moment was bracketed by two scholars: a legendary critic, several of whose books were still considered classics, and the local Mr. Chips, a man who had all he could do to not let alcohol and loneliness undermine his legacy. Two men with nothing in common but an innate generosity. Both disposed, for reasons at once mysterious and profound, to think better of people than perhaps they deserved, whereas her own tendency had always been to think less of them. Bellamy had tried to warn her. He'd seen how skilled she was, how coldly persuasive she could be, that she would use the study of literature to distance herself and build a fortress around her heart. Maybe he even foresaw how things would go for her and Robbie, how she'd win every argument in their marriage until finally there was no marriage left.

"I'm sorry," she said, when Tom Newhouse finally released her from his bear hug. "I must look awful."

"You've looked better," he conceded. "*I've* looked better. We've *all* looked better." Then, after a beat: "So James *Cox* didn't write that essay."

"Oh, I don't know. He might've," she admitted. "But no, I don't think so." It was the same accusation she'd made before, but it felt different this time, and Newhouse now seemed willing to accept it.

"Well, *shit*," was all he said.

"You were right about one thing, though," she told him. "I *am* a good dancer. Or I was. When I passed my prelims, Robbie invited everyone in the department to come out and help us celebrate. His band played, and they were so great that night. There's this one song I used to sing with them . . . Jefferson Airplane's 'Somebody to Love'?" It was clear Newhouse had never heard of either the song or even the group, but the very thought of Grace Slick had her on the verge of tears. "We ended up at a biker joint around three in the morning where I danced on the bar."

"That must have been something," he said. "I wish I'd *been* there."

"Yeah, well, you missed it," she told him.

"Hey," he said, planting a kiss on her forehead. "Just because I wasn't there doesn't mean I can't remember it."

Robbie's car was in the drive, and when she got out she could see her husband and son through the dining room window, Robbie opening the pizza box, Marcus closing his eyes, breathing in, re-creating, for all she knew, every single detail of the pizza parlor that he supposedly loved. So this, she thought, was heartbreak. She'd read about it but wasn't sure she wanted to get any closer and had long suspected that epiphany was overrated. Even now her inclination was to remain right where she was with a pane of glass between herself and her husband and child, safe from them and they from her. The night she'd just told Newhouse about, Bellamy had been there, and when the bar closed they'd all adjourned to a truck stop and ordered huge breakfasts. Waiting for the food to arrive, they argued as only happy, drunken grad students can, about which was the greatest lyric poem ever written. You couldn't nominate a poem unless you recited it first, start to finish, from memory. Only then were you allowed to make your case for its greatness. Robbie had surprised her by doing "Kubla Khan" in its entirety, to wild applause. When it was Bellamy's turn, he'd chosen "Windy Nights," a children's poem everyone but Janet remembered. He emphasized its childish iambic downbeat by slapping the table so hard the water glasses jumped, and by the time he finished, the entire group was weak with laughter.

"Okay, okay, okay. Now explain," someone insisted, "why that's the greatest poem ever in the English language."

"Because," Bellamy said, suddenly serious, his eyes full, "when I speak those words aloud, my father's alive again."

He left the following year, as predicted, back to the Ivy League, but not before he'd recommended Janet for a prestigious postdoctoral fellowship, a much-needed port in the academic storm.

Why had he granted this favor? Maybe it was mostly for Robbie's sake. Though Bellamy never gave any indication, she'd come to believe that he'd arrived at the F-lot in time to see her flee. If so, he apparently hadn't held her cowardice against her. Was it possible that with this fellowship he wanted, as Tom Newhouse did later in a different place and context, to express his optimistic view that in the end she'd be okay? And if that was what he'd truly believed, could she be certain he was wrong?

Tomorrow she'd dig up the journal Bellamy had loaned her all those years ago with those essays she'd stubbornly refused to read. She already knew what she'd find in them. In his would be the man they'd all known, his human presence tangible in every word. Truly authorial. What he learned from literature and life had made him hungry for more, and it was this hunger that drew people to him. Robbie had wept when he read her his obituary from the *Times*, the same year she'd accepted her tenure-track position here, and it was Robbie who'd wanted to name their son in Bellamy's memory. She'd argued for a host of other names, most originating in her family or his, but could never make him understand. "What's wrong with 'Marcus'?" he kept asking, until she finally gave in.

In the other essay she'd find what Bellamy had noticed in hers, an absence. An implied writer. A shadow. A ghost. "But I *do* exist," she'd told him that day, however meekly, fearing he meant to convince her that even *that* wasn't true, when in reality he was merely urging her to discover that last elusive thing, a self worth being, worth becoming and finally worth revealing. Yet, even though she knew what awaited her in those essays, she would at last read them. She owed Bellamy that much. He'd given her an assignment, and she intended to finish it. After which, she suspected, he would haunt her no more.

Robbie was now bent over the dining room window, trying to peer out. He'd no doubt heard her car pull in and was wondering what she could be doing out there *in the dark and wet*. He'd set the table for three. Tonight they'd eat pizza. Tomorrow she'd figure out what the hell mincemeat was. Then Thanksgiving. After that, who knew?

Voice

The World of Others

The Biennale group—most of whom, like Nate, hailed from central Massachusetts—has taken over thc small, three-and-a-half-star hotel in *sestiere* Dorsoduro. Nate, fearing his social skills might have atrophied after so many months of self-imposed solitude, is standing by himself in the busy lobby and doing his level best to escape notice or, if that fails, to feign innocence, strategies that until a year ago came naturally. What happened with the Mauntz girl changed all that.

Or did it? He wonders if people actually see him differently now, or if he's just seeing himself differently. Maybe it's his own low self-esteem that people are picking up on, self-recrimination his new default mode. Earlier, in baggage claim at the airport, after a single glance Julian had demanded to know what was wrong. When Nate, surprised, asked his brother what he meant, Julian just shrugged, his own default mode annoyance morphing effortlessly to indifference. "You look all uncunted," he explained.

"All *what?*" Nate said, thinking he'd misheard. Though he was the English professor, it was Julian who'd always been in love with language, especially clever or mischievous turns of phrase that identified their speaker as cool. Pushing seventy, his brother still considered himself hip.

"Uncunted," he happily repeated, apparently having a favorite new word. "Unhinged, unmoored," he continued helpfully, "untethered, unraveled, befucked."

Amazing, Nate thought. Thirty seconds into their first face-to-face conversation in several years and he already wanted to strangle the man.

Of course it was entirely possible that Nate's appearance had nothing to do with his brother's reaction. Maybe Julian heard about his disgrace from Brenda, to whom in a weak moment last spring Nate had confessed everything. She'd sworn she wouldn't tell his brother, but possibly she'd then thought better of it; Nate almost hoped this was the case. Better for Julian to know already than to see that debacle written all over his brother's face. Because if Nate's mental state was so uncuntedly obvious, he might as well give up now. The rest of the Biennale group, otherwise all strangers, would twig this in short order.

Stop, Nate chides himself. Because hasn't he just traveled halfway around the world in the hopes of escaping precisely this kind of thinking? He is *not* a monster. He's not and the fact that he's felt like one the last twelve months doesn't make him one. Nor can people see inside him. They can't know the truth unless he confesses it. And what *is* that truth, anyway? Okay, without meaning to, he harmed someone. Just how badly, he might never know. And it's clear he also harmed himself. Still, people live with such things and much worse, Nate knows. They have no choice. *He* has no choice.

Nearby in the lobby, Klaus, the leader of this Biennale tour of Venice and then Rome, is telling a story about the offspring of fifteenth-century prostitutes who were conscripted to sing at Mass because of their angelic voices. Since many were grotesquely deformed by venereal disease, they were carefully situated behind opaque screens to safeguard the finer sensibilities of the patrician Venetian faithful, lest their uncouth appearance divert those superiors' attention from the divine. Hearing this, Nate again finds himself thinking about the Mauntz girl, though it's not immediately clear why. What did these unfortunates—however heart-wrenching—have to do with a troubled American girl six centuries later? Was it starting all over again? A year ago his thoughts had labored along on some unending loop where everything—overheard conversations, song lyrics, scenes from movies—reminded him of what had happened with the Mauntz girl. Going to ground had helped, at least for a while. Muting the noise of the outside world had also turned down the volume on voices in his head, a much-needed relief. Was it a mistake to allow the noise of life back in? If so, it's too late to correct now. For the next twelve days, unless his courage fails him and he locks himself in his room, he will be back in the world of others. He will see and be seen.

Scanning the crowded lobby, he notices the two women standing near the elevator. The taller one is attractive in an anxious, deer-in-the-headlights way, but unluckily, it's her squat, plain companion with whom he makes accidental eye contact. Realizing what's about to happen, he looks around for his brother, but he's still deep in conversation with Bea, the woman who organized the trip. The good thing about Julian—maybe the only good thing—is his lifelong ability to reduce Nate to a welcome state of insignificance. Coming in from the airport, Julian spent the entire trip talking to the water taxi's driver. He loved chatting up strangers. People with whom he had an actual connection were a different story. His endless silences were the reason, or one of them, that Brenda had cited for divorcing him.

Sitting there, listening to the two of them shout at each other over the roaring engine and the boat's slapping maddeningly against the waves, Nate understood that yet again he'd made the mistake of expecting too much of his brother. His flight had arrived late, and when he saw on the monitor that Julian's would be early, he'd decided to wait. It was only forty-five minutes, and they could share a taxi and spend the half an hour catching up. His all-too-predictable reward was to be told he looked "uncunted" and then ignored. Nor should he have been surprised when, climbing out of the taxi, Julian turned to him in his most offhanded manner and said, "You don't mind falling on this particular grenade, right?" He hadn't had a chance to stop at the ATM at the airport, he explained—*Sure you did* was on the tip of Nate's tongue—and he'd pay Nate back that evening when the group went out to dinner.

At any rate, as the two women approach, weaving through the crowd, Nate knows he's on his own. The plain one arrives first, thrusting her hand out, much as a man would, and announcing that her name is Evelyn, or, if he prefers, Eve. Nate, wondering why on earth he should have a preference, takes the proffered hand and pretends delight to be met. Eve's hair is cut sensibly short for a woman her age—early sixties, Nate figures, though he's never been much good at guessing women's ages—and she's wearing something like a tracksuit, except nicer and maybe even expensive. The general impression she conveys is of a woman who once upon a time cared about how she presented herself to men, but woke up one morning, said fuck it and was immediately happier. She is also, Nate fears, one of those women who's confident she knows what's in the best interest of others. Seeing someone who obviously prefers to be left alone, she's all the more determined to include him in whatever awful group activities she's contemplating. The word she probably uses to describe whatever she has in mind is *fun*. It won't be, of that Nate's certain.

Her companion—whom she introduces as Renee—offers a lovely contrast. Tall and slender and coltishly awkward, she's dressed in a long, flowing skirt and a sleeveless silk blouse, a colorful shawl draped over her fragile shoulders. Unless Nate is mistaken, paralyzing anxiety is this woman's more or less constant companion. Her hands are restless birds, anxious to take flight. And when she offers one, he hesitates, fearing it might not be possible to grasp something so delicate without damaging it. But of course this doesn't happen, and he suddenly feels a surge of gratitude so powerful he's able to envision a future, a whole new life—one devoted to reassuring this lovely woman that there is absolutely nothing to fear. An odd thought for a man in these circumstances to have but, given Nate's personality, not all that surprising, either. He's always gotten out ahead of himself where attractive women are concerned; he wishes it were otherwise, but it isn't. He's noticed that in general things prefer to remain as they are.

"So," Evelyn says, the intros now complete, "are you an art lover or a Venice lover?" Apparently this Biennale group is divided equally along these lines.

Nate takes a deep breath and explains, alas, that he belongs to neither camp. He knows exactly nothing about art after Pollock. He has traveled some, having served as director of his former college's junior-year-abroad programs in Salamanca, Lyon, Cork and London, his favorite, but never to Italy. More than once, when the chill and damp of England or Ireland got to him, he'd considered hopping a cheap flight to Cinque Terre or Rome or the Amalfi Coast, but soon recognized these as mere impulses, and he'd never acted impulsively. He's feeling, truth be told, woefully unprepared for both the Biennale and Venice. He's tried to prepare for the latter by reading some Henry James and Ruskin. (What an insufferable ass he must sound like, Nate thinks, dropping Ruskin's name as if these two women would know who the hell he was, and the world were populated solely by English professors.) Maybe because it's been so long since he's talked to anyone, this personal information gushes out like a torrent from some abruptly breached dam. He wouldn't blame them if they turned on their heels and fled. Indeed, he almost wishes they would. "Oh, and I reread *Death in Venice* on the plane," he adds, "which failed to cheer me up."

He hadn't really intended this remark as a joke, but that's how it's received, at least by Evelyn, who brays loudly in appreciation. Her companion offers a smile that's both lovely and difficult to categorize: the smile of someone who perhaps hadn't meant to, who'd fallen out of the habit and is surprised to learn that her facial muscles still work.

"All right, then," Evelyn proclaims, as if by his witticism Nate has passed some muster. "When we get to the restaurant, *you'll* sit with us."

And so, since Julian seems to have completely forgotten that he's even here, Nate does. Loud and boisterous, the group takes up two large tables set for ten in the otherwise empty restaurant. His brother is seated next to Bea and her husband and a round, humpbacked man named Bernard at the far end of the second table, and he chats them up as effortlessly as he did the driver of the water taxi. Studying Julian, Nate decides that he doesn't know about the Mauntz girl. Even *he* wouldn't be so unfeeling as to abandon him to strangers on their first night in Venice if he knew what Nate had recently been through, would he?

Over the course of the meal, Nate learns a good deal about his new companions. Both women are divorced. Evelyn, a few years older, gave her husband his walking papers some time ago and seems unambiguously pleased with this decision. She now refers to her ex, whom she presumably once loved enough to marry, as "the Wanker," a term she apparently picked up from watching the BBC cable channel. Renee's divorce is more recent and, Nate gathers, more ruinous to her frail self-confidence. Evidently the unstated purpose of this trip is to reintroduce her to the wider world, from which she's voluntarily withdrawn, which gives them something in common. When the subject of his own marital status comes up, Nate admits he's a career bachelor. Never even come close? Evelyn wants to know, probably trying to ascertain if he's gay. Well, as a younger man he was engaged to a woman named Brenda, he tells them. (*What happened?*) She married his brother instead. (*No!*) Yes, in fact, though the marriage didn't last. (*You must be a very forgiving man.*) Nate doesn't think so, but doesn't mind if they do. It's true that he's never held a grudge against either Julian or Brenda. They didn't mean to fall in love, it just happened. And anyway, Nate says, in hopes of changing the subject, his true love has always been Jane Austen. This makes Renee look momentarily hopeful, until the name rings a bell and she realizes she's made a mistake. Jane Austen is someone famous and dead. She, too, Nate can tell, would like to be dead, and thus beyond such social gaffes. Whereas Nate would like to take her in his arms and tell her everything's okay. He marvels again at his need to say such a thing to a woman he barely knows—the very thing, in fact, that most days he struggles to convince himself of.

At some point during dinner Nate realizes that he's drunk too much red wine, which isn't recommended in conjunction with his antidepressant, and that he doesn't much care. He's having an excellent time, his first in what seems like forever. His food actually tastes good, and the Chianti, well, he can't get enough. Is it possible that at long last his depression is lifting? Or maybe the doctor who diagnosed him is full of shit and he's just been in a funk. He knows now that taking Ambien was a huge mistake. Yes, it had allowed him to sleep, but also made him morose and deepened his sense of personal failure, as well as rendering him too sluggish to extricate himself. So it might be time to quit taking the mood medication as well. Because tonight, in the company of these two women, he's actually flirting with happiness, or at least its possibility. No sooner does this occur to him, however, than he wonders how much longer it can last, what will cause it to fizzle, precisely the defeatist attitude he's determined to banish once and for all. This, he realizes, is what he'd hoped to explain to Julian in the water taxi. Not what happened with the Mauntz girl, but that for the last year he simply hadn't been himself and that he was determined to shake off his lethargy and once again enter the world of the living. He's tired of hiding. At this, he again glances over at the second table, just as his brother whispers something to Bea, who replies, "Oh, that's a splendid idea." When she gets to her feet, Julian helpfully calls for silence by tinking his wineglass with his spoon, and Nate's heart sinks. He should've known better than to ask how much longer his newfound sense of well-being could last. To pose that question was to invite its speedy answer. The group will reconfigure over dessert so those who haven't had a chance to introduce themselves can do so.

"Rats," says Evelyn, when this is announced. "And we were

having such a good time. Okay, everybody, let's act invisible. Maybe they'll leave us alone."

It's too late, though. All the other chairs are scraping back, and a moment later Nate feels a heavy hand on his shoulder. He doesn't even need to look up to know it's his brother's.

But guess what? To Nate's amazement, both the warm glow from the wine and a renewed sense of possibility accompany him to the next table, where he finds himself seated beside a woman who's just received an urgent text from her cell-phone carrier about her escalating data fees—apparently triggered by her daughter e-mailing her a dozen photos of her new grandson. Nate, who for this trip has traded his ancient flip phone for a snazzy new "smart" model and received a tutorial in its use, shows her how to turn off the phone's roaming feature and is promptly celebrated with a toast. Asked again to account for his presence on the tour, he repeats what he told Evelyn and Renee, including the bit about how reading *Death in Venice* on the plane had failed to cheer him up, and is rewarded with more appreciative laughter. Part of him, though, is still back at the first table, where his brother, to judge from the hilarity there, is a hit. Nate can't help noticing that the lovely Renee's smiles, hopeful but tentative when he was there, are now more frequent, confident and radiant, though it's possible some of this might be in response to the charismatic Klaus, who's been coaxed into repeating his story about the children of the fifteenth-century whores, their lovely voices rising up from behind the screens.

On the walk back to the hotel, Bea falls in step alongside him. Evelyn and Renee and Julian are up ahead, arms linked, his brother in the middle, their laughter echoing off the moldering Venetian walls. "I've known her most of her life," Bea whispers.

Apparently she noticed that during dessert his attention kept being drawn back to the other table. "She's a lovely woman."

"Yes," Nate agrees, realizing only then that she's talking about Evelyn, not Renee. There is, of course, no way to clarify this confusion, and at any rate Bea happens at this moment to notice that the humpbacked Bernard has fallen behind and is angling across the *campo* in the wrong direction. "*Yoo*-hoo!" she calls. "Over here, Bernard! *This* way."

Later, in the middle of the night, a siren wakes Nate up, and for several moments he's disoriented, his throbbing head still back in Massachusetts. Rising, he goes over to the window, half expecting to see flames reflected in the canal below, but the water is black and still as death. Did he have the fire dream again? If so, it's the first time in many years. When he and Julian were boys, their mother fell asleep with a lighted cigarette and burned down the shabby house they were renting, nearly killing all three of them in the process. Since then, sirens always make him think of fire. Actually, the book he'd read on the plane wasn't Mann at all but one about the famous fire at La Fenice, the Venice opera house. Why had he lied about that, especially to so little consequence? He wonders if lying—the *habit* of it—might be part of what's afflicted him. Once diagnosed with it, he read up on clinical depression, which is generally attributed to a chemical imbalance in the brain, an explanation he finds less than satisfying. But then English professors are probably drawn to moral and symbolic diagnoses rather than medical ones.

Returning to bed he lies awake, trying to recall what that siren—still wailing in the distance—is all about. At some point during dinner or on the walk back to the hotel, somebody—was it Klaus or Bea?—said something about a siren, but what? Finally, it comes to him: *acqua alta*. This had also been noted in the pamphlets he'd been given when they checked into the hotel—the high-water siren that sounded in anticipation of flooded streets. Odd that his instinct upon hearing the siren had been to fear fire when the actual threat was water. Not just incorrect but diametrically so. Strange, too, that a man so desperate to rise from a dark place should travel thousands of miles to a city that's sinking into one.

He's about to fall back asleep when his new phone vibrates on the nightstand, its screen eerily illuminating the room. The device suddenly inquires whether he wants it to make use of his current location. Unable to make sense of this unprompted question, he powers the phone completely off, its screen darkening at the exact same moment the siren outside stops wailing, filling him with sleepy wonder at a linkage that's simply not there.

Speaking of linkages, his last waking thoughts are of the prostitutes' children who sang so beautifully. How did they feel about being hidden behind those screens? Did it seem a kindness that their voices alone should represent them to the world of others? Why should these privileged others be spared the deformity its victims had no part in causing? Is it better to be known whole or to conceal what makes us unworthy of love?

Buddies

Nine-thirty the next morning finds the Biennale band once again filling the tiny hotel lobby. Klaus is giving them their marching orders, stressing his intention—no, his *determination*—to run a tight, efficient ship. Having led this group before, he knows all too well that they require a firm, authoritarian hand. Apparently part of his shtick includes being endearingly insulting in the manner of gay men, though Nate isn't certain the others recognize him as gay, just witty and urbane and a snappy dresser. Not, in other words, from central Massachusetts.

They're only here for four days, Klaus reminds them, and there's much to see and do. Therefore. Each morning they will be leaving the hotel *promptly* at nine-thirty. Anyone who isn't in the lobby will be left behind, and won't they be sorry! Because this is *not* London or Berlin. They won't be able to hail a taxi out front. Many of the venues they'll be visiting are well off the beaten path, and Venice is a labyrinth whose streets are famously full of water. Personally, Klaus informs them, he'll consider this leg of the tour a success if nobody ends up floating facedown in the Grand Canal.

This is an attempt at humor, of course, and it gets the expected laugh. Though Nate chuckles along with the rest, the joke sends a chill up his spine. Lying in bed this morning, hungover and wide-awake an hour before the alarm, he studied the schedule of daily activities they were given at dinner, trying to square it with the people he met there. A few appear fit enough, but others strike him as medical emergencies waiting to happen. Both hump-backed Bernard and the orange-haired, chain-smoking woman who stops to catch her breath at the foot of each new *ponte* are genuine heart-attack candidates. Then there's the extremely elderly couple who, when at rest, lean into each other shoulder to shoulder, forming the letter A; if either were to move quickly, a broken hip would be the likely result for the other.

This morning the whole jet-lagged group appears even more vulnerable than they did the night before. This pessimistic assessment suggests to Nate that today is going to be one of his down days. Last night's flirtation with optimism seems just that: a flirtation. In his pocket is the pill he takes with lunch each day to ward off despondency. Is it possible that, under the influence of too much Chianti, he actually contemplated forgoing the medication his doctor told him was essential to his recovery?

If Julian doesn't hurry up, Klaus is bound to use him as an object lesson. When heading down to the lobby, Nate had stopped by his brother's room, but Julian growled through the locked door that he should go on by himself, he'd follow in two shakes. That was fifteen minutes ago. It's entirely possible that Nate's knock woke him up, and if so, there's a good chance he went right back to sleep. True, his voice hadn't seemed sleepy, but that didn't mean anything. Even as a boy Julian had been a master of sounding awake when he wasn't, of pretending to be up and about even as he burrowed under the covers. "I'm just tying my shoes," he'd tell their mother when she called up to him from the foot of the stairs. (Why did she always believe him?) Nate is about to ask Giancarlo at the desk to ring Julian's room when he appears on the stairs.

"How perfectly divine you could join us," Klaus says jovially.

"Divine I'll grant you," Julian says, ignoring Nate's wave so he can join Renee, who is standing shyly at the outer ring of the assembled group. "*Perfectly* divine is pushing it a bit." A charismatic himself, Julian doesn't take to others of that ilk, and though Nate finds Klaus to be cultured, extraordinarily well read and far more knowledgeable on a wider range of subjects than his academic colleagues used to be, Julian seems to dislike him on the grounds of flamboyance. It's never before occurred to Nate that his brother might be homophobic.

"So, then," Klaus says, ignoring Julian's remark. "Are we all buddied up?"

That's the other thing Klaus insists upon, to ensure that no one is left behind as they move from exhibit to exhibit. And if this doesn't work, he threatens they'll be required to hold on to a rope like preschoolers.

To Nate, a buddy system makes sense, and for most it won't be an imposition. There are several older couples, as well as half-a-dozen women like Evelyn and Renee traveling as companions, so these are already buddied. As of course Nate and Julian are de facto as brothers. He does feel bad for the singletons, though. It seems unfair that they be required first to search each other out and then be responsible to and for a stranger. That Nate himself might become one of them doesn't occur to him until Renee raises her hand and announces that Evelyn, whom Nate hadn't noticed was missing, woke up feeling under the weather and she's decided to sleep in, though she may join them for lunch if she feels better. Which means Renee is buddyless. For about half a second. That's how long it takes for Julian to steal a march on his brother.

"Looks like you drew the short straw," Bernard says when he shakes Nate's hand on the street. They'd been introduced at Bea's table the night before, but the man hadn't said a word beyond hello, so they might as well be complete strangers. Perhaps because Bernard is so round shouldered and hunched over, Nate is surprised that his voice is so deep and robust.

"No worries," Nate tells him, "I'm not exactly the longest straw myself." He intends for this remark to be self-deprecatory, but it doesn't land right. Without meaning to, he's conceded Bernard's status as the group's shortest straw. As they begin walking, Nate, for something else to say, poses the question Evelyn asked him last night: "Are you here for Venice or contemporary art?"

"I'm here for my wife," Bernard tells him. "She's the one who loved this place."

Noticing the verb tense, Nate says, "I'm sorry . . . did she—"

"Last winter," the other man says. "Sudden. She booked this trip and died before the check cleared."

"That's terrible."

Bernard shrugs. "Everybody dies."

"I'm sure they would've refunded—"

"I have to stop talking now," Bernard tells him abruptly. "I can either talk or walk. Not both."

The first exhibition, on the fourth floor of an abandoned warehouse, fills that very large room, the floor of which is covered, several inches deep, with dark soil. Exactly how dirt is to be construed as art is not immediately clear to Nate, and the artist's statement—an obscenity-laced, left-wing political rant—might have been expected to shed some light, but instead muddies things further. For this artist, *Dirt equals art* apparently wasn't a sufficiently slippery equation; he chose *dirt equals politics equals art*. Nate, cursed with a highly practical imagination, finds himself wondering how all that soil got up to the fourth floor and, once there, who spread it. Had the artist thought of this laborious process as "installation"? How would the result have differed in the hands—wheelbarrow?—of a lesser talent? More bizarre still, according to Klaus, there is a precedent. A couple years before in New York, another conceptual artist covered the floor of his Chelsea loft with dirt, and this exhibit could be taken as a scathing critique of it or else as an homage. Near the exit is a small sign stating that the work isn't for sale. Seeing this, Bernard snorts but makes no further comment.

As they walk to the next venue, which Klaus assures them will be equally provocative, Nate's thoughts wander to his brother, who's up ahead with Renee. Since becoming her buddy, he hasn't left her side. Nor has he apologized to Nate for abandoning him so unceremoniously. Indeed, beyond a gruff hello there in the lobby, he's barely spoken a word. Did Nate somehow manage to offend him? When, at baggage claim? In the water taxi? At the restaurant? He could ask, of course, but to what reasonable end? Julian would just deny anything's wrong and want to know why the hell he was forever internalizing everything. Incredible, really, that Nate could ever have imagined two such inherently different, even diametrically opposed, men reconnecting after so long an estrangement. Still, it's a shame, right? Because they are, at least as Nate sees it, all each other has. There are no other siblings. Neither having fathered children, they're the end of their family's line. But who knows? Maybe Julian doesn't see it that way. His life might be rich and full. Unlike Nate, he's always made friends easily and may have more than he knows what to do with. Lovers even. In a world of social networking and Facebook "friending," Julian might consider blood relatives as vestigial as tonsils or appendixes, whose original purposes have long been forgotten and that can be excised without consequence. What particularly troubles Nate is that he can do little more than speculate. He knows next to nothing about his brother's life. He is never home when Nate calls, though maybe he is standing right there by the ringing phone, staring at the caller ID. Granted, he usually calls back in a few days, explaining that he's been "straight out" or "tits back," or some other Julianism, but he never elaborates, and his curtness conveys all too clearly that Nate is as much a bother as a brother.

Which begs an obvious question: why, against reason and experience, does he continue to hope that things will ever be different? That this time he'll not only love Julian, which after all is his blood's duty, but also *like* him. They've always been temperamental opposites, Nate instinctively striving for peace and harmony, Julian thriving on confrontation, seldom right but never in doubt, much less self-doubt, his brother's lifelong weakness. What he's been banking on, really, is time. Aren't people who share the same bundled genetics supposed to become more alike as they age? Maybe Julian's gruff manner masks sympathies he's unable to give voice to. It's possible. Doesn't Nate himself secretly envy the very qualities that make Julian such a dick? Women actually *like* the man, at least for a while. Even they don't seem to know why. His charm—Nate has to admit his brother *can* be charming—is gossamer thin, a triumph of style over substance, and females drawn to him all eventually realize he's an empty vessel. There would be comfort in this except that even after they finally *do* come to their senses, these same women invariably blame themselves, not him. Sure, he's a self-centered jerk, they concede, but he never pretended to be otherwise, right? And if his wake is strewn with the casualties of his narcissistic carelessness, well, they should've known better. Julian, Teflon coated, always gets a pass.

Whereas Nate himself is made of something stickier. Though modest and thoughtful, unfailingly considerate and an excellent listener—all traits women are reputed to value in men—he somehow ends up disappointing them far more profoundly than Julian does. Though they never explain precisely how he fails to measure up, they leave little doubt that he does. Apparently they prefer an empty vessel to one so full of whatever it is they refuse to name. The Mauntz girl was different, of course, but so was their relationship. She belongs in another whole category. In her case he knows exactly what he did wrong, though it's of little use except to underscore that it's probably a mistake to seek clarity when what's vague are your own moral failings.

Mulling all this over, Nate doesn't immediately notice when Bernard, just as he did last night, falls behind. Even in this gimpy, long-in-the-tooth group, he is particularly pathetic. Though it's nearly sixty degrees out, warm for northern Italy in November, he's wearing a parka, and underneath it a tweed jacket, and underneath that a sweater and a shirt and an undershirt. What little remains of his hair is stirring, frondlike, in the breeze.

"Are you okay?" Nate asks when he catches up.

"Peachy," Bernard replies. "Don't worry about me."

But if something happens it'll be Nate's fault, so he calls to Julian and Renee, who are some fifty yards ahead at the crest of the next small bridge. The others are farther along, mid*campo,* clustered around Klaus, who's paused to point out something architecturally or historically significant. "I'll be right back," he promises Bernard.

When Nate trots up, his brother regards him in a way that suggests he's been expecting just such an unwelcome intrusion and says, "What's up, Prof?" His demeanor implies a firm conviction that nothing possibly could be.

Prof. How the word rankles. For Julian it's always been a term of gentle derision, the clichéd implication being that cloistered, academic life leads inevitably to an ignorant innocence in worldly matters. Teaching, his brother maintains, is a profession you gravitate toward if you're modest and thoughtful and considerate and a good listener—a natural haven to old women of both genders. It's possible, of course, that his mockery stings because it's linked to Nate's own self-doubt, his secret fear that he's led a life other than the one he was intended for, following the wrong trajectory entirely. He'd put himself through college and graduate school working summers for a contractor named Handscombe, a surprisingly contemplative man who specialized in restoring old houses. For some reason he took a shine to Nate and, instead of having him hang drywall day after day, mentored him in the trade, teaching him carpentry and masonry as well as basic plumbing and wiring, marveling at his aptitude for all these tasks, especially since he'd grown up largely without a father. "Why don't you stay on?" he suggested one summer a couple weeks before Nate would return to grad school. "You're good at this. You seem to enjoy it."

Which was true, he did enjoy the work. There was something straightforward and appealing about driving a nail, fitting a pipe. You couldn't pretend a job was well done if it wasn't. In grad school people could and did argue that bad books were good and vice versa. Any persuasive case—no matter how wrongheaded at its core—was widely admired. Not so in Mr. Handscombe's world, where shoddy work meant the pipe leaked or the wall fell down. Though Nate wouldn't have admitted it at the time, the rhetorical tools he employed during the school year weren't nearly as satisfying as the actual ones dangling from his tool belt in July and August. Even better, by the end of the summer his body was tanned and strong. Back then, naturally, these truths hadn't seemed at all evident. What kind of man chooses physical labor over a contemplative life? It's possible, though, now that he thinks about it, that Julian might have liked him better, or respected him more, as a maker of things you could touch.

Say this for Julian, a career salesman: he's lived the life he was meant to live and followed the *only* trajectory that truly suits him, from start to finish. He's sold cars, time-shares, stocks, television advertising. Indeed, people are always impressed by the wide range of things Julian has sold, but as he likes to say, selling is selling. It's all about knowing people better than they know themselves. Figure out who they are and what they really want, and they're yours. Julian tends to make a fist when he says this, as if inviting people to imagine being in his cruel grasp. Knowledge is power, he maintains, though apparently not the sort that bestows upon you a Ph.D. in English. Julian claims his head is full of the kind of algorithms Google would pay millions for, but in Nate's opinion it isn't just algorithms he's full of. And he disagrees that his brother can sell anything. He's known the man a long time, and he's only ever sold one thing: Julian.

"Bernard can't keep up," Nate now informs his brother.

Julian snorts at this, seeming neither surprised nor concerned. "Morning of day one and already our vaunted buddy system's come uncunted."

"Oh, dear," Renee says, one avian hand fluttering up to her mouth, and for a moment Nate thinks she's reacting to the vulgarity, but no, it's the sight of Bernard trudging toward them with his head down, as if deeply apprehensive about his footing, the uneven stones still slick from last night's *acqua alta*. Breathing hard, he pauses at the base of the bridge.

"Bernard?" she says. "Are you feeling okay?"

"I'm fine," he insists, though it takes all his remaining breath to make this dubious assertion, and it's a long moment before he completes the thought. "I just can't walk as fast as the rest of you."

"It's that goose-stepping German's fault," Julian says, unable as always to show sympathy for one human being without expressing contempt for another. "Where the hell did they all go?" he adds indignantly, surveying the now-empty square.

Nate points at the alleyway into which the last of the Biennale group is disappearing. "They went thataway."

"Well," his brother says, "somebody should run on ahead and get Herr Mengele to slow the fuck down."

"I could . . . ," Renee begins, but Nate can tell she doesn't want to be the one.

"Nah, let the professor go," Julian says. "He's the one who saw where they were heading."

Which is true, yes, though since he'd just shown them which *calle* their party entered, they're all, from a purely informational standpoint, on an equal footing.

"We'll keep Bernard company," his brother assures him, as if consideration for others were his raison d'être.

And thus Nate is dismissed. Scuttling dutifully across the *campo* he feels the entire weight of the long history they share and how little has changed between them over the decades. Even when they were kids, Julian resented him tagging along. Often, at their mother's insistence they would leave home together only to have Julian and his friends give Nate the slip. Later, of course, he would deny it, boldly claiming it was Nate's fault they'd gotten separated. He'd been right there one minute and gone the next, impossible to keep track of and certain to disappear if you didn't give him your undivided attention—already a consummate salesman, Julian's protestations of innocence so convincing that even his brother half believed them.

But other times, he has to admit, Julian wasn't so bad. If not for him, what would Nate have done after their father's desertion? "We're better off," his brother insisted every time Nate confessed how much he missed him. "He was a bum. Good riddance." And when none of his own friends were around or he was bored, Julian played games with him and even helped with his homework. It was only later, in adolescence, that Nate began to discern a clear pattern to his behavior. What at first glance seemed to be kindness or affection on Julian's part would later be revealed to be self-serving, causing Nate to wonder if he was capable of genuine empathy or if their father's defection, their mother's growing abstraction, hadn't caused him to harden.

Which probably explains his initial suspicion when Julian invited him on this trip. According to Julian, the tour was sold out, but if Nate was interested, he knew the woman in charge of the whole shebang and could have a word with her. But yesterday night in the lobby, Bea had greeted Nate as the tour's savior. There'd been several unexpected cancellations due to illness and injury, she told him, and for a time it had looked like the trip would have to be called off. True, two other couples had come on board after Nate, but it was *his* participation that provided the necessary critical mass.

Of course it's possible she and Julian simply remembered things differently. Maybe she's one of those women who like to make other people feel important. More likely, though, this was yet another instance of Julian being Julian. There was nothing his brother enjoyed more than giving the impression that everyone was in his debt when it was actually vice versa. Regardless, the discrepancy between these accounts immediately confirmed Nate's original misgivings, and while he knew it was petty he couldn't help wondering how many other people his brother had solicited before leaning on him. It wasn't difficult to imagine Julian impatiently scrolling down his Contacts list and inviting Nate only after everyone else had been crossed off. And an even-more-cynical inference might be drawn: Julian is involved in some can't-miss development in Florida or South Carolina or Arizona and wants to offer the other members of the Biennale tour an opportunity to get in on the ground floor. In fact, it wouldn't surprise Nate to learn that the real reason Julian came on this tour is to pitch whatever he's presently marketing to people with enough disposable income to afford a fortnight in Italy.

Which would mean that as far as his brother is concerned, Nate's just another mark.

But why entertain such thoughts? Even if Julian has ulterior motives for inviting him, does it necessarily mean he's totally without warm brotherly feelings? People have lots of moving parts, and trying to reduce motives for simplicity's sake is always dangerous. The fact that Julian's selling doesn't mean Nate's necessarily buying. The sad reality is that they're both old men. Why not let past grievances go?

Lost in parallel labyrinths—the maze of his own thoughts and Venice itself—Nate doesn't immediately comprehend that he's somehow managed to mess up even this errand. Rounding each subsequent corner, he expected to come upon Klaus and the rest, but entering another large, empty *campo* he realizes that he would've done so by now if he was going to. Somewhere he must have zigged when they zagged. Though he can't understand how, they've disappeared. Which means there's nothing to do except retrace his steps back to where he left Julian and Renee and Bernard, admit his failure and accept his brother's silent scorn.

But when he arrives at that *campo* they, too, have disappeared. In its center he stands by the statue of a man who appears to be sitting on a tall stack of books. Something is burning nearby, and its acrid taste burns like panic at the back of Nate's throat. Then he remembers that after dinner, before turning in, he and Julian exchanged cell numbers. When he calls, though, he's sent directly to voice mail, and in that moment he is visited by an awful certainty: he doesn't just dislike his brother, he *hates* him. He imagines telling Julian, with Renee and Bernard looking on, that he is today what he's always been—a selfish, arrogant asshole.

Except the pleasure in doing so would be fleeting and the harm, at least to himself, long lasting. Renee would look at him with new eyes, and he'd see in her sad, frightened expression the belief that if she'd chosen him instead of Julian, he would've ended up hurting her. Even Bernard would turn away in disgust, just as his academic colleagues had done when rumors about the Mauntz girl began circulating

The antidepression pill is still in his pocket, and he swallows it dry.

The Mauntz Girl

He'd noticed her in the gym the year before she enrolled in his seminar. Neither attractive nor unattractive, she wouldn't have stood out except for how fiercely she swam against the current of campus life, steely will and bottomless need seemingly poised in Manichaean balance. She worked out early, sometimes arriving at the athletic center before daybreak, probably crossing paths with hard-core party types—the jocks and sorority girls—staggering back to their dorm rooms. Nate, who since retiring from full-time teaching had become increasingly insomniac, would occasionally get to the center a few minutes before it opened, and there she'd be, patiently shivering outside the entrance—her thin, thrift-shop clothes inadequate to the frigid early morning temperatures. Silently they'd wait for the custodian to unlock the doors, just the two of them, their nearness an intimacy. More than once Nate thought about introducing himself to this strange, seemingly friendless girl, so they could pass a minute or two in pleasant conversation before being allowed inside. But he was a man in his sixties, and a stranger to her. If he spoke it might weird her out. Still, it seemed a shame. Her willful unawareness seemed so purposeful it would've hurt his feelings had a terrible question not occurred to him: was she a *mute*?

Unlike other girls who frequented the gym dressed in designer athletic outfits and expensive sneakers, the Mauntz girl actually worked out, training with the grim determination of a professional athlete. After forty-five minutes or so, her threadbare T-shirt, always the same dingy gray, was as drenched with sweat as an overweight man's would've been. She never listened to music on headphones or watched television while she exercised, just plodded resolutely upward on the StairMaster, floor after imaginary floor. Nate felt sorry for her. Despite her dogged efforts, her body remained boxy and thick in the middle, much like his own had lately become. As a young man, working summers with Mr. Handscombe was all it had taken for him to round into physical form. How awful it must be for a twenty-year-old to be surrounded by others in the prime of their young lives, girls who could play drinking games with the boys into the wee hours, confident they'd be able to repair the damage on the lacrosse field the next day.

That spring, about a week before the semester ended, she had an accident on the StairMaster. Nate was in the locker room when it happened, but he heard the commotion outside. "Some girl," a guy explained when Nate inquired, had fallen and hurt herself pretty badly, though she was refusing all attempts to help her. Later that week he saw her moving painfully across the quad on crutches, the other students giving her wide berth as if she'd contracted something that might be catching. Then the following autumn, she turned up in his seminar.

Her name was Opal Mauntz, and she must've decided to sign up at the last moment because it was penciled in at the bottom of his computer printout. Had she realized he was the man from the gym? (If she'd ever noticed him there, she'd given no sign.) His Jane Austen course was less popular than ever, its enrollment having declined incrementally through his semi-retirement, fewer students knowing anything about him. Those who took the class now were mostly majors who needed to fulfill a period requirement they'd been putting off. Next fall the department would probably offer it to the new nineteenth-century hire who'd apparently expressed interest.

The young woman who belonged to the penciled-in name arrived after seven other females and one male had already staked out positions around the oblong seminar table. They were poring over the syllabus he'd just distributed, groaning over the fact that four papers would be required instead of the standard three and that these would be rigorously "workshopped," when the strange girl from the gym entered without apology for being tardy. Rather than joining them at the table, she dragged a chair over to the far wall, angling it so that when sitting she wouldn't have to look at anyone. Normally Nate wouldn't have permitted such rudeness. On first days he usually took a few moments to remind everyone that seminars were different from other classes, their success dependent on each student's investment not just in the topic but also in one another. He would not be lecturing. Discussions would go wherever the group took them. What prevented him from providing the usual drill had less to do with Opal Mauntz's behavior than that of the other students, who'd shared a knowing glance when she entered. Nor were they apparently surprised or offended when she isolated herself in their midst. Clearly, they knew something he didn't.

He got his first inkling as to what that might be when at the end of class, after the others had left, the Mauntz girl wordlessly presented him with a document from the health center, which stated that the bearer had difficulties with physical proximity and should be allowed to situate herself however she chose to in a classroom setting. Nor should she be required to speak. It was a medical issue, the document implied, and if he had any questions or concerns he should contact the dean of students.

Nate, who had a history with Greta Silver, nevertheless called her as soon as he got back to his office. "What can you tell me about Opal Mauntz?" he asked.

"Ah, right," she said, "Opal."

Nate waited for her to elaborate. When she didn't, he said, "She's in my seminar."

"I know. I tried to talk her out of it."

"Thanks. May I ask why?"

"To this point she's taken only women professors."

"It's come to this?"

"Opal is a special case."

"All our students are special," he reminded her. "It says so right in the student handbook."

"Opal . . . ," she began. "I have to be careful here."

"Can the girl speak?"

"Yes, I believe so." Greta sounded grateful to be asked a question she could answer.

"You believe so?"

"Yes, she can speak. I've just never heard her."

"You're saying the problem isn't physical, then?"

"Umm . . . she's had a difficult life."

"In what respect?"

"In every respect."

"Can you be more specific?"

"There are privacy considerations."

"You're suggesting she's been abused?"

"I'm not suggesting anything."

"The health-center document she gave me said you were the person to talk to."

"I understand, and I'm sorry. I can assure you she's not violent."

"I never thought she was, but how am I supposed to proceed? This is a seminar. There are only eight other students."

"Nate," she said after a long beat. "This is going to sound harsh and unfeeling, but pretend she's watching you on television from a remote location."

"Does the poor girl have any friends?"

"I don't think so, but that seems to be her choice," she said. "Opal isn't . . ."

"Like everybody else in the world since the beginning of time?" Nate suggested. "Because if she doesn't want friends, that's what she'd be."

She sighed. "I've already told you more than I should've."

"You haven't told me anything." He could imagine the dean massaging her temples with her thumb and forefinger.

"This much I *can* tell you," she said finally. "Just being here? On campus? You have no idea what it means to her. None."

Whatever the Mauntz girl's problems might be, they weren't evident in her first paper, which was by far the best in the class. Three weeks into the term she'd still not spoken a word and remained physically isolated, her expression a mask of grim concentration, her head cocked like a dog listening to a sound only it could hear. Perhaps because the discussion was otherwise so lively, Nate found himself unintentionally following Greta Silver's advice to pretend the girl was watching the proceedings on closed-circuit television. The problem was that when he did remember her it was always a shock. She felt doubly real then, her presence a rebuke. It troubled him to recall how after she fell on the StairMaster last spring, she'd refused both help and comfort from onlookers. Then again, had anybody really tried? Shouldn't *he* try? Though she wasn't "participating" in any conventional sense, he was convinced that Opal Mauntz was fully engaged in everything that went on in the seminar. Sometimes he saw, or possibly imagined, the hint of a smile, especially when he responded to her classmates' comments in a particularly probing manner, as if she knew precisely what he was after. She seemed attuned not just to the discussion but to his methods, his unwillingness to let glib comments go unchallenged. And now, his intuition was validated by her brilliant essay.

Over the years Nate had his share of fine students, a few even gifted, but never really the one who justifies a career, and as he read that first essay with mounting excitement it occurred to him that the Mauntz girl might be just such a student. How cruel it was that he wasn't allowed to speak with her. On the other hand it was also possible he was wrong, that on the basis of a single essay and perhaps a nonexistent smile, he was projecting onto her blank silence his own yearning, as if it were within her power to refute his growing conviction that he should've accepted Mr. Handscombe's offer of a whole different destiny that long-ago summer.

Except for Opal's, that first batch of essays was depressingly dismal. Their authors weren't stupid—the classroom discussions had proved that much—but the writing was breathtakingly incoherent. All their academic lives they'd been cutting and pasting from the Internet—a phrase here, a sentence there—a pastiche of observations linked by little more than general subject matter. Individual sentences, lifted from their original context and plopped down in a foreign one, varied wildly in tone and style. Given a list of transitional phrases—*but, rather, on the other hand, while, hence*—the essays' alleged authors would've been helpless to choose the one that correctly expressed the relationship between juxtaposed assertions, had any such relationship by chance occurred. Whole paragraphs were maddeningly free of both mistakes and meaning. By contrast, Opal's thoughts, having sprung from the soil of a single, fertile mind, flowed elegantly from each to the next. Her sentences were carefully constructed to accommodate quotations, not just accurately but gracefully, from the primary text. She never used block quotations as filler, like her lazy classmates. Okay, there were errors, as well as spots where her thesis might have been bolstered, but here was an intelligence that was truly engaging. She wrote as if the book she was addressing mattered and somehow squared with her experience of the world. Here, for want of a better word, was a *voice*.

Handing back the students' essays, especially the first batch, was invariably an unpleasant duty, marking as it did the end of the academic honeymoon. They'd all been getting along so well, pretending to be the best of friends, and now this. A *grade*. Having briefly thought that *this* class might be different, they now understood it wasn't. Betrayed again. Sarah Griffith, an English major to whom Nate, on the very first day, had felt a visceral aversion, seethed with undisguised resentment at the generous B minus he'd given her instead of the C plus she deserved. Normally that would have irritated him, but not today. Opal's reaction was the only one he cared about. He wasn't sure exactly what he expected from her, perhaps a slight amplification of the smile he'd suspected whenever he refused to praise an idle observation in class. Whatever her response might be, he'd purposely put her essay on the bottom of the stack so he could savor it. How odd, he realized when he finally handed it to her, that *he* should be anxious and so let down when she barely glanced at the A he'd circled at the top of the page before stuffing it into her backpack. It was almost as if he himself had been given a failing grade or, worse, that she actually *had* just been streaming the class on her computer.

His custom when returning graded work was to circulate a conference sign-up sheet for those who wished, in theory, to discuss in greater detail the strengths and weaknesses of their work, though in practice these conferences amounted to little more than an opportunity for students to dispute their grades. While the page was slowly passed around the table, Nate excused himself and stood before the mirror in the men's room and gave himself a good dressing-down. According to Brenda, his ex-fiancée, this was the abiding pattern of his life, especially with females of the species. He expected too much. He got his hopes up. Sensing this, women invariably fled. Okay, it wasn't like he had a romantic interest in Opal Mauntz, but was it possible the same principle applied here? There was no denying he'd gotten his hopes up. How else could they have been dashed so devastatingly?

The talking-to must've taken longer than he thought, because when he returned to the classroom it was empty, the sheet placed thoughtfully on top of his briefcase . . . on it was a wonderful surprise. He hadn't expected Opal to sign up for a conference, but there was her name! And she'd selected the last slot of the day, which in his experience suggested the student anticipated having more to discuss than the allotted half hour would accommodate. And just that quickly he forgot the scolding he'd just given himself. Tomorrow, he thought, at long last she would speak.

The following day, unfortunately, delivered only bitter disappointment. At first he thought she might simply be late, then that she might be pacing outside in the hall, trying to work up the courage to knock, though when he went out to check the corridor was empty. He waited until her entire half hour elapsed before tossing his things into the briefcase. To boost his spirits, he reminded himself that over the course of the afternoon he'd done some excellent work with the other students. He'd reassured each of them that while their first effort wasn't all it might've been, he wasn't discouraged, and they shouldn't be either; he had every confidence they were up to the task. He even spent a few minutes at the end to inquire after their families and ask about their plans for after graduation. It wasn't easy, but he somehow even managed to feign goodwill toward Sarah Griffith, who began by asking him to explain his criteria for assessing grades and wondering if his expectations were in line with those of his colleagues, whose estimation of her talents was rather loftier than his own.

But of course it was now obvious that the first eight conferences had been merely rehearsals for the only one that really counted. He'd broached their personal lives and future plans so he'd be able, in good conscience, to ask Opal Mauntz about her own. As they talked, he'd mostly tuned them out, his thoughts running on ahead to that last half hour. He cautioned himself more than once that she might prove disappointing. It was possible she'd panic, clam up, say little more than hello and thank you. If so, he was prepared to bear the brunt of the conversation. Think of it, he told himself, as an opening gambit. They had the rest of the semester to establish trust. Mostly he wanted to assure her that whatever her personal challenges, everything would be all right. Life was long and could get better. He was there if she ever wanted to talk, and, yes, there even if she didn't. Starting now, whether she wanted one or not, she had a friend. He would somehow make her understand she was not alone.

Damned foolishness. Crumpling the sign-up sheet, he started to toss it in the wastebasket, then reconsidered, smoothing the page out on his desk so he could stare at Opal Mauntz's name, the curious back slant of her handwriting. A whole new set of inferences now occurred to him. She hadn't selected that last time slot because she wanted more time with him. Her fellow students had just grabbed the earlier ones, and she'd taken the only slot left. Back in her dorm room she'd probably read the lavish praise of his end comments and concluded—hell, he'd *said* as much—that she didn't even need a conference. She must've thought, Why waste his time? And she was right, it would've been a waste, because what could he have said to her? Keep up the good work? She had no need of such advice. No need, apparently, for the larger gift of friendship he'd been prepared to offer. Was it possible he'd actually allowed himself to imagine brief snatches of a conversation between them? *I noticed you outside the gym . . . I was glad you were there . . . I wanted to say hello . . . Normally I can't talk to people, but you looked nice and I thought maybe with you . . .*

Bloody old fool. What had he been thinking?

Feeling resentment welling up inside, he quickly tamped it down. After all, it wasn't the poor girl's fault. Okay, she might at least have phoned to say she wasn't coming, or, if she really couldn't bring herself to speak, zipped him a quick e-mail (though he'd indicated on the syllabus that he preferred not to communicate electronically). Well, he thought gloomily, snapping his briefcase shut, that was that. She was, for all intents and purposes, gone. He had to reconcile himself to the fact—physical realities aside—that he had only eight students, an unacceptably low number for an undergraduate course. Next year, in place of the Austen seminar, he'd be offered a section of comp, an indignity that put him in mind of e. e. cummings's Olaf, who from his knees declares there is some shit he will not eat. A better man than Nate, who, God help him, would probably eat it standing up, for the simple reason that autumn's days grew paradoxically both shorter and longer, each with fewer daylight hours than the one before, even as those same hours were ever harder to fill. But of course there was no point in despairing over next year's class when he'd barely begun this year's. He would just have to accept what couldn't be altered or improved.

And the following Tuesday, there she was, still voiceless and apart. Why, despite his every resolution to put her out of his mind, did she now somehow seem *nearer* than before? And she wasn't really voiceless, in point of fact. She had spoken to him through her essay and would continue to do so. With that in mind he tried his best to address his remarks to the other students, those who actually responded, however inadequately. But try as he might his attention continued to drift back to the Mauntz girl. Sarah Griffith, noticing this, rotated in her chair to regard her silent classmate, then turned back to him with her eyes hooded, her lip curled.

Uncunted

Thoroughly buddyless, Nate spends the morning at the Scuola San Rocco looking at the Tintorettos and trying to imagine the world in which they were created. What was that line from Arnold? The Sea of Faith . . . like a girdle unfurled about the world? Something like that. How comforting it must've been to know that everybody was proceeding from the same basic assumptions about God and creation and arriving at the same conclusions about the eternal existential questions: Who are we? What is our purpose? Yet Nate suspects the shared belief that nurtured Tintoretto must've been every bit as constraining—girdle, indeed—and mean-spirited as the balkanized academy of his own experience, as well as, apparently, the world of contemporary art. In Renaissance Venice, placing the Virgin and infant Jesus anywhere except the exact center of a painting was heresy, akin to suggesting, as Copernicus did, that the earth revolved around the sun and not, as the pope insisted, vice versa. Contemporary Venetians would have regarded such impiety an assault on public virtue, every bit as outrageous and indefensible—not to mention far more dangerous—than hauling a half ton of dirt up four flights of stairs, dumping it on the floor of a decaying warehouse and calling it art. Renaissance painting and architecture were both designed to make the individual feel inconsequential in the grand scheme of things, which to them was, well, grand. Was it the loss of this grandeur, and of the faith that was its foundation, that led to the fragmentation of today's world, to postmodern silliness, art as a sight gag? Possibly, though Nate has little affection for Tintoretto's muscle-bound figures, their heavy, brutal limbs foreshortened to emphasize their relentless determination to climb up and away from Mother Earth. Even his graybearded elders look ripped and ready for battle, which might be why Nate, feeling paunchy, leaves the Scuola San Rocco feeling bullied.

Noon finds him in the Piazza San Marco, sipping a staggeringly expensive cappuccino in an outdoor café and watching the tourists feed pigeons in front of the Doge's Palace. He keeps expecting to see his brother and Renee cross the square, with slow-footed Bernard—no Tintoretto elder, he—trailing in their wake. After all, their chances of reconnecting with Klaus and the others before lunch are no better than his own, which means they, too, are probably wandering around the city, killing time. The sun warming his face, Nate begins to relax, and his resentment toward the three of them—why hadn't they stayed where he left them?—to dissipate. Actually, there's no reason at all to be annoyed with Bernard, who hasn't asked anyone for anything. Or, for that matter, with kind Renee, either. And Julian, well, the prevailing wisdom seems to be that he's just being Julian, so let it go.

According to his new phone's locator app, Trattoria Giacomo, where the group will have lunch, is nearby, only a five-minute walk. Arriving early would make him appear anxious, as if he'd been lingering there all morning, unable to function on his own, and he doesn't want that. On the other hand, it would be good to get there before his brother does. More gratifying by far to join the others in worrying about Julian and Renee and Bernard than to have them worrying about him. The impression Nate would prefer to cultivate among his new acquaintances is that of a man no one needs to fret about, and at the moment, having just spent twenty dollars on a very small cup of coffee, that's exactly how he feels. At twelve-thirty, when he tries his brother's cell one last time and again is sent directly to voice mail, he decides it might be a good idea to at least locate the restaurant. If the others aren't there yet, he can take a leisurely stroll along the Grand Canal until one o'clock.

Not a bad strategy, except the restaurant isn't there. He has no trouble finding the right small, bustling square, which is home to several other restaurants, just not Trattoria Giacomo. Though it's embarrassing to solicit directions to one restaurant in another, he has little choice. None of the waiters he asks, however, has ever heard of the place. Nate tries to make sense of this but simply can't. In the interest of demonstrating that he's not a lunatic, he shows the waiters his phone, enlarging the map so they can see the little teardrop that fixes the establishment he's searching for *exactly* where they're now standing. They are uniformly impressed with the phone, how prettily its excellent graphics represent their little *campo*, but as to this Trattoria Giacomo he's looking for, they can only shrug their shoulders.

Ten minutes later and three *campos* over, he runs across a shopkeeper who nods enthusiastically when Nate again names the restaurant. The man sketches a diagram in the air before them: a right, a left, then a hump, which Nate takes to mean a bridge, then another right—directions that when followed dead-end at a major canal. Backtracking, he consults another shopkeeper, who's also heard of Trattoria Giacomo but claims it's much farther away, and his directions bear no relation to the last set. Only the result is the same. No restaurant. Worse, Nate's no longer even sure which *sestiere* he's in. The streets are virtually empty, which means he's well off the beaten path, but where, exactly? Which beaten path is he off and how goddamn far? When his phone inquires, as it did late last night, if he wants it to make use of his present location, he clicks YES, but the map that then fills the screen is inexplicably of his college town in Massachusetts. Clicking out of the app, he continues to stare at the fucking thing, utterly mystified, as if awaiting further instructions. On the off chance that he entered the name of the restaurant wrong, he types it in again, more carefully this time, but the aggravating little teardrop reappears in the same *campo* as before. Substituting *ristorante* and *osteria* for *trattoria* yields the same result. A trickle of nervous perspiration tracks between his shoulder blades.

Initially concerned about arriving early, he's now a good forty-five minutes late. Why, he wonders, his earlier resentment returning with a vengeance, hasn't Julian called *him*? Obviously, Nate thinks bitterly, because now he'll have the lovely Renee all to himself. But this cynical inference doesn't really hold water, because for all intents and purposes Julian already *has* her to himself.

Nate had *his* chance last night but frittered it away. This morning, when he came downstairs and saw Renee standing by herself in the lobby, he thought about going over and maybe picking up where they'd left off at dinner. It then occurred to him that they'd actually said relatively little to each other. It was open, direct, no-nonsense Evelyn who'd carried the conversation, making everything seem easy. Still, why conduct an autopsy? Let. It. Go.

There's only one thing to do and that's head back to Saint Mark's. At least from there he should be able to find his way back to the hotel. His lower back, he realizes, has begun to stiffen. Sciatic nerve, an old problem. In the next large *campo* he sees the ubiquitous bent arrows pointing toward major Venetian destinations—Ferrovia, Rialto, Accademia—and follows the one for San Marco into a dark, empty *calle,* then another and another, crossing *ponte* after goddamn *ponte,* his lower back now throbbing. Gradually the streets become crowded again, which means he must be getting close, though nothing looks even remotely familiar. Every time he rounds a corner he expects the *calle* he's on to open onto the piazza, and every time he's disappointed. Is he somehow going around in circles? He hasn't felt so completely untethered—*uncunted,* his brother's word, is suddenly a tiny malignancy in his unruly brain—since what happened with Opal Mauntz. Could the two be related? It's a crazy question, of course, further evidence, were any needed, of a disordered mind. Yet he can't help wondering if there was some lesson he failed to learn from that whole ordeal that might explain why he's lost again now. Jesus, he thinks, his fucking phone is right. Physically he's in Italy, but part of him—some ludicrous little Google-Schmoo self—is back home in Massachusetts trying to . . . what? Is this what it feels like to lose your mind? His eyes fill with hot, angry tears. Has he really traveled halfway around the world in order to come completely unglued among strangers?

What he needs to do, and right quick, is pull himself together. Concentrate on the here and now. For instance, is he still on course for Saint Mark's? How many *campos* has he hurried through without even checking the bent arrows? If he can just find the piazza, maybe he'll be able to relocate the relaxed, confident Nate who'd sipped expensive cappuccino there. He'd gladly spend twice as much—no, ten times—to reclaim that emotional tranquility.

In the next square there's an attractive restaurant with outdoor tables, and seeing it Nate knows he's finished. He can go no farther. His shirt is drenched with sweat, his sciatic nerve pulsing to the beat of his respiration. It's hard to believe, but he's been looking for the Trattoria Giacomo for over an hour. The others will already have ordered, and probably finished their first course. To show up now, in this condition, would be beyond humiliating. Better to have a quiet lunch alone. He'll order a small carafe of prosecco and a simple plate of pasta. Gather himself.

When he sets his phone down on the café table it rings, as if a flat surface is all it's been waiting for. "About time," he says, touching the green ANSWER icon. "Where are you?"

"Bethesda," says a familiar voice. "Where should I be?"

"Brenda?" She's the only person he knows who lives there, but why would she be calling him? Surprise, pleasure and confusion struggle for ascendance. "It's good to hear your voice."

"So, how did it go?"

"How did what go?"

"He hasn't asked you?"

"Who?"

A deep sigh on the other end of the line seems to sum up his long-ago fiancée's myriad frustrations with him. "I'm sorry, I thought you were calling about Julian."

"But I *didn't* call you."

"Right. My phone rang. It said: NATE CALLING. I answered and there you were. But if you claim you didn't call me, okay."

"This new phone has a touch screen," he explains. "I must've—"

"Yeah, okay, but here's my question. Why am I there to be touched?"

It takes Nate a moment to understand what she's asking. "They take the data from your old phone—"

"You're missing my point."

This strikes him as entirely possible. "You want me to delete you?"

"No," she says. "What I want is for you to . . ."

He waits, curious as to how she'll finish the sentence, but isn't entirely surprised when she suspends the thought by saying, "Okay, you didn't *mean* to call me. Fine. So, I can hang up now?"

"Please, don't," he says, failing to keep the desperation out of his voice. He feels a powerful urge to tell her everything. That he's lost. That his very reason is under siege. "I need to talk to you . . . to someone . . . I've—"

"You've come all uncunted," she says.

Is his head going to explode? Because it really feels like it might.

"Or so your brother claims."

"When did you speak to Julian?"

"Last night."

Suddenly, a brainstorm. "Are you two getting back together?"

"That's hilarious."

"Oh," he says, relieved. "I guess I—"

"Leapt to an absurd conclusion?"

"So, what does Julian want to ask me about?"

"I promised I wouldn't say anything until he broaches the subject himself. For what it's worth, I'm not sure it's a great idea."

"He's barely said two words to me. It's almost as if he doesn't want people to know we're related."

"Honestly, you two," she says, and when he doesn't react to that, turns the subject back to him, as if all this talk about Julian's behavior is masking the real subject. "Look," she says. "Did you ever see a doctor?"

"I did. They put me on a mild antidepressant," he says, trying to sound rational. He's glad now that he hadn't blurted out everything. "I'm feeling better now."

"You've been able to put it behind you, then? That business with the girl?"

Has she, he wonders again, broken her promise? Last night, when Julian reported that he appeared "uncunted," did she tell him about the Mauntz girl? Because that might explain why Julian's treating him like this. "Sure. You bet. Water under the *ponte*."

She chuckles. "That's pretty good, actually. Water under the *ponte*. You always did have a sneaky sense of humor. Women like that, you know. Are you seeing anyone?"

"No, why?"

"It would be nice, is all."

"You know, I've always wondered," he says, feigning nonchalance. "After you and Julian split up? Was there any possibility for us?"

"Nate." The exhaustion is back in her voice.

"Hell, we could try even now," he continues, knowing all too well that he shouldn't. The need is just too great.

"Tell me something. Because I'm genuinely curious. What are you picturing right now?"

"I don't know what you mean."

"In your head. How are you picturing me? Because I'm an old woman."

True, he wasn't picturing an old woman. Not a young one, either, at least not exactly. Actually, now that he thinks about it, he hadn't been *picturing* her at all.

"Nate?" she says. "Are you still there?"

"Right here."

"See, this is kind of what I was getting at before. On your new phone, which list am I on? Contacts or Favorites."

"Umm—"

"Because I really *shouldn't* be on your Favorites list. You see my point? What really worries me is that after all these years I'm still one of your Favorites. It's balance I'm talking about here. Equilibrium. Okay?"

And then she's gone, the line dead. Has she hung up, or did the phone make another executive decision and disconnect her? Maybe it really is a smart phone. Maybe it knows that if it permitted the conversation to continue he'd only make things worse, that he'd begin blubbering like a pathetic old man. He just sits there, staring at the phone until a question pops onto the screen: RETURN TO FAVORITES?

"Nate?"

Bewildered, he can't immediately source the voice, and when he finally glances up at the woman standing at his elbow he thinks for a lunatic moment it must be Brenda, his ex-fiancée, magically transported all the way to Venice to illustrate what she was telling him earlier—that she's become an old woman. But then he blinks and sees it's Evelyn, from last night. His sluggish brain had her back at the hotel, in bed with a runny nose and a box of tissues, yet here she is.

"Aren't you coming in?" she wants to know.

The depth of his confusion must be obvious, because when he doesn't respond she sits down next to him. "Is it bad news?" she says, nodding at the phone he's still holding.

He's about to say no, then thinks maybe it's simpler and—who knows?—even more truthful to agree.

"Someone died?"

"Yes," he tells her, surprised by this ridiculous lie, by his need to tell it. Yet another falsehood that serves no conceivable purpose.

"I shouldn't intrude," she says, "but may I ask who?"

"A former student," he hears himself say, because of course the Mauntz girl is not water under the *ponte*. "A brilliant girl, but broken."

"Broken how?"

"She couldn't . . ." He stops, suddenly unsure of how to continue, somehow lost, simultaneously, in both the past and the present. "How did you find me?"

Now Evelyn looks confused. "I just noticed you sitting here . . . on my way in," she tells him.

And just that quickly, some small vestige of order and sense is restored to the world. The sign for the restaurant, obscured by its awning until he sat down, comes into focus: TRATTORIA GIACOMO. Difficult though it is to credit, it appears he's actually *at* the very place he's been looking for so helplessly.

"The conversation you were having looked so serious I thought maybe you'd come out here to take the call. But then inside, the others said they hadn't seen you."

"We got separated."

She nods. "So I heard. They only just got here themselves. Do you need a few minutes? Shall I tell them you're still on your call?"

Nate thanks her, says he'll join them momentarily.

Rising, she says, "What was her name?"

He considers telling another lie, inventing some other girl, but he's too tired. "Mauntz. Opal Mauntz. She was the brightest student I ever taught. I feel . . . responsible."

Evelyn rises to her feet and puts a hand on his shoulder. "Nate?" she says. "It's going to be okay. *You're* going to be okay."

"You think so?" Because honestly that doesn't seem likely.

"I do," she assures him. "Can I tell you a secret?"

"Why not?"

Though there's no need, she whispers, dramatically, "I wasn't really sick this morning. Just hungover."

He finds himself smiling, mostly at her extraordinary kindness.

"And *you,*" she continues, "are in charge of making sure that doesn't happen again. You think you're up to it?"

"I'll do my best."

"I'll help in any way I can," she tells him, "but, really, it all comes down to you."

When she's gone, his phone vibrates. There's a new map on the screen, a new teardrop, indicating his current location: Campo San Zaccaria, Venice, as well as the name of the restaurant he's about to enter. And a message: YOU HAVE ARRIVED.

A place near the end of the long table is waiting for him between Evelyn and Bernard, across from Renee and Julian. Except for his brother, who greets him with his customary gruffness, everyone seems delighted he's rejoined the group. Better yet, no one seems either alarmed by his appearance or to be harboring suspicions about his sanity.

Over a first course of saffron risotto he learns what transpired that morning. Apparently someone from the main group noticed the missing four. Bea's husband was then dispatched to find them while Klaus and the rest stayed put. Julian and Renee and Bernard were quickly located in the *campo* where Nate had left them, and together they waited for him to return, concluding when he didn't that he must have linked up with Klaus and the others. When it turned out he hadn't done that either, they had little choice but to resume the morning's schedule of activities.

Asked about his own morning, Nate explains that he spent most of it among the Tintorettos at the Scuola San Rocco, then sipping expensive cappuccino in the Piazza San Marco. He even mentions that his phone sent him on a wild-goose chase, though he plays the whole ordeal as comedy, which in fact is how he's already begun to see it. By the time he finishes, however, he notices that Julian's face has become alarmingly red. It looks like he's either having a heart attack or trying to set a Guinness record for holding one's breath.

"Julian?" he says. "Are you okay?"

He appears to give the question serious thought before saying, "Why don't you just tell me to fuck off?"

To the others, Nate can tell, this seems to come completely out of nowhere. They just sit there, slack-jawed. Nate is surprised, too, but in a different way. His brother has somehow managed to intuit the truth about his morning, that he actually spent it wallowing in a series of bitter sibling resentments, some of which reached back to their childhoods.

"Because that," his brother continues, "I could at least respect."

"I have no idea what you're talking about."

"Fine," Julian replies. "Be that way."

"Be *what* way?"

But Julian apparently has nothing further to say, just applies himself to his risotto.

And in a heartbeat Nate is as furious as he can remember ever being. "Julian," he says, trying to keep his voice steady, "if anyone's got a right to be angry here, it's me. Why is your phone off? Didn't it occur to you that I might be trying to reach you?" He holds out the Recents screen on his phone log, five calls to Julian's number. "Look how many times I tried to call you."

"Bullshit," his brother says, refusing to even glance at the screen. "My phone's been on the whole time."

And indeed, when he shows Nate his own Recents log, there's no trace of his calls. Which only proves, Nate concludes, that he'd somehow deleted them. But the performance? Nate can't help but admire it. When it comes to faking righteous indignation this man has no equal.

"Okay, how come you didn't call *me*?" Nate says, trying not to sound peevish. The worst part of being around Julian is that he immediately reverts to being the little brother, a child who has to appeal to adults for justice.

"I did. And left three different messages." He turns to Renee here. "Didn't I?"

Nate now brandishes his Recents screen—no calls, no messages. This time Julian deigns to look, and when their eyes then meet, Nate sees that same dark thought—that the phone has been edited—occur to Julian. Not to be outdone, Nate entertains a new, contradictory suspicion, that his brother hadn't really called at all, only pretended to, just so that Renee, overhearing, could verify it.

"Try calling me," she suggests now. Clearly, the heated conversation has unsettled her. "Maybe there's something wrong with your phone."

Nate, thinking she's speaking to him, is about to ask for her number, but Julian evidently already has it in his phone and is anxious to demonstrate there's nothing wrong with *his*. He touches the screen, and a moment later Renee's purse rings. To Nate's surprise she fishes the phone out and actually answers it, as if the caller might be someone other than Julian.

"Hi," Julian says, in his best salesman's voice, directly into his phone, though the person at the other end of the line is sitting right next to him. "This is Julian speaking. Tell my brother he never could lie worth a shit."

"Umm," Renee says, and for a moment Nate thinks she's going to do as instructed, but then he sees she's looking at Bernard, who's slumped over sideways in his chair. His fork clatters to the floor.

By the time the water ambulance arrives, Bernard is conscious again. He tells the EMTs (with Klaus translating) not to worry, that this happens from time to time. He has low blood pressure and it's been too long between meals. But his voice is not robust like it was this morning, and he's very pale. The consensus is that he should go to the hospital and get checked out. Also that someone from the Biennale group should accompany him. Nate presupposes that as the only one fluent in Italian Klaus will assume this duty, but then the rest of them would miss out on the afternoon's exhibitions they'd all paid for. Bea offers to go, but somebody points out it should probably be a man. Everyone's looking at Nate, who is, after all, the sick man's buddy.

And so when Bernard, assisted by two medics, is lowered into the bobbing ambulance, Nate follows, his stomach protesting audibly. He'd eaten only a few bites of risotto, which he now realizes was delicious. The next course was to have been grilled branzino, his favorite. Still, it's perhaps just as well that he and Julian go to neutral corners and think things over. And that the others apparently consider him sufficiently competent and trustworthy is a vote of confidence that buoys his spirits. As the ambulance pulls away, he watches them file back into the restaurant. Evelyn and Renee pause to wave goodbye, and Nate wonders if his brother, under the circumstances, will relent and offer a conciliatory wave, but of course he doesn't. Is it possible Julian was telling the truth, that he really did try to call him this morning? Doesn't Nate owe him the benefit of the doubt? And what was it Brenda had let slip on the phone—that there was some mysterious subject that Julian was anxious to broach? What was that all about? She said she didn't think it was a great idea, which probably meant it was just another of his financial schemes, but on the other hand, maybe not.

Chastened by doubt, he calls Julian again, prepared to apologize for the misunderstanding, if that's what it was, and to suggest they have dinner tonight, just the two of them, and hash things out.

But the call goes directly to voice mail.

The Littlest Dean

A month into the term, Nate heard someone climbing his front porch steps late one afternoon, and a moment later the doorbell rang. The day before he'd seen two clean-cut young men carrying Bibles in the neighborhood, so when he answered the door he expected to see missionaries. So out of place was the dean of students on his porch that he didn't recognize her until he saw her trademark red roadster parked at the curb.

"Greta," he said, unable to conceal his surprise. She was carrying a split of red wine, which made him smile. A good dozen years younger, Greta Silver was still attractive. She might even have qualified as voluptuous if she hadn't been so tiny. Arriving on campus thirty years earlier as an assistant dean for student affairs, she was immediately dubbed "Dean Barbie" by the kids, and the name stuck. To Nate she looked like someone who ought to live in one of those model homes where the furniture is scaled down to give the false impression of spaciousness. In her extremely small hand the half bottle looked regulation size. Only when transferred to Nate's own hand did it seem comically minute. Who brings a split of wine as a gift?

"Wow," she said, taking a seat in his front room. "This is *nice*."

He understood her amazement, of course. This working-class neighborhood was in decline and had been from the time he'd moved in. His was one of the few cared-for houses on the block.

"You were expecting . . . ?"

"No," she said quickly, embarrassed. "It makes sense. I guess I never thought . . ."

He wasn't sure he wanted to know exactly what "makes sense" and why, so he let her off the hook. "Shall I open this?"

"I don't think you'll be able to pour it otherwise."

He glanced at his watch. "Bit early?" he ventured, as it was four-fifteen.

"Clearly you've never been a dean of students."

When he returned, she was standing next to his reading chair, browsing his bookcase, or pretending to. On an end table was the second batch of essays from his Austen seminar, the last of which he'd just finished marking up. Opal Mauntz's was on top, and Nate had the distinct impression that while he was uncorking the wine Greta had been reading either the essay itself or, more likely, his copious comments. The topic of her essay was "The Overlooked Male," and it was even more impressive than her first effort, almost as if she was determined to show him that he hadn't been critical enough of that earlier paper, that she could do even better. At the top of the essay he'd emblazoned an A plus.

"I'm sorry," Greta said when he handed her a glass, and for a moment he thought she might confess to snooping. "You'd just made yourself a cup of tea."

He would've liked to deny this, but the cup sat there next to the essays, still steaming.

"I didn't mean to insult you before," she said, returning to her chair. "It's just . . . if you showed somebody this room and asked them who lived here, they'd never guess a bachelor."

"My brother claims I was born an old woman."

She nodded, her brow knit. "I didn't know you had a brother."

Nate opened his mouth to say something about Julian, then decided not to. "That car at the curb?" he said, trying a different tack. "Not many would guess it belongs to a dean of students at a liberal arts college. And a woman at that."

"Women don't get to have midlife crises?"

"Sure, but don't you worry someone will report its present location to said dean's husband?" Because frankly Nate did. He and Greta had dated briefly back in the day, but she'd broken things off before their relationship reached the point where he felt comfortable enough to ask her over. The reason she'd given was Barry, the head of campus security, whom she'd been seeing prior to Nate. According to some, it was Nate who'd provided him with the motivation he needed to propose. At any rate, not long after Nate had been given his unconditional release, they'd gotten married. That would have been the end of the story if Barry hadn't been both jealous and inordinately curious about just how far things had progressed between the two of them. Nate suggested she put his mind at ease, but she apparently considered her husband's jealousy "sweet." The man put Nate in mind of a dog that belonged to a family that lived across the street when he was a boy. They'd assured Nate that he didn't bite, but this evidently meant that he didn't bite *them*. The first chance the miserable little cur got, he bit Nate on the ankle, and then every time Nate passed, always on the other side of the street, the animal regarded him darkly, as if the business between them was unfinished. Now, whenever their paths crossed on campus, Barry gave him that same look.

"He's in South Carolina," Greta said. "Not that he cares much where I park these days."

Nate took a sip of wine and offered a fervent prayer that she didn't intend to elaborate.

"So, how are things going with Opal Mauntz?"

Since this new subject was only slightly more welcome than the last, he considered carefully how and even whether to answer. From his point of view, things weren't going well at all, the poor girl still alone on her island, ignored by her classmates and, Nate felt certain, in dire need of a friend. Worse, he was ashamed to admit he'd followed Greta's hard-hearted advice about how to treat her.

"It's a simple question, Nate," she said, when the silence dragged on.

"I know," he agreed. "It's the answer that's complex."

"I don't see why it should be."

"Read this," he said, handing her the most recent essay.

Greta took it reluctantly, deepening Nate's suspicion that she'd already taken a look, though it was possible she didn't consider the girl's written work germane to their discussion. To Nate, it was the heart of the matter. Noting the grade on top, she flipped quickly through the text, then lingered thoughtfully over his end comments before dropping the essay in her lap and studying him openly. "Is something amusing?"

"Well, you did exactly what *they* all do. Students. They start with the grade and skip straight to the rationale for it, as if both were unrelated to everything in between."

"Nate. Correct me if I'm wrong, but you wanted me to read this so I'd know Opal Mauntz is brilliant and special. I already knew that."

"But she doesn't speak."

"That's not true," she said, holding up the essay like exhibit 1. "She's speaking in this. To you."

"It's not enough," he said. "You must see how wrong it is to have a voice and not use it."

"You want to *hear* her speak."

"Of course I do."

"Then she hasn't?"

"Not a syllable."

Greta actually seemed relieved to hear this, and Nate could feel his anger and frustration with her rising dangerously.

"And you've had no contact with her outside the classroom?"

"Of course not," he said, but then realized this wasn't quite true. "Some mornings I see her at the gym. She works out early. So do I."

"Is that a coincidence?"

"That should go without saying."

"And you don't . . . *speak* there."

"Oh, for Christ's sake, Greta," he said, allowing his voice to rise. "What is this about?"

"There's been talk," she said.

The sip of wine he took was too large, and he felt himself nearly gag in swallowing it. "Remember when you first came to campus?" he said. He was crossing a line now, and he knew it. "You were only a couple years older than the seniors. There was talk then, too."

He expected her to be furious, but all she did was meet and hold his gaze. "In one instance it was true, in fact," she said. "Repeat that and I'll deny it."

They sat in uncomfortable silence for what seemed like forever.

"One of your other students came to see me."

Nate didn't have to be told which. Sarah Griffith. The girl who'd noticed his interest in Opal when he returned that first set of essays.

"And I've reached out to a couple other students from the seminar."

"Reached out."

"You're not accused of anything at this point," she conceded. "But everyone seems to agree that something's off."

"What does *off* mean?"

"*Amiss. Subtext* was the word they seemed to be searching for. They said it's like you aren't really talking to anyone else, just pretending to include them."

"Maybe *they* aren't really listening. Just pretending to."

"Are you hearing your*self* right now? How defensive you sound?"

In truth he was, and only his justifiable outrage at her insinuations prevented him from admitting as much. Instead he asked, "Has it occurred to you that you could be wrong about this girl?"

"Yes, it has. Has it occurred to you that *you* might be?" When he had no immediate response, she set down her wineglass, unsipped, as far as he could tell. "It may not seem like it, Nate, but I'm actually on your side in all this."

"You're right, it doesn't seem like it. But that's hardly the point. It's Opal Mauntz's side we should both be on."

"I'm thinking about removing her from your class."

"You have no such authority."

"I'm responsible for the safety of all our students."

"And you think I'm a danger to Opal Mauntz?"

"Has it occurred to you that she might be a danger to you?"

This surprised him. "You said yourself she wasn't violent."

"There are other dangers."

"What are you suggesting, Greta?"

"How long have you taught here, Nate? Have you ever known another student who labored under so many challenges?" She gave him a moment to digest this. "Why is she here, Nate?"

"She's brilliant," Nate said, now surprised by how naïve this sounded.

"But why is she *here*?"

"You tell me."

"Have you ever seen a list of the college's mega-donors? No? You might want to have a look." She rose now, smoothing her skirt. Nate knew he should rise, too, but he wasn't sure he trusted his legs. "And while you're in research mode," she went on, her hand on the doorknob, "you might want to read up on Asperger's syndrome."

"Are you saying that's what's wrong with Opal?"

"I'm suggesting you open your eyes," she said. And then she was gone.

Fire

The hospital is crowded and they have to wait forever. A physician finally listens to Bernard's heart and lungs, and peers into his eyes. He speaks very little English but has the utmost confidence in his limited vocabulary, so after the physical exam is concluded, their ensuing conversation, at least to Nate, resembles a game of charades. He half expects each hard-won understanding to be celebrated by either Bernard or the doctor enthusiastically tapping the tip of his nose, then holding up two fingers for *second syllable*. The doctor doesn't seem terribly troubled by Bernard's fainting. Yes, his blood pressure is low, but not alarmingly so. After all, he is not a young man, *and* he has pushed himself physically more than is his habit, *and* he has just flown across the Atlantic, *and* he has gone too long without food. He recommends salt tablets, less exertion and frequent snacks ("fruit in-a the pocket") in between activities. Nor does he rule out the possibility that the Biennale itself might have caused Bernard to faint. "Art?" he says, waving the exhibits away contemptuously. "Pah! Titian? Art. Bellini? Art. Giorgione? Art."

"Tintoretto?" Nate offers hopefully when the doctor's voice falls.

"Art!" the man thunders. "Biennale? Is no art!"

It turns out that both the ambulance and the consultation services are provided to tourists at no charge. "Amazing," Bernard says when they are so informed. "Our own government won't pay for our health care, but the Italian government does."

In a water taxi back to the hotel, Bernard says he's going to rest until dinner. Nate, too, is worn out, but after missing the morning's exhibits he feels he should at least try to link up with the others. When he calls his brother's cell, though, once more it's voice mail. "Julian?" he says when he's invited to leave a message. "It's me. Again. I don't know if you got my last message, but let's have dinner tonight. I'm sorry if I've done something to upset you. Let's sort it all out, okay?"

He hangs up as the taxi glides beneath the Rialto Bridge. "Question," he says to Bernard, who was clearly listening. "You spent the morning with my brother. What do you make of him?"

Bernard appears to give this serious consideration. "Well," he says finally, "I'm trying to think if I've *ever* liked anybody named Julian."

There's a *farmacia* across the *campo* from the hotel, so Bernard tromps off to buy his salt tablets. It's now late afternoon, and Nate decides he'll take a short nap, maybe dispel the last of his jet lag. According to the schedule, the others are due back at the hotel at six and are free to make their own dinner plans. Before he can head upstairs, however, he's summoned by Giancarlo at the front desk, who lowers his voice confidentially, though only the two of them are in the lobby.

"You . . . brother," the man begins, his demeanor one of profound embarrassment.

"Julian?"

"Yes-a," he agrees, apparently pleased that Nate doesn't intend to deny the relationship. "He say . . ."

And here he pushes a document, still warm from the printer, across the counter. It's in Italian, of course, but Nate recognizes it as his brother's hotel bill. They'd all paid half of their stay in advance, with the rest to be settled upon arrival. He and Julian each provided a credit card when checking in. Yet it seems—here Giancarlo shrugs—there's a problem with his brother's.

"He say . . . ," he repeats, his face the color of Chianti.

When Nate hands him his own card, the man lights up. "*Grazie*," he says, beaming with delight and mutual understanding. "*Perfetto*."

Only when Nate is up in his room does it occur to him to be puzzled. Having more than once had problems himself with credit cards in Europe, he first assumed that Julian has failed to inform the company that he'd be traveling abroad. But he's too experienced to have forgotten such a detail. He's also vain about the sheer number of cards in his wallet, and all their impressive colors—gold, silver, platinum, black. Surely one of them would have worked for such a modest amount.

But never mind, he tells himself. After all, it's pretty far down on the list of things he and his brother need to get to the bottom of tonight, assuming Julian hasn't already made dinner plans with Renee. That possibility would have troubled him if he weren't so utterly exhausted. But he's asleep before his head hits the pillow.

And for the second time, Nate dreams of fire. This time there's screaming—his mother's, of course, and his own, and perhaps even Julian's. The fire itself has a voice, a high-pitched shriek so loud that when he jolts awake Nate can't quite believe his ringing phone is the only sound in the room. Though the wooden shutters are open to the cool Venetian night, he's in another flop sweat, his undershirt soaked through. He swings his legs over the side of the bed and shakes his head, trying to dispel the aura of the dream and unwilling to answer the phone until he does. According to his watch, it's nine-thirty, but how could that possibly be? Judging by how groggy he is, he must've slept deeply—but for five and a half hours? Have the others returned to the hotel and gone out again without him? EVELYN CALLING, his phone tells him. When he says hello, there's a slight hesitation on the other end of the line, as if the caller had been about to hang up. "Nate?"

"Yes."

"Is Julian with you?"

He wonders stupidly why Julian would be in this room when he has a room of his own, then says, "No, he isn't."

"We're afraid something's happened to him," she continues. "He said he was going to the gents, but that was over an hour ago, and the waiter says there's no one in there. We don't know what to do."

"I don't understand. Where are you?"

"At the restaurant."

"Which one?"

"The Gondolieri. You were supposed to meet us here two hours ago. Julian said he e-mailed you the directions."

Nate checks his phone. Three e-mails have come in while he slept, but none of them are from Julian.

"And I sent you a text."

He's about to tell her he didn't receive that either when he notices there is indeed a text message. *Not lost again, I hope? Forget the name of the restaurant? Gondolieri. Once again, the wine is flowing. Have you forgotten your promise to keep me sober?*

"I'm sorry," he tells her. "I fell asleep."

"Nate?"

"Yes?"

"Can you tell me what's going on? Your brother's very angry with you. Did something happen?"

She means now, today, in Venice, but because the fire dream's still so fresh in his mind Nate makes a connection that might not have occurred to him otherwise. Yes, Julian *is* angry and has been forever. He was seventeen at the time of the fire, and he never forgave their mother her criminal carelessness. Even that first night at the hospital, when they didn't know for sure—with third-degree burns over half her body—whether she'd live or die, he'd already made up his mind. In fact, he was so intent on blaming her that he didn't even notice when the medication wore off and she cried out in pain. "It's her own fault," he insisted angrily. "You *know* she drinks herself to sleep every night. You've *seen* the cigarette burns in there. On the nightstand. The bedspread. Her fucking *pillow*. That's how she falls asleep, night after night. It's like she's been *trying* to kill all of us."

What Nate remembers most vividly is that his brother's anger seemed directed as much at him as their mother. As if Nate's sympathy for her, his refusal to be angry, somehow made him her accomplice. "But she never meant for anything like this to happen," Nate, then fifteen, had argued, because that, surely, was true. Okay, maybe she was depressed and maybe there were times when she wanted to die, but he simply couldn't accept that she ever wanted *them* dead. That Julian actually believed she did was almost as upsetting as the fire itself. What he needed more than anything, he remembers thinking, was for Julian *to stop acting like this*. Unfortunately, you only had to glance at him to know he had his own needs right then, and Nate's didn't come into it.

All night long and well into the next day their mother screamed, sometimes calling out their names. Did she even know they were alive?

"Don't you *dare* go in there," Julian told him sternly, as if he'd voiced an intention to. They'd been told, of course, that due to the risk of infection it would be several days before they'd be allowed to see her, but it wasn't this prohibition Julian was cautioning him about. Rather, he was warning Nate against *wanting* to go in there, against *wanting* to comfort and be comforted, against *wanting* to touch and speak, against *wanting* to forgive.

So, yes, Evelyn, Nate would like to say, you are correct. Something *did* happen between them, something that's made them fundamentally distrustful of each other, that's undermining every impulse toward brotherly affection. Sure, it happened fifty years ago, but nothing's changed. Julian is still seething, still furious with Nate for being so . . . for being *himself.* As if he could be otherwise. As if by being himself he's demonstrating unnatural, perverse obstinacy.

According to Evelyn, Julian had seemed out of sorts right from the start of the evening, his agitation becoming more pronounced when Nate failed to arrive at the restaurant. Renee suggested that maybe one of them should go back to the hotel and see if he was there. Maybe he never got Julian's e-mail. Hadn't he indicated at lunch that something was wrong with his phone?

But Julian insisted this was bullshit. There was nothing wrong with the goddamn phone. Something was wrong with *Nate.* He'd always been a passive-aggressive little shit, and this was just an attempt to embarrass him publicly. When asked exactly what there was for him to be embarrassed about, though, Julian wouldn't say, and as the evening progressed he grew increasingly morose, refusing to allow himself to be drawn into the conversation. Finally, when dessert was served, he rose from the table and said he was going to the men's room. Worried when he didn't return, Renee phoned him, but the call went directly to voice mail.

"She's very upset," Evelyn adds, when Nate admits to being baffled by the particulars of his brother's behavior. "And I'm worried, too. I know it's silly, but I can't get what Klaus said earlier out of my head. About how we'd be lucky if somebody didn't end up floating in the canal? You don't think Julian's suicidal, do you?"

The idea of Julian taking his own life is laughable, and Nate's about to say so when he, too, is visited by the mental image of Julian's body floating lifeless in the black water. Shaking it off, he suggests that she and Renee stay put, that he'll leave now, and it shouldn't take more than ten minutes to get to the restaurant. Then, whatever this is about, they'll figure it out together. Evelyn gives him backup directions in case his phone's locator app fails again, but when he types in *Gondolieri Ristorante,* a map pops up that correctly puts him at the hotel and the restaurant on the other side of the Accademia Bridge, right where it's supposed to be.

In the lobby, when Nate steps out of the elevator, Giancarlo seems embarrassed again and motions for him to come over to the desk, but whatever he wants it will have to wait. Despite the hour the bridge is bustling with tourists returning from dinner and Nigerians selling knockoff handbags. Nate takes the stairs three at a time right to the top, pausing there to catch his breath. Directly below, a man standing in the back of a water taxi looks for all the world like his brother. "Julian!" he calls, but the man doesn't react. He shouts again, louder this time, as the taxi slides beneath the bridge. Just as the figure disappears, is there an instant of recognition? Nate hurries over to the other side of the bridge, but when the taxi emerges again, no one is standing in the back.

A Learned Man

It was Thursday afternoon when the dean visited, so Nate had a long weekend to consider the wisdom of his plan for Monday afternoon's class. Though he'd neatly parried her thrust, Greta Silver's suggestion that he might be dangerously mistaken about Opal Mauntz did bring him up short, and on the off chance that she might be right he went online to read up on Asperger's. He already knew enough about the syndrome not to be terribly surprised by what he found. Like the Mauntz girl, most Asperger's sufferers struggled with social interaction, often avoiding eye contact and failing to make friends, even refusing to speak to people they didn't like. And like Opal their emotional range often appeared stunted. What was surprising, though, were the secondary symptoms; AS victims were frequently wedded to inflexible routines and many were physically clumsy, which of course brought to mind both the girl's single-minded doggedness on the StairMaster and her injuring herself on it. Still, he reasoned, wasn't this litany of symptoms—suggestive as it seemed at first glance—rather like those character descriptions as defined by astrological signs, broad enough to apply to an incredibly wide range of people? Didn't his other students exhibit at least a few of these same indicators? Wasn't Sarah Griffith, for instance, essentially devoid of empathy and concern for others?

More tellingly, as Nate saw it, there was another cluster of symptoms that didn't fit with what he'd observed in Opal Mauntz at all. Many AS sufferers not only spoke but in fact exhibited extreme verbosity, giving long-winded lectures on subjects of interest only to themselves. Others possessed abnormally large vocabularies but used pet words in rambling, incoherent sentences, "word soups" devoid of meaning. Nuance escaped them;

ambiguity angered them. Preferring straightforward nonfiction, where facts could be controlled, people with Asperger's often saw little merit in fictional narratives. For them, Jane Austen would be a minefield, and writing about her with precision and elegance and grace would be impossible. Yet that was exactly where Opal Mauntz excelled.

Still, much as he would have liked to reject Greta's diagnosis out of hand, he simply couldn't and was moreover aware that as dean of students, she might know things to which he had no access. To make matters more complicated, AS sometimes overlapped with other syndromes, causing its victims to be that much more difficult to diagnose and treat. What particularly angered Nate was the dean's disinterest in reading the girl's essay, her stubborn determination to focus on his own behavior rather than Opal Mauntz's plight—however they chose to define it. Her threat to remove her from the seminar had the unintended consequence of stiffening his resolve, as did what he'd learned about her father, an alum of the college. A wealthy investment banker with residences in Manhattan, London and the Bahamas, he'd joined the board of trustees a decade earlier, and though he seldom visited the college in person, attending most board meetings by teleconference, he'd made several staggering donations. His daughter's threadbare clothing had initially led Nate to believe she must be a scholarship student, not from one of the richest families on the East Coast, but now it was hard not to see her self-presentation as a repudiation of her father and everything he stood for. And while that scorn might have been abstract and political, what if it wasn't? Why, until this semester, had Opal Mauntz not taken a single course with a male professor? Was it possible she not only loathed her father but also feared him? This was pure speculation, of course, yet Nate felt a pattern was emerging, one that compelled him to reconsider his assumptions. Maybe Greta Silver knew more about Opal than he did, but what if she knew—or suspected—less? What if she was really more worried about Mr. Mauntz than his daughter? Or if the advice she'd been giving him—to pretend Opal wasn't there—wasn't just wrong, but dangerous. Maybe what the girl needed most was to understand that there were men in the world who could be trusted.

It rained hard all weekend, stripping the trees of their last foliage, though on Tuesday the sun came out, and by the time Nate arrived on campus the crisp autumn air was redolent of burning leaves. Greta's husband, apparently back from his travels, was supervising the blaze. Leaning against his university pickup, he watched, unblinking, as Nate pulled into the faculty lot and walked across the quad to Modern Languages, as if the professor represented a greater danger to the college than wind-borne sparks. Had Greta told him about her visit?

In his office Nate took his fourth antacid tablet of the day and reminded himself, as he'd been doing all weekend, that there was nothing pedagogically unsound about the prose workshop he meant to conduct during the second half of today's class. In the first, they'd discuss *Northanger Abbey,* the next Austen novel on the syllabus, but since Wednesday marked the beginning of fall break, many students were already halfway out the door, and few in his seminar would have started the reading. So in the final forty-five minutes, prior to his handing back their essays, they'd examine in detail two substantial passages from the most recent batch, excerpts he'd selected and retyped without authorial attribution. Was it the very necessity of this exercise, he wondered, that prompted his students' deep, nearly universal resentment of it? They understood and grudgingly accepted that their arguments were supposed to be persuasive, their theses clearly articulated, their supporting evidence effectively marshaled. They'd all taken and passed the required composition course where these principles had been drilled into them. Still, most of his students, even the English majors, were content for their meaning to loiter in the shadows of their murky prose, as if clarity were a responsibility shared by both writer and reader. His prose workshops flew in the face of their unshakable conviction that the essays they turned in were a private matter strictly between them and him, sort of like therapy or confession. "What if you were taking a painting class?" he inquired when they made this claim. "Wouldn't your work be public—and an implied object of criticism—from the start?" If you couldn't discuss the specifics of good writing in an English class, then where? To assuage the worst of their fears, he was careful to preface each session by reminding everyone that he'd chosen these particular passages precisely because the problems they highlighted were so common. Predictably, they were not persuaded. Because this *wasn't* a painting class and because having their shortcomings, whether unique or not, put under a microscope was humiliating. If they'd known when the workshops were coming, they'd have skipped class en masse.

None of this, however, was why he was eating antacids today. His misgivings—okay, they were grave ones—derived from the fact that today's iteration would be different. For one thing he'd never conducted a workshop in a seminar; they were far more effective in survey courses with students drawn from a variety of academic disciplines, allowing the various writers' anonymity to be mostly preserved. Here, since many of the students—setting aside Opal Mauntz—would've discussed their proposed topics in advance of actually writing the essays, anonymity was a transparent ruse. More important, the second excerpt he'd selected was from the essay that Greta Silver had declined to read. It was difficult to justify putting such an accomplished piece of writing on the worksheet. What was there to say about it except *This is what you should be striving for*? On the other hand, the passage eloquently answered the question that had been stumping B students from the beginning of time: *Why isn't my B an A?* Surely on these grounds alone its inclusion could be justified. The others would know the work was hers, sure, but what of it?

Of course the real problem was that he'd chosen Sarah Griffith's essay for unflattering comparison. But really, could you blame him? She, more than any of the rest, seemed to feel entitled to an A grade she couldn't earn, and when she didn't get it, her conclusion was that her professor's unreasonably high expectations had cheated her out of it. Why not demonstrate how wrongheaded this was to both her and her classmates, most of whom actually seemed to admire her pretentious, awkward, jargon-riddled prose? Besides, in addition to his many valid reasons for putting the Griffith girl's work under scrutiny, there was an ugly personal motive as well: it was she, Nate was certain, who'd gone to the dean to complain about his behavior.

But never mind. In all probability, he thought, rising from his desk chair and gathering his things, his anxiety was groundless. In the end these prose workshops never ended up as rigorous as planned. When push came to shove, he'd remind himself that the writer was only nineteen or twenty and could hardly be blamed for the culture of carelessness he or she had grown up in. Invariably, the poor kid's hangdog, mortified expression identified him as the offending author, and then Nate always relented, unwilling to cause him any serious embarrassment. The same thing would probably happen today. He'd measure Sarah Griffith's reaction to being selected, and if she appeared more apprehensive than indignant, he could always tone down his remarks by emphasizing, as he generally did, that in and of themselves any mistakes you could correct with a pencil were relatively minor, significant only when their cumulative effect undermined the whole. His purpose was merely to prove how something good, with a little fine-tuning, could become special, which after all was the goal.

In the doorway to the tiny office he shared with an adjunct poet, who was away this term on a visiting-writer gig, Nate paused to wonder, not for the first time, if he'd stayed too long. The college had been good to him. He'd been decently paid, fairly treated. Why hadn't he made a clean break like the rest of his retiring colleagues? Was it possible that the dean's visit last week wasn't about the Mauntz girl at all, but simply because he'd overstayed his welcome? Had he, without meaning to, become the guest still seated when the rest of the dinner party pushed back their chairs to go home, the one who ignores the yawns of his host, pours himself one last glass of port and takes his leave only when he glimpses the hostess in her terry-cloth robe turning off the kitchen lights and heading upstairs?

Indeed it was possible. But it was also possible his mistake had been in accepting the dinner invitation in the first place. He'd been a competent, dutiful teacher, but not—he knew deep down—a really good one. He often liked individual students, but in a classroom of forty or fifty, his spirits routinely plummeted. As a young professor he'd tried to convince himself that over time he would cleave to the work, or at least come to see it as vital and necessary, as turned out to be the case, but he knew he'd never be a natural, and so his fear that he just wasn't cut out for academic life festered. When finally granted tenure, he'd celebrated, like many of his colleagues, by buying a house. These properties were all close to campus, many within walking distance. They bought as much house as they could afford in neighborhoods where their children could enroll in the best schools. The house Nate bought in the poor, working-class hamlet was a good twenty minutes away—even more in winter—and was in such ruinous condition that his peers shook their heads and wondered if he'd lost his mind. Not one suspected that the place appealed to him not *in spite* of how much work it needed but *because* of it.

That house had excellent bones, though, and over the next decade he methodically restored it, usually working alone, though he'd hire a scholarship student when a task required an extra pair of hands. It always surprised him how much he enjoyed these students' company in a nonacademic setting, and they appeared to enjoy his as well. They invariably remarked on how different he seemed when dressed in jeans and work boots, with a tool belt around his waist and his tweed jacket hung on a hook in the mudroom. They didn't say they *liked* him more then, or that he was better at teaching carpentry or plumbing than romantic poetry, but he could tell that's what they meant. The same day he was promoted, in an irony no English professor was likely to miss, he received a letter from Mrs. Handscombe, who was writing to tell him her husband had fallen off a roof and broken his back the previous spring; he'd survived that, but later contracted an infection and died. Going through his things, she'd run across an old photograph of the two of them and wanted Nate to know that over the years her husband had often wondered if he was enjoying his life as a man of learning. Had that been *her* phrase, he wondered, or her husband's?

But what did it matter when the error in judgment had occurred? In any case, he decided, closing the office door behind him and starting down the deserted corridor toward the seminar room, this would be his last year. Even if he were offered a course next fall, he'd decline. It was time. Which made this, with only five weeks left, his last seminar and that much more important. What difference did it make if he'd never been a natural? He'd learned to do the job, and in the time remaining he would do it as well as he could. Why, now that he was on the brink, should he be timid? Normally, he didn't read the passages on the worksheet out loud, but today he thought he might. *Hearing* words could be instructive. The tongue often tripped precisely where the mind stumbled, and elegance was as much a function of the ear as the eye.

Really, though, it came down to this. He was determined that the others should hear Opal Mauntz's voice, even if it had to come out of his own mouth.

Batshit

So, then, it's even worse than what he's been fearing all along. He's losing his mind.

Really, what other explanation is there? Because the man slipping under the Accademia Bridge can't have been his brother. From the restaurant it's an easy walk back to the hotel, and on such a lovely night there's no reason for Julian to take a taxi, and where else, at this hour, would he be going? Therefore, if it *wasn't* Julian he saw, then Nate's mind is playing tricks on him. His senses are no longer to be trusted. Also supporting this thesis there is, well, the whole day, starting that morning with his inability to locate his entire troop, then getting lost trying to find the restaurant, not to mention the phantom phone call to his ex-fiancée. And finally, after inviting his brother to dinner to hash things out, falling asleep for five hours and missing dinner entirely.

If he *is* losing his mind, then much of this behavior makes a certain kind of sense. His subconscious, somehow, is now in charge. Earlier, desperate and lost, he'd wanted to talk to Brenda, so the back of his brain managed to phone her without troubling the front. And she was right to chide him about still being on his list of Favorites after all these years. And while falling asleep for five hours this evening might be attributed to jet lag, a far-better explanation would be that part of him feared a confrontation with Julian, who as always would emerge triumphant. Though he sometimes hates his brother and maybe even wishes him gone, he's also terrified of being utterly alone in the world, so after Evelyn mentioned a body floating dead in the canal Nate's subconscious had restored Julian to life by placing him, hale and healthy, in a water taxi. These events all add up to a case study in avoidance; he's alternately blamed his own phone, his brother's phone, and Julian himself, but it's time to face the ugly truth. At the airport Julian had taken one look at him and known something was terribly wrong. Odd that the loss of his rationality, a ghastly possibility earlier in the day, should be so exhilarating now, but it is. Because if he's really batshit, then he's also off the hook. He can stop feeling responsible for his failures, past and present. Surely a drowning man, exhausted and alone in a sea of self-doubt and recrimination, is at some point allowed to welcome the water into his lungs.

If he's crazy, then it follows that the world is sane. By the time he arrives at Ristorante Gondolieri, he reasons, rational order will probably have been restored without any assistance from him. If for some reason Julian did momentarily go off the rails, there'll be some perfectly logical explanation. After all, his brother is not a young man. Perhaps before leaving the States he was given some new medication that's interacted badly with something else he's taking. By now he's had the opportunity to reflect on his boorish behavior, realize he owes his dinner companions a profound apology and has returned, hangdog, to offer it. Even his abrupt disappearance from the restaurant will somehow turn out to be perfectly sensible. Maybe in the men's room Julian realized he'd left his wallet at the hotel and went back for it, made a wrong turn and got lost. Hadn't much the same thing happened to Nate himself? Right now, over grappa, Julian's probably explaining, to great comic effect, how it all played out.

But no, when Nate arrives, he can see from the restaurant's foyer that except for the waiters, busily turning the chairs upside down on nearby tables, it's just the two women inside. He almost doesn't recognize Evelyn, who instead of one of her signature tracksuits is wearing a sleeveless black dress and a necklace and, unless Nate's mistaken, makeup. Renee looks different as well, though in her case it isn't the attire. She usually gives the appearance of being on the cusp of a panic attack, but now she looks like whatever she's been dreading has come to pass. Both women seem genuinely relieved to see him, and this causes Nate's newly identified inner lunatic to grin maniacally. They wouldn't be so pleased if they knew the man who stood before them was in fact completely uncunted. (For the first time, his brother's terminology seems appropriate.)

"We're sorry to drag you here," Evelyn tells him. "We should've just gone back to the hotel."

"We didn't know what to do," Renee adds.

Clearly, they're under the misguided impression that *he* will, and their faith in him stirs something like regret, because he's always wanted to be someone women could depend on. He should probably confess to these two that he's merely feigning competence, but they've apparently had a rough evening and he can't bring himself to disappoint either of them further. Why not pretend a little longer?

So, though a waiter has apparently done this already, he locates the men's room and checks the stall to make sure that his brother, for reasons unknown, isn't hiding in it. Then he goes outside and surveys the square in case Julian has fallen asleep on a bench or isn't smoking yet another cigarette alongside the small canal. And, yes, he even glances in the canal itself for any floating bodies. Finally, going back inside the restaurant, still faking competence, he asks Evelyn what he imagines a movie detective might—whether Julian said or did anything peculiar right before leaving the table.

"Actually, it was all rather peculiar," she admits. "He said several very cruel things to Renee."

"Like what?" Nate says, because while Julian certainly can be mean-spirited, it really is out of character for him to be anything but charming to an attractive woman he isn't married to.

"It was probably my—"

"No," Evelyn says sternly, as if to a child. "It was *not* your fault." She waits until she's sure Renee doesn't intend to challenge her on this point before turning her attention back to Nate. "There's no need to repeat the actual words."

Something about how Evelyn says this suggests she plans to tell him later, just not now, in front of her friend. "Was he, like, joking?" Nate says. "I mean, trying to be funny?"

"No," Evelyn insists, apparently certain of this much. "He was trying to *hurt her feelings*."

"I don't really think he—" Renee tries to interject.

"Don't make excuses," Evelyn says, taking her hand. "You know I'm right."

"It's just . . . ," she says, utterly bewildered. "He was so nice the rest of the day . . ."

"I know, sweetie. I know how much you liked him," she says, "but Nate's here now and you like him, too."

Renee regards Nate seriously, as if to determine whether this can be so, then says to Evelyn, "We shouldn't have come."

"That's not true," Evelyn tells her. "Remember what you said this afternoon? About what a good time we're having?"

"Julian thinks there's something wrong with me."

"There isn't."

"So does Nate."

"He thinks no such thing," Evelyn assures her when Nate is caught flat-footed and misses his cue to testify on Renee's behalf. Actually, despite Evelyn's assurance to the contrary, he's begun to wonder if there *is* something wrong with the woman, as she appears to be unraveling faster than Nate himself. Was it only yesterday that he'd imagined falling in love with her, devoting the rest of his life to making sure she knew that everything would be okay? What a batshit pair they'd have made.

"Besides," Evelyn is saying, "remember we agreed that it doesn't matter what other people think? It's what *you* think that counts?"

One look at Renee and you know the reverse is true. "Can we . . . ," she pleads with her companion, as if Nate were not present. "Can we, please?"

Can they what? he wonders. The way she's holding her knees together makes it look like she needs to pee.

"You want to go back to the hotel?" Evelyn says, somehow understanding her friend's actual need.

Renee nods, choking back a sob. “And when we get there, can I take one of my pills?”

“Of course you can,” she says, and the intimacy between the two women is suddenly so private and profound that Nate has to look away.

Back at the hotel, he steers the two women into the tiny elevator, telling them he’ll take the stairs. Not wanting to alarm Renee, he doesn’t tell them he’s going to stop at his brother’s room. If Julian’s there, whether Nate’s subconscious mind wants to or not, he means to get to the bottom of things, once and for all.

“Call me in the morning?” Evelyn says as the elevator door closes, and to Nate, though he’s no longer able to put much faith in his own conclusions, the invitation seems sincere, rooted in genuine fondness. How lovely she looks in her black dress, he can’t help thinking. How has he managed to miss that loveliness until now?

Arriving at his brother’s door, Nate knocks, gently at first, then louder, listening for sounds of stirring inside. “Julian?” he says. “If you’re in there, please open up. I know it’s late, but please . . . I need to talk to you. Julian?” He puts his ear to the door, but only for a moment, because he immediately imagines his brother doing the same thing on the other side, and that idea’s too creepy. The silence within is perfect.

Downstairs in the lobby again, Nate gently rings the bell at the front desk until a sleepy-looking Giancarlo emerges from the back, rubbing his eyes. “I’m sorry to disturb you,” Nate says, “but can you tell me if my brother has returned to the hotel?”

For some reason this question elicits from the young man an

even-more-profound embarrassment than his earlier one over Julian's credit card. *"Signore,"* he begins, producing from beneath the desk another official-looking document. "You brother . . . ," he continues, but then words fail him. When he pushes this new paper toward him, Nate sees in the upper-right-hand corner a drawing of a water taxi, and the significance of this hits him right between the eyes, everything becoming, in that single image, painfully clear. He's *not* insane. The man in the water taxi *was* his brother. "He's gone, isn't he."

Giancarlo grimaces with sympathy. "I try to say to you before. He check out-a."

Nate looks at his watch. By now Julian's at the airport, possibly even on a flight back to D.C.

"He say-a . . . you pay. I hope is okay?"

The restoration of his sanity should be a relief, even cause for celebration, but somehow it isn't. Indeed, what Nate feels is closer to dismay than elation. Having accepted, perhaps even embraced, the idea of lunacy, not to mention the sense of emancipation that trailed in its wake, he's reluctant to switch gears again so quickly. Because if he's not crazy, he's also not off the hook. If he's in his right mind, then it's his moral duty to expel the metaphorical water he's so recently welcomed into his lungs, to push painfully for the far-off surface and emerge yet again into burning air. He hands the man his credit card and tells him not to worry, it's fine, really, it is.

"Goo-da," Giancarlo says, wiping imaginary perspiration from his brow. "Be-cow-za. If *signore* don't pay?" He points at himself. "Giancarlo. *He* pay."

Bacon

In the run-up to fall and spring breaks it was not unusual for impromptu parties to spring up in the quad, so when Nate heard sounds of revelry in the seminar room, he assumed they must be coming from outside. Stepping in, he fully expected to see his students, those who hadn't already departed early for the break, hanging out the open windows and shouting encouragement to their partying friends below. Not Opal, of course. No social reciprocity for her—not with people her own age and certainly not, he was reluctantly coming to understand, with her teachers. If Greta Silver was right, there was simply no room in her syndrome for his good intentions, much less his almost pathological desire to help her discover a normal life that would include touching and being touched, speaking and being spoken to. Sadly, Opal would be in her usual seat, situated so as to preclude bearing witness to a life she'd never share, her gaze, as always, directed inward.

But no. Entering the seminar room, he saw that the revels were being conducted right here. Sarah Griffith had climbed up on the chair he himself usually occupied at the far end of the oblong table and was tossing—he could scarcely believe his eyes—strips of raw bacon to her classmates at the other end. Each time she threw another, they lunged for it, yelping like dogs, their expressions so ravenous he half expected them to devour it on the spot. What they were actually doing with it was even stranger. Kneading and massaging the bacon strips until their hands glistened, they then ran their fingers through their hair, slicking it back, shiny, against their skulls. The air in the room was redolent of smoked pig.

"Professor!" exclaimed Cody, his lone male student, who appeared delighted by his arrival. "You're just in time!" The others also seemed pleased to find him in their midst, as if they'd forgotten altogether that this was their Jane Austen seminar. Immediately, a chant sprung to life—"Grease him up! Grease him up!"

Several of the girls were on the lacrosse team and had relatively short hair, which they'd now fashioned into glistening pompadours, and this gave them a rather terrifying, androgynous look. This was especially true of Sarah Griffith. Cody had tried his best to achieve a similar effect but had little to work with, his blond head cropped too close. "Release your inner Elvis, Professor!" he suggested.

Griffith—making no move to climb down from *his* chair!—made an imaginary microphone of her shiny fist and began singing, her normal, husky alto now scarily baritone, "He's a hunka, hunka burnin' love." The others joined in, expressing the same, no doubt ironic, opinion. "Hunka! Hunka! Hunka! Hunka!" they howled, until Griffith climbed onto the table itself and strutted its length to her accustomed seat at the other end. Only then did the chanting stop. Most amazing, to Nate, was that they were so clearly pleased with themselves, not in the least ashamed of their behavior.

"Uh, Professor," said Cody, when he finally joined them at the table. "Don't be shocked, but"—here he lowered his voice confidentially—"we've been drinking."

"All of us," said the shyest girl in the class, who seemed anxious that he understand, should he feel disapproving, that they were all, if not innocent, then equally guilty.

"And Jane Austen?" said the girl sitting next to her. "Could we give her a pass? Just for today?"

"The thing about Jane?" said Sarah Griffith, indicating the copy of *Northanger Abbey* he'd placed on the table. "She never once in her whole life went to a bacon party. It's kind of tragic, really."

"She's a hunka, hunka burnin' love," someone sang, but the joke had run its course and this time no one joined in.

"So," Cody said, suddenly embarrassed, as if he'd just looked down and discovered he was naked. He pointed at the two strips of bacon left in the package. "You gonna grease up?"

What he was being offered, Nate realized, was membership in their drunken society, which was, in its own stupid way, kind of sweet. If he accepted, if he gave in to the moment and ran greasy fingers through what remained of his hair, his relationship with these students would be fundamentally and permanently altered. It was, he realized, a perverse, twisted version of what he'd often wished for, the kind of acceptance and appreciation that can be conferred upon a teacher only by his students. By the time they all returned from fall break, everyone in the college would have heard how Professor Wilson had attended a bacon party and there revealed a side to his personality that no one had suspected. It was the kind of story that would be told for years, maybe even become part of his legacy, how he would be remembered on campus. The choice was his. Without realizing it, he'd picked up a strip of bacon and could feel its warm grease being released onto his fingers.

What he would try to recall in the long months that followed was just how strong the temptation had been. Would he have actually joined in their idiotic fun if he hadn't just then thought of the Mauntz girl? That, of course, made it impossible, and in his hesitation, when he glanced in the direction of the chair she always occupied, apart from the rest, Sarah Griffith read his mind. "She won't be coming," she said, with what seemed great personal satisfaction.

And just that quickly he was full of dread. "Why not?"

"We heard she had an accident," Cody said.

"What kind of accident?"

"She fell off a StairMaster."

"Again," someone added.

"On her head," said someone else.

"They had to call an ambulance."

"I guess some people never learn," Sarah Griffith concluded.

What occurred to Nate then was that he was the only one who, in the midst of the revelry, had forgotten Opal. The others—all of them—had been waiting for him to notice she wasn't there. Their terrible silence now made this clear. Worse, far worse, was a second realization—that her absence was actually responsible for their high spirits. As they saw it, Opal—and people like her—kept the world from being a fun place. They understood that the Opal Mauntzes of the world—the damaged, the poor, the snakebit—existed, much like third world countries did. They comprehended, too, at least abstractly, that such unfortunates were owed sympathy, understanding, perhaps even assistance. At some later date, a few of these same students—for some reason he suspected it might be Cody—would come to embrace empathy and even moral obligation. Others, like the Griffith girl, would end up living in the world's gated communities, aloof, at a safe distance. Ironically, she and those like her would have, as did Opal Mauntz herself, "proximity issues." Their expensive educations would prove a waste of time. Of *his* time.

And so, instead of "greasing up," Nate took those strips he'd been given, together with the rest of the package, and deposited it all in the wastebasket.

"Uh, Professor?" said Cody, slow to grasp that the party was over. "That was perfectly good bacon."

A hush fell over the room, and Nate allowed this uncomfortable silence to abide before announcing that if no one was prepared to discuss *Northanger Abbey*, then they would proceed to the only other item on the day's agenda before adjourning. Normally, the distribution of a dreaded worksheet would have elicited a communal groan, but today there was just the sound of rustling paper as the handouts were passed around the table. Noting that Sarah Griffith's essay was excerpted there, the other students, one by one, glanced over at her warily, and when Nate began to read her passage aloud she interrupted him. "I can read it," she said, twirling her greasy pompadour with her index finger, her voice rich with confrontation. "I mean, everybody knows it's mine, so why not? Then you can explain why it's a piece of shit."

"The purpose of the workshop—" he began, but she'd begun reading and there was nothing to do except wait for her to finish. When she did, she tossed the sheet of paper toward the center of the table, where it caught an updraft and skittered off onto the floor. "Like I said. A piece of shit. But hey! The second one's much better, right?"

"Yes," Nate heard himself say. "Yes, it is."

At this Sarah Griffith rose and began gathering her things. "So," she said. "Just to summarize . . . Jane Austen is great. Opal Mauntz is great. The rest of us suck. *I* suck."

A fair assessment, Nate couldn't help thinking, and he might actually have said so if at that moment the door hadn't opened and, to everyone's astonishment, Opal Mauntz entered. She was wearing a wool stocking cap pulled down low over her forehead and very dark glasses that weren't quite large enough to conceal completely her facial swelling. She was limping badly, and it took almost a minute to arrive at and then settle herself in her usual chair.

Sarah Griffith was first to recover from this surprise. "Hey, Mauntz," she called. "Good news. You're on the worksheet."

If the girl heard this, she gave no sign.

"I just read mine out loud," Sarah Griffith continued. "You want to read yours?"

"Sarah, please," Nate said, unable to take his eyes off the other girl.

"No, really. Share with us, girlfriend. We're all dying to hear from you."

Later, Nate wouldn't remember getting to his feet, but he must've. Even as he approached her he understood this was a mistake. Better to remain at the table with the others, at the distance Opal herself had established as safe, but that would've meant he was *with* the others, no? That his sympathies were with *them*? And he couldn't bear that she should think that. Or that *they* should. He registered, if only distantly, their confusion and alarm as he approached the poor, broken girl.

Though she'd canted her head away, he now could see her split lip, also grotesquely swollen, and there was a spot of dried brown blood in her ear canal. The idea that this blood would remain where others could see it and she couldn't seemed to Nate insupportable. "Opal?" he said, without expecting a response. "Opal, you shouldn't be here."

She should be in the hospital was what he meant, but the words were no sooner out of his mouth than he heard their other meaning, that she had no business in his Jane Austen seminar, no business at the college, no business out in the world. And it must've been this meaning that she heard because why else would she have turned to face him then, something she'd never done before, and remove, in a gesture he could interpret only as defiance, both her stocking cap and dark glasses. Was it the sight of her, of the full extent of her injuries, that caused the other students to offer up a communal gasp, or the fact that he'd extended his hand to brush, as lightly as he knew how, her swollen, purple cheek?

"Professor! Don't!" he heard Cody shout, but of course it was too late. He'd already reached out. Wasn't that—despite repeated warnings about what the consequences might be—what he'd been doing from the start? Reaching out? Wasn't that what you were supposed to do for any human in need? Though in the instant the backs of his fingers touched the skin of her cheek, he understood that he was making, had *already* made, the worst mistake of a career that was itself a mistake, not only by failing to comprehend what this girl needed, but also by confusing her need, her bewilderment, her inability to kick down life's barriers, with his own. Both of these profound errors of judgment were immediately confirmed by the keening yowl that issued from deep in Opal Mauntz's throat, the voice he'd been so determined to summon from behind the blank screen of her grotesque face, now gushing forth like blood from a wound that would not close anytime soon.

Ink

There's a small wine bar at the far end of the *campo* that's open late, which is good, because Nate discovers that, along with his sanity, his appetite has been fully restored. In fact, having eaten nothing since a few forkfuls of risotto at lunch, he's suddenly famished.

He'd like to confirm his suspicions about his brother, which he could do by calling Evelyn, but it's quite late. It's only twenty minutes since he put the two women in the elevator, so he doubts they could be asleep yet, but given what she and Renee have been through with Julian, he's hesitant to disturb them further. Though he could satisfy his curiosity by calling Brenda, she wouldn't be happy to hear from him, not twice in one day. Over the years her advice to him has been simple and consistent. To move on. And now the time has come to follow it. So he thinks again of Evelyn, who, unless he's mistaken, will be pleased to hear his voice, even if it wakes her. And indeed, answering on the first ring, she does seem pleased. It's hard to tell for sure, however, her barely audible whisper suggesting that Renee has indeed drifted off.

"My brother skipped out on the check, didn't he?" he says.

"I wasn't going to say anything, but yeah."

"I'll make good on that," he assures her.

"I'm not worried."

Which makes him smile. People are like paintings, he thinks; they exist in real time and space, but also in the eye of the beholder. Julian, who's known him all his life, took one look at him at the airport and saw cause for alarm. Evelyn, who's known him for all of twenty-four hours, sees an entirely different man and isn't worried. Is it within his power to prove her right, his brother wrong? He will make it his business to find out.

"Julian's gone," he tells her, explaining that he's taken a water taxi to the airport. "I'm pretty sure he's broke." He hopes it's not true, but the known facts—the denied credit card, Julian's inability to broach the subject directly, Brenda's unwillingness to say anything until he did—all suggest that this whole Venice trip is nothing but an elaborate head fake. Brenda had admitted as much. She knew Julian as well as anyone, understanding all too well how hard it would be for him to ask Nate for help. His entire life he's been the wheeler-dealer, lording his various worldly successes over Nate, relentlessly poking fun at his brother's poorly paid profession, as well as his financial timidity when offered opportunities for greater reward. Asking for help now would be tantamount to an admission that Nate has come out better in the end. Worse, it would be admitting to an even-more-damaging truth: people had stopped buying Julian.

"What will you do?" Evelyn asks.

"I don't know," he tells her. "Whatever I can, I guess." It will depend on how much help his brother needs. That he needs money is a safe bet, but how much? It's also possible he needs a place to stay until he can get back on his feet. That would explain Brenda's remark about Julian's proposal not being, in her opinion, a great idea. "How's Renee?" he asks.

"Out like a light," she says, "but I still should keep my voice down."

"And how are *you*?"

"Disappointed, mostly. I bought a new dress, and the man I was hoping to impress didn't even notice."

"Maybe he's not worth the effort."

"Yeah, but what if he is? Maybe he deserves another chance. Maybe he's just lost. He got lost earlier today, actually. Of course in Venice, that's allowed." She must've heard the music in the bar, because then she said, "Where are you?"

"That little place across the *campo*. As you know, I missed out on dinner."

"Order me a glass of red. Something expensive."

Hanging up, he enters her number into Favorites, where it belongs, and deletes Brenda's, which doesn't. Seeing his ex-fiancée's name disappear makes him even more ravenous, and when his pasta comes he inhales it, pushing the plate away just as Evelyn, in one of her tracksuits again, walks in. As she comes toward him he can't help smiling, finally recognizing her for what she is, the overlooked woman. That he, a Jane Austen scholar, has been so blind to her shames him. Still, that he's blind to her no longer just might be grounds for hope.

"Oooh, yum," she says, sliding into the booth and taking a sip of the Barbaresco he ordered for her. "Will we always drink expensive wine?"

"Probably not. Only one of us is now."

She smiles, then grows serious. "Poor Renee. She was doing so well. Now this."

"What did Julian say to her?"

"He asked if somebody dropped her on her head when she was little."

"What in the world would have provoked that?"

"Oh, he'd been going on about you, how you'd always been passive-aggressive, and this was all about you trying to humiliate him in front of us. Renee said no, she couldn't believe that. You were a nice man, and this had to be a big misunderstanding."

"I'm really sorry," he says, and he is, especially knowing it was Renee's defending him that had precipitated Julian's cruelty.

"The worst part is, it's exactly the sort of thing her husband used to say." There are, Nate notices, tears in her eyes. "Renee's always been a little . . . she's not slow, exactly, just . . . defenseless against unkindness. She doesn't understand it. She gets flummoxed." She dries her eyes on a bar napkin and just that quickly is herself again.

"You're a good friend," Nate tells her.

"No choice. She's my sister."

"Really?"

She regards him gravely now.

"I'm sorry. Did I miss that?"

"Couldn't you tell? We're twins." He half believes this until she bursts out laughing. "Of course we're not *twins*."

"Oh."

"Nate? For future reference? When I tell you things that can't possibly be true, I won't be mad at you if you don't believe them."

"That would make you unique among the women of my experience."

"If it makes you feel better, your brother didn't twig it, either. I'm pretty sure he concluded we were lesbians. Maybe I should let my hair grow out."

"Um," he says, aware that he might be about to make one of his catastrophic mistakes with women, "while we're setting the record straight?"

Evelyn does look genuinely worried now. "There's a wedding ring in your pocket?"

"No."

She takes a deep theatrical breath, then another sip of wine. "Okay, let me have it."

"Well, I haven't been entirely honest. In fact, the very first thing I told you was a lie. About how I read *Death in Venice* on the plane?"

"And it failed to cheer you up."

"The book I actually read on the plane was about a fire at the Venice opera house."

She just stares at him for a long moment. "What else you got," she says, "because so far I'm not impressed."

"And then this afternoon, when I was on the phone and you asked me if I'd gotten bad news, I told you a student of mine had died."

"And he didn't."

"She."

"Oh."

"I'll tell you about her sometime," he says, "but not tonight."

"Maybe in Rome," she suggests. "By then we'll be fast friends."

"I should warn you it's a very sad story, and I don't come off at all well."

She doesn't say anything for a long moment, but then rummages around in her purse. "I want you to see something," she says. She's holding up a lady's makeup compact, which she pops open and hands over, as if she expects him to powder his nose. "Look at your face."

He hesitates, almost afraid of what he'll see reflected there. On the other hand, he's coming to trust this strange, kind woman, so he takes the compact, and the face that looks back at him is, well, his own, neither ugly nor handsome, no longer young but hardly a ruin, either. He can find nothing remarkable in it, no particular reason for any woman to be attracted to it, though, by the same token, no reason to be repulsed. The only thing out of the ordinary—it's probably just the dim lighting in the restaurant—is that his lips, for some reason, appear bruised.

"Smile," Evelyn suggests, and when he does he finally sees what she's getting at. On the waiter's enthusiastic recommendation he'd ordered the squid-ink pasta, thinking the ink would be *in* the noodle, whereas what came was ordinary spaghetti drenched in a salty, pitch-black sauce that's not only darkened his lips but ringed his teeth. The overall effect is gruesome in the extreme. "Sometimes," Evelyn says, handing him a cloth napkin, the end of which she's dipped in her water glass, "things aren't nearly as bad as they appear."

Ash

That night Nate sleeps soundly for the first time in what seems like forever. Near dawn the *acqua alta* siren wails again, but for once it fails to penetrate his slumber until the moment it ceases. Blinking contentedly in the dark, he sees that the shutters, which he's forgotten to latch, have blown open. The room is chilly, but under the covers it's cozy, and from where he lies in bed he can see the first hint of gray in the east. His first thought is of Eve—since it suddenly matters, he's decided he prefers Eve to Evelyn—and how he'd hurt her feelings by not noticing her dress. A week ago such a failure would've driven him even deeper into self-imposed solitude. Now, perhaps because she's gone on record as saying they'll be fast friends by Rome, he feels hopeful he can make it up to her. Having agreed to call her this morning, he'd like to make good on that promise right now, though of course it's too early. He'll wait. But for how long? He hates to think of her awake, perhaps rethinking her conviction that he's worth the effort. If he allows himself to fall back asleep, the time will pass more quickly, but what if, like yesterday afternoon, he sleeps too long?

Before he can resolve this thorny issue, his phone, which he set on silent before falling asleep, suddenly comes to life, as if its awakening were somehow tied to his own. JULIAN CALLING, it says, but when he answers, the line is dead, and pressing RETURN sends him yet again to voice mail. "Julian," he says, then pauses, unsure of how to continue. Should he scold his brother for his treatment of Eve and Renee? Or apologize for not intuiting his financial distress? As he did last night before falling asleep, Nate wonders exactly where Julian is. Back in D.C. already, having caught a red-eye? Or still at Marco Polo Airport, having spent a sleepless night in a straight-backed plastic chair, waiting for the first flight out this morning? It's possible he's boarding now. Who knows? Maybe the flight attendants have asked everyone to power off their devices, and his brother's compliance somehow triggered the call. Why their phones should each be able to communicate with the rest of the world but not with each other is still deeply mysterious, though perhaps apropos. "I have no idea where you are," Nate says, adding, "but that's been true for a long time, and it makes me very sad. I miss you. Maybe you feel differently, but could we at least agree to clear the air? I'm tired of being angry at you."

Later this morning he'll have to tell the others that Julian is gone and make some sort of excuse. He should probably cut his own trip short and return home, find his brother and somehow make things right, but he knows he won't. For the first time in a long while he actually *wants* something. He wants to see Rome. He wants to see it with the Biennale group, which has been, without exception, kind and welcoming. Julian? He'll mend *pontes* with his brother later, those that can be mended. Right now, for the next week or so, he means to mend himself.

When there's a low knock at his door, his heart sinks. Having placed his brother at a distance, he would hate for him to be just feet away, his mood, as always, volatile. Still, he'd rather have it be Julian than Eve, come to tell him that her sister's had a bad night and is in no condition to continue on the tour, that there's a water taxi bobbing in the canal below and she's come to say a quick goodbye. Because in that scenario their friendship will be nipped in the bud. Each, for the other, will be forever associated with a trip to Italy that should have been wonderful but somehow ended badly.

About the last person he expects to find at his door is Bernard. The man's dressed as he was yesterday, in layers—overcoat, sport coat, sweater, shirt, undershirt. This morning, in the crook of one arm, is a box just large enough to contain a football. "I need a favor," he says without preamble, and Nate is again surprised by his powerful baritone.

"Are you feeling poorly . . . ?"

"I'm fine. This"—here he jiggles the package—"will only take a minute."

"Okay if I get dressed first?"

"I insist."

Downstairs, the front desk is unmanned, the lobby hushed and empty, the rest of the Biennale flock still safely tucked in their beds. Out in the street, Nate expects Bernard either to turn left or head straight across the *campo,* because a right turn sends you down a dark narrow alley that dead-ends abruptly at a canal. But that, it seems, is where they're headed. The only sound is their footfalls on stone, that and Bernard's already labored breathing. "Did I mention," he says, "that what we're about to do may be illegal?"

"If you did, I missed it," Nate tells him.

Though the siren has stopped, the water's still high, in places lapping over the wall, which means that Piazza San Marco is flooded, a sight Nate wouldn't mind seeing. A barge laden with fresh produce chugs toward them. "Let's let these guys pass," Bernard remarks, deepening Nate's misgivings. On deck three men dressed in work clothes acknowledge the two of them with a tip of their caps, probably having concluded that they're awaiting a water taxi. When the barge is out of sight, Bernard hands Nate the box. "I'm sorry, but you're going to have to do this," he says. "I already tried and it's no go."

Inside is a plastic receptacle, and Nate knows what it contains even before he removes the lid. He thinks again of Julian, how he wanted no part of scattering their mother's ashes. There was no earthly point in his coming all that distance, he'd argued, and it wasn't like flinging a few handfuls of ashes was a two-man job.

(The present circumstances suggest otherwise, Nate can't help thinking.) Not long after their mother was finally released from the hospital, she and Julian had a serious falling-out, after which he moved away, eventually settling in Atlanta. Nate never knew exactly what hurtful things had been said, but over the next few years he urged his brother to make things right. Their mother was never the same after the fire, recovering neither her physical nor mental health. Part of what ailed her, he felt certain, was Julian's refusal to forgive her carelessness, continuing to blame her for what *might* have happened as if it actually *had*. He tried to make him understand that she blamed herself even more than Julian did, but his entreaties fell on deaf ears. Sure, Julian would call her over the holidays and again on her birthday, but every time she asked if she was ever going to see him again, he only said, "Ma, we've been through this."

Nate had done his best to soothe her. Julian was just being his stubborn old self, he said; eventually he'd come around. You couldn't withhold forgiveness forever, especially when the person you refuse to forgive is the only one who was actually harmed. But his mother didn't believe that stubbornness or forgiveness had anything to do with it. Her burns, she told Nate, were what Julian couldn't bear: having to witness the shiny, hairless skin stretched taut along her neck and cheek. Julian was ashamed of her, she maintained—ashamed and afraid, as if her grotesque appearance were genetic, something he'd grow into himself over time. Nate didn't want to believe it. After all, Julian was his big brother, once his defender against school-yard bullies. Julian, afraid? But when she died and Nate called to say that she was gone, her suffering over at last, he could hear the relief in his brother's voice, as if now he could finally get a good night's sleep. And when Nate mentioned it was her wish to be cremated, Julian's response was a nasty chuckle. "Well, that makes sense, I guess. Might as well finish the job, right?"

Unless Nate was mistaken, their own estrangement can be traced to this precise moment in time, though doubtless the seeds had been planted earlier, when their father left and Julian insisted they were better off without the bum. His brother's angry defiance took the edge off the terrible longing Nate himself couldn't help feeling. Julian seemed to intuit when Nate was most vulnerable, because out of the blue he'd say, "Who needs him?" and though Nate wanted to say, *Me,* he did admire his brother's courage. Their mother's passing, though, was different. What Nate had earlier taken for proud self-reliance seemed to have morphed into something darker, more akin to callous detachment than bravery. If Julian truly felt he was better off without their mother, then maybe it was only a question of time before Nate got written off as well.

"Is there anything you want to say, well, before . . . ?"

"It's all been said," Bernard tells him.

So Nate pours the contents of the urn into the lapping water, thinking as the ash sinks out of sight that in a sense Klaus was right. Just as predicted, one of their number has ended up in the canal. He's not sure tapping the urn against stone to free the last of the grit is proper etiquette, but he does so anyway, then puts the lid back on and hands the empty receptacle to Bernard, who regards it sadly. "In the end," he says, "we don't amount to much, do we?"

Nate remembers thinking the same thing when he scattered his mother's ashes, so he's about to agree, though it then occurs to him that Bernard isn't just talking about people who have been reduced to ash by heat and flame. "I cheated on her, the poor woman," he confesses. "Not just once, either. With a woman she knew. From our church. For a long time I told myself she didn't know, but I'm pretty sure she did." When Nate can't think of an appropriate response to this unwelcome revelation, Bernard continues, "I know what you're thinking. There were *two* women willing to have sex with this guy?"

"I wasn't—"

But Bernard waves his unspoken objection away. "No, it's okay. I had a hard time believing it myself."

"Did you love her?"

"Which do you mean?"

The one whose ashes I just poured into the canal, Nate would like to say, because the other man's inability to perform this intimate duty implied not just sincere guilt but also love, didn't it?

"Same answer in either case," Bernard tells him. "I don't know. I should be able to say I did or I didn't, but both feel like a lie. Maybe that's why I say we don't amount to much. Feel free to talk me out of that, if you want."

What surprises Nate most is how much he'd like to. Because face it, since Opal Mauntz he has harbored this same dark conviction, and there's been no one to try to talk him out of it—no wife, no brother, no son or daughter, no friend. Now suddenly there's Eve, and while it's a heavy—not to mention unfair—burden to place on a woman he didn't even know two days ago, she gives every indication of being the right woman for the job. Last night, talking to her at the wine bar, he felt as if he'd been taken off a ventilator he hadn't even known he was on, capable once again of filling his lungs on his own. It seems only fair that he offer Bernard, another shallow breather, the same service. After all, they're buddies, right?

"Anyhow, I think we're done here," Bernard tells him. "I've

already experienced an Italian hospital. I think I'll skip the jail. If you're up for coffee, there's a little place by the bridge that opens early."

Nate tells him that sounds fine, and together they go back up the narrow *calle*.

"I can't talk, though," Bernard reminds him. "I can walk . . . or talk . . . but not both."

That suits Nate fine. He can use the silence to marshal his evidence, plot his strategy. He might, for instance, tell Bernard about last night with Eve, how he'd looked in her compact mirror, his teeth ringed with black, a monster out of a horror film. But he thinks probably not. This morning the story feels too easy, its moral—that things sometimes aren't as bad as they look—too pat. Because a man doesn't have to be a monster, or even a bad man, to harm others, or to be a profound disappointment to himself. Better—not to mention braver—to tell Bernard about Opal, what he'd done and why, about her removal from the campus to a mental facility where her worsening condition could be treated and monitored, her college days over. Nate's remaining ties to the college had been quietly severed midterm, another professor brought in to complete his seminar. He will tell Bernard all this, not because the story refutes his conviction that in the end human beings don't amount to much, but rather because, as Nate has belatedly come to understand, life is, seemingly by design, a botched job.

Halfway to the Accademia Bridge, Bernard stops, Nate assumes, to catch his breath, but his head is cocked, like a dog's, listening. "What the hell is that dinging?"

Nate, deep in thought, hadn't noticed. "My phone," he says, taking the stupid thing out of its holster.

And there they are, his brother's e-mails and voice messages, a good dozen of them, the idiot server having apparently seen fit to deliver them at last. Too late? Maybe not. Perhaps their belated arrival means that whatever the problem was, it's now solved, that he and Julian can communicate, can hear each other's voices at last, proximity no longer poisonous.

"You need to rest a bit?" Nate asks Bernard.

"No, I'm good," the man assures him.

"Okay, then. We'll go slow."

Bernard nods. "You bet your ass we will."

Intervention

Thirty-two degrees, according to the dashboard thermometer, so . . . maybe. In warm weather the garage door dutifully lumbered up and over the section of bent track, but below freezing it invariably stuck and you had to get out, remote in hand, and manually yank the door past the spot where it caught. Within a few degrees of freezing, though, it was anybody's guess, so Ray pressed the remote and opened the driver's-side door, prepared to get out if he needed to. When the door shuddered past the critical point and up along the ceiling, he closed the car door again, noticing as he did so that Paula, his wife, was watching him with her O *ye of little faith* expression.

Pulling inside, he made sure to leave her enough room to get out. *Two-car* was how the garage had been described when they bought the house. Ray, himself a realtor and all too familiar with such dubious representations, had squinted at the phrase in the listing information, then at the garage itself. It was probably true it could hold two small sedans, but with anything larger you'd need to pull the first car in at an angle to have enough space for the second vehicle. He'd considered calling Connie, the seller's agent, on this, but he liked her, in particular how she confessed right up front that she'd just gotten her license. She seemed genuinely terrified of saying the wrong thing, of disclosing something that by law wasn't supposed to be mentioned or of failing to disclose something else that was mandatory. She'd gone into real estate, she claimed, because she liked helping people find what they wanted, and she seemed blithely innocent of the fact that most people had no idea what that was, especially the ones who were defiantly confident they did. Ray doubted she would last long and wasn't surprised when, a year later, he ran into her and was told she'd embarked upon a degree in social work.

Anyway, Paula had loved the house and didn't want to see the not-quite-two-car garage as a problem, though she conceded they'd probably have to find someplace else for the lawn mower and the other stuff they usually stuck in there. She argued they'd be okay if they went slow and paid attention, especially at backing out. When for the record Ray expressed grave doubts about this as a long-term solution, she asked, "What are you saying? That we're careless people?"

Well, no, but they were human and there was no app for that. A person could be careful most of the time, maybe eighty percent, if you really worked at it. The way Ray saw it, human nature was flawed, almost by definition, pretty much a hundred percent of the time, which left a sizable margin for error. For nearly a year, though, they waged a successful battle against such cynicism, until one day Ray misjudged and sheared off his side-view mirror. A month later Paula—okay, okay, she admitted, she'd been in a hurry—backed into the metal track the garage door slid on, warping the runner and taking out a taillight. The two accidents, in such close proximity, represented a genuine *I told you so* moment, but Ray'd given it a pass. He and Paula had been married for close to thirty years, thanks in large part to a mutual willingness to let an arched eyebrow do the heavy lifting of soliloquy.

Tonight, though, as the garage door rattled closed behind them, palsying violently the last few feet before finally slamming down onto the concrete floor, he knew there'd be more than her eyebrow to worry about. His wife hadn't spoken a word during the ride home from the restaurant, and when the garage light went off, plunging them into complete darkness, she made no move to get out.

"You hurt Vincent's feelings," she said finally.

"He had it coming," Ray said, referring to how they'd tussled briefly and pointlessly over the check. After all, it was Vinnie's sixty-fifth birthday they were celebrating, plus there were two of them and just one of him, and his halfhearted grab was really just an attempt to get in a final political dig. "This is the least I can do, bud," he said. "From now on you're paying for my health insurance."

"You forget we're Democrats," Ray responded, placing his credit card on the tray. "We think people are entitled to health care. We're happy to contribute to that end." A lifelong Republican, Vinnie had reluctantly voted for Obama but was now suffering buyer's remorse. (*The guy's not a realist . . . another Jimmy Carter . . . doesn't know how the world works.*) It had made for a trying evening.

"I'm not talking about the check," Paula said. "I'm talking about his offer."

"Which I thanked him for."

"'Thanks, anyway,' was what you said. It sounded like 'Mind your own business.'"

"That's how I meant it."

Truth be told, he'd been out of sorts from the start. They'd gone to La Dolce Vita, or, as Vinnie called it, Dolce Vita's, his favorite place, pretentious and overpriced à la Vinnie. Ray and Paula had purposely arrived a few minutes early, but of course he was already there, ready to rise from his chair with a flourish and gather Paula in. "Hey, baby," he said, as if it was still the fifties and they were all Rat Packers. "Is this stiff treating you right?"

Paula tried gently to extricate herself from his embrace, assuring Vinnie as she always did that Ray was treating her fine, but with everyone in the dining room watching them, Vinnie wasn't about to surrender either the pretense or the woman.

"I only mention it because we could run away, just the two of us." All of this sotto voce. "Someplace warm, with our own private cabana? Call me."

Vinnie in a nutshell: *Call me*. You need a table at Babbo? *Call me*. You need Red Sox tickets? *Call me*. You need to get your dog trained? *Call me*. You don't have a dog? *Call me*. Because Vinnie always knew a guy. Sometimes from the old neighborhood, sometimes from prep school or maybe his university fraternity. Guys who normally didn't do favors, but for Vinnie . . .

Only when Paula promised to call if Ray turned into a lout did Vinnie release her and turn to the patient witness of this recurring lunacy, and Ray extended his hand. Vinnie swatted it away, offended, as if handshakes were insulting to guys who shared deep emotional bonds without getting swishy about it. "Get outa here with that," he said, pulling Ray into one of his hugs. "How's every little thing? You okay?"

Ray, anxious to be seated, said he was right as rain.

"We need to hit the links," Vinnie said, making a Johnny Carson golf swing. "I'm not saying I'm giving you strokes, I'm just saying."

Then he spun back toward Paula, imploring, arms extended wide like a crooner's, to take in the entire restaurant. "What do you think? Best table in the house? That's how things would be every night if you were with me."

He's just lonely since Jackie died was how Paula excused such outrageous behavior, to which Ray always responded that, yeah, sure, Vinnie *was* lonely. The mistake would be to conclude that he was *just* lonely.

"He's your friend," she reminded him now in the dark garage. "He cares about you. If he knows a good surgeon—"

"Not *good,*" Ray corrected her. "The *best.* Vinnie always knows the *best* guy. You'd have to be crazy to go to anybody besides Vinnie's guy."

"But that's how he *is.* He's just being Vincent. People like to feel important. What's so wrong with that?"

Ray would have liked to tell her but couldn't, though it did put him in mind of his uncle Jack, whom he hadn't thought about in years.

"Is this how it's going to be, then?" she said.

"What do you mean?"

"I just don't see why you have to act like this. What does it get you?"

By now his eyes had adjusted to the dark enough to see that hers were glistening. "Paula," he said. "What are we talking about?"

He knew, though.

"What I'd like to get through to you is that in this particular circumstance . . ." She paused, seemingly poised between all-too-understandable fear and something closer to anger. "Being you, going about things the way you usually do, isn't always a good thing."

"I should become somebody else?"

"Yes," she said, taking him by surprise.

"How come Vinnie gets to be Vinnie, but I don't get to be me?"

"Vinnie's not the one who—"

"I already told you, I'll do whatever you—"

"What I *want* is for you to swallow your pride."

"Fine," he sighed, because it was ridiculous to be sitting there in the cold damp garage, their visible breath fogging the windshield. "If he wants to put me in touch with this Boston guy, fine. Now, can we go inside?"

He took her silence as permission to open his door, and he did—too far, dinging yet again the rear panel of his parked SUV.

Which felt like what? Vindication was the far-from-comforting answer, but that's what it felt like.

The following morning Ray was startled awake by a car horn, half-a-dozen loud, angry blasts as the unseen vehicle roared by the house and up the street, and for the second time in the last twenty-four hours he thought of his long-forgotten uncle Jack. Tall and thin (hungry looking, he seemed to Ray), Jack was straight haired, loose limbed and handsome, a contrast to their father, who was several inches shorter and thicker, his face dimpled (attractively, Ray felt at the time) from a childhood disease, his hair an unruly bird's nest. Even when he wasn't working in the mill, he always dressed in rugged work pants, coarse gray shirts with dual breast pockets and ankle-high, steel-toed boots, whereas his brother wore sharply creased slacks, white button-down shirts and shiny black shoes. Looking at the two men, you'd conclude that Uncle Jack was the more prosperous, but apparently he owed everybody.

Though he lived in nearby Skowhegan, Ray and his brother,

Bill, rarely saw their uncle, whose visits were as dramatic as they were unexpected. Their purpose was always the same—to get their father to invest in one of Jack's many schemes, each pitched as the investment opportunity of a lifetime. Their father always listened politely and without comment, as if to the radio (no need to look at it, either), while his brother explained how this new deal worked, how it would make them both rich, how a small outlay of funds today would put him on the ground floor tomorrow. Hell, in a matter of months he'd be able to quit his sucker job at the mill and be his own boss for once. Their uncle's cadences rose and fell in great waves, and at various points Ray would think he was winding down, but then he'd remember something else. "Hey! Wait, I almost forgot the best part!" Eventually, though, it was impossible to ignore his sibling's lack of visible interest, and he'd say, "So what do you think, Big Brother?"

What Ray's father invariably thought, or at least said, was that, no, he didn't think he was interested. Did he want to think it over? No, no, that wouldn't be necessary. So his answer was final? Yes, it was. What was so perplexing was not that his father declined—he always did—but that he offered his brother so little in return for his wonderful enthusiasm. After all, it took Uncle Jack a good half hour or more to detail how great this idea was, how you couldn't lose, really, if you thought about it. If their father had misgivings, small or large, why not express them? Or at the very least offer some general excuse. Why not tell his brother he was sorry but just didn't have the money? How would Uncle Jack, who'd never had any himself, have known any better? Or he could've reminded his brother *he* wasn't a bachelor, that he had a wife and two young boys to think about and couldn't risk what little they had on an adventure, no matter how tempting. Instead, unless Ray's memory was playing him false, the impression his father conveyed was that, yes, he *did* have money. He just wasn't going to give any to his brother. His refusal to say why could mean only one thing: Uncle Jack was himself the reason.

Their uncle hadn't been a man to take such rejection lying down, and this was where the drama came in. Nearly five decades after hearing the last one, Ray could still recall almost verbatim the furious tirades their father's cool rebuffs always occasioned. *What is it with you, Tommy? You* like *standing in lines? You* like *waiting for somebody to decide what your share is? Because while you're standing out front with the schmucks, waiting for scraps, the smart people are slipping in the back, and taking what's theirs. You were in the army, for God's sake. You saw how things work. You know what this country we fought for is all about? It's the land of back doors and secret handshakes. People didn't stop drinking during Prohibition. They just stopped going in through the front.*

Another time Uncle Jack had grabbed the phone book and shaken it in his brother's face. *You know what's in here, Tommy? The numbers they want dummies like you to know about. All the important ones are unlisted. There's two kinds of people in the world, Big Brother. The ones who know the unlisted numbers and the ones who don't. You know what they call the ones who don't? Chumps. Your average chump spends his life wondering why his luck never changes. See, that's what* makes *him a chump. He thinks it's luck. But here's the thing. If somebody gave your average chump an unlisted number, he'd write it down and call it. He might be a chump, but he's not a complete moron. You? You're no average chump, Tommy.* No sir. *There's nothing average about you. Somebody comes along and lets you in on the score, offers you the unlisted number, you say,* No thanks, *I'll just wait here in line with the other chumps.* At this point, he dropped the phone book in their father's lap. *When* you *want something, you consult your damn phone book.*

Much as Ray and his brother Bill enjoyed their uncle's riffs, it was his thrilling dismounts they really looked forward to. He always blew out of the house violently, as if on a sudden gust of wind, the door slamming so hard their mother's figurines leapt on the shelf. Outside, he'd take the porch steps in a wild, imprudent leap, one time hitting an icy patch and ending up on his ass. Turning his key in the ignition of whatever beater he happened just then to be driving, he'd rev the engine until it screamed, then pop the vehicle in gear and lurch away from the curb on squealing tires, leaning on the horn all the way down the street, as if each blast were yet another insult.

Except of course for the last time. What on earth had caused their father to explode that day when he'd always been so unflappable before? It had been August, Ray recalled, so maybe the heat? They'd been out on the porch—Ray and his brother, their father and uncle—all four of them drinking tall glasses of their mother's fresh-squeezed lemonade. As usual Uncle Jack was holding forth about how rich they'd be, how you'd have to be blind not to see how much moola—one of his uncle's favorite words—was waiting there to be made. And also as usual his father had said no, he didn't think he was interested, and was promptly called a fool and asked—rhetorically, Ray now understood—what the hell was wrong with him. Did he *like* slaving away in the mill for peanuts?

Here, though, came the memory glitch, everything fast-forwarding to Uncle Jack sprawled flat on his back and their father, who'd come flying out of his chair, on top of him, pummeling him with his fists and grunting *Shut . . . up . . . shut . . . up . . . shut . . . up,* the word *shut* timed to the impact of his right fist and *up* to his left. Their mother, who'd been in the kitchen when it started, was suddenly there on the porch (for some reason Ray remembered the faded floral pattern of the dress she was wearing) screaming for their father to *stop, stop, please stop, you're killing him.* Neither Ray nor Bill had ever seen their father disobey a direct command of hers, but now he just kept punching, as if he were too far away to hear her pleading. He stopped only when Uncle Jack went limp, his eyes rolling back in their sockets. Had there really been as much blood as Ray remembered? There must've been, because Ray recalled feeling so light-headed that he thought he might faint. *This,* he also thought, this torn skin leaking blood, was what their mother didn't want them to see when dogs fought in the street and why she sometimes turned off the evening news.

"Hello?" Paula had materialized at the foot of the bed, dressed and ready to head into the gallery, staring at him as if she'd been standing there for a long time.

"Sorry," he said sheepishly. "I was elsewhere."

"Here," she said. "Right here is where I need you."

Half an hour later, showered and dressed, Ray pulled into the driveway of the house where he was meeting his clients, the Bells, for what promised to be a wasted day. On the other hand, it had been months since he put a property under contract, and weeks since he'd even *shown* a house, so motion, however useless, was better than nothing. The juggernaut recession had landed the coastal housing market in the doldrums. A few million-dollar-plus properties on the water had sold to the sort of buyers who were immune to economic hardship, and some low-end listings were moving lethargically. The vast middle lay inert. According to his brother, who lived forty miles inland, it was even worse there.

The first house he was showing, one of his own listings, was situated on a gentle rise two streets back from the ocean. Nicki, the reluctant seller, was a friend of Paula's and had recently lost her job as an office manager at a nearby call center. The property offered what realtors euphemistically called "winter views," an intermittent sparkle of blue water among the stark black trees. A *two-car-garage* sort of view, Ray thought, getting out of his SUV, and today, since the distant sea was the same gray as the sky and the patches of dirty snow, not even that good.

He'd gotten here fifteen minutes early so he could bring up the heat inside and, more important, let some light in. Nicki's house was dark, its murk intensified by too much wood paneling and densely flowered wallpaper. He'd urged her to steam off the latter and give the walls a coat of white paint, but she claimed—sounding like this was his fault—not to have the money. If the house didn't sell soon, she kept warning him, the bank was going to begin foreclosure proceedings. For the moment she was living with friends in Portland while looking for work there, but she called at least once a week to wonder out loud what the problem was. "I don't understand," she kept saying. "It's a *nice house*."

The problem was you couldn't tell that by looking at it. The house wasn't only dark, it was *cluttered*. A hoarder by nature, Nicki'd boxed up everything she owned and just left the boxes sitting there, as if their location would remind her of their contents and all those precious memories. What they contained, according to Paula, who'd spent the better part of a week helping her pack up, was a decade's worth of impulse Internet purchases from QVC, Overstock.com and eBay. Though Nicki seldom cooked, her kitchen was equipped with a high-end pasta maker, a bread-making machine, a Mixmaster and a deluxe slow cooker, as well as several complete sets of expensive pots and pans and too many gadgets to count. She had an espresso machine the size of a snowmobile. Another room was full of gym equipment—treadmill, StairMaster, rower, ab machine—though she exercised even less frequently than she cooked. When her father, a well-known academic, died, she'd built floor-to-ceiling bookshelves in the spare bedroom and moved his whole library in, though she confessed to Paula that most of his books were highly specialized and on topics that held no interest for her. When Ray suggested culling rather than taking them all with her, she was mortified. "They're *books,* Ray. Only Nazis throw books away." He felt compelled to point out that "actually, Nazis burned books," but Nicki proved deaf to this nuance. Also to his every attempt to explain the psychological effect of clutter on prospective buyers, how hard it was to imagine the absence of something you were staring at and had to figure out how to get around. "These are my *things,* Ray," she objected. "You're talking about my *things.*" As if when you looked up *thing* in the *Oxford English Dictionary*—one of the books she'd inherited from her father—you'd discover the word's numerous sacred connotations. Last week, before heading to Portland, she'd reluctantly agreed to rent a small storage unit and move out some of these *things* so the property would show better, but Ray would have given odds she'd done no such thing.

He was inserting the key to the mudroom door when his cell vibrated. "Okay, we're lost," Cliff Bell said without preamble, as if he'd known this was coming right from the start.

The Bells were cultural refugees from Texas who'd apparently vacationed in Maine last summer and taken to heart the state's license plate motto: THE WAY LIFE SHOULD BE. That happened pretty often, actually. Something in the Zeitgeist, Ray supposed. "If things get really bad," people said, "we'll sell everything and move to Maine," as if it were a foreign country. Liberals came fleeing conservatives, libertarians fleeing government, traders fleeing Wall Street, film people fleeing LA, everybody fleeing the nation's collective culture, as if there were no cable TV or Internet access north of Boston, and by means of geography they could escape Snooki and hip-hop and Sarah Palin and bird flu. One rough winter, followed by a blackfly-rich June, was usually sufficient to send such folks scurrying back to wherever they came from. Not always, though. Vinnie, who'd fled Palm Beach with his wife nearly a decade ago, was still hanging in. After her unexpected illness and death left him all alone in their big house on the lake, Ray assumed he'd hightail it back to Florida to be closer to their grown children, but so far he'd shown no such inclination.

How was it possible, Ray wondered, for his Texans to be both lost and fifteen minutes early? From where he was standing he could see the back of the B and B where they were staying and, up the street, a Taurus that was inching in his direction.

"Are you in a red Taurus?"

"Is this piece of shit a Taurus?" Ray heard the man ask, his phone somewhat muffled by his chest. Then, to Ray, "Yeah. How'd you know?"

"I'm looking at you. Waving." He waved.

The car stopped abruptly, as if the driver feared he was being sighted through the scope of a high-powered rifle. "That you on the hill?"

"That's me."

"You're joking, right? Four hundred K for *that*?"

Ray heard the man's wife offer a strong suggestion. That Cliff Bell should shut up was the gist of it. Either that or they had a pet named Fuck in the car, and it was the dog or cat she wanted her husband to silence.

As soon as they got out of their piece-of-shit Taurus, it was clear that Cliff Bell and his wife were in the middle of an argument that had come up with the sun. "That's not what I'm saying," he was telling her as they approached. Then, extending his pudgy hand to Ray, he said, "You people ever hear of a grid? Go right, go left? That sort of deal?"

"I'm Cheryl," his wife said matter-of-factly, as if she'd stopped waiting for her husband to introduce her decades ago. She had the stronger grip and seemed to know it. She also seemed to understand that without even trying, or perhaps because she wasn't, she still exuded sex. Another portly, balding man might have been grateful for such a companion, but Cliff Bell seemed to resent her. Probably thinking: How fair was it that other men still wanted to fuck his wife when no other women wanted to fuck *him*.

"Cliff doesn't like for things to go all twisty on him," Cheryl explained, regarding the man in question sternly. "This isn't the Panhandle, Streak. There are obstacles here that even you have to go around. Mountains. Large bodies of water. Things you can't just put your hard head down and plow through, like you're used to doing."

"Lordy, Lordy, Lordy," he sighed, clearly hoping that Ray, by virtue of their shared gender, might commiserate. "Not even ten o'clock yet and already my balls ache like it's four in the afternoon."

"The phrase 'You can't get there from here' was invented in Maine," Ray said, trying to extend the correct amount of sympathy. From long, bitter experience he knew better than to be drawn into a marital feud. "You might want to invest in GPS if you decide to move up here."

Cheryl chortled at this suggestion. "Really?" she said. "You think that would solve the problem, do you?"

Having lived his whole life, except for college, in Maine,

Ray had limited experience of Texans, but he'd never met a man from there he liked. The women, on the other hand, were invariably entertaining, having apparently concluded that only a well-lubricated sense of humor was likely to make life with such assholes bearable. Despite his small statistical sample, Ray was pretty sure the Bells wouldn't require him to rethink this sweeping generalization.

"How about I meet you around front?" he suggested, pointing. He hated to leave them alone, even briefly, fearing their argument might escalate, but he was determined to let some light into Nicki's house before allowing them inside.

"Stand out here in the freezing cold?" Bell said, pulling his jacket collar up against the wind. "Sure, we can do that."

Inside, even in the dark Ray immediately saw it was just as he'd feared: cardboard boxes—tall, wobbly towers of them—everywhere. Worse, the heat wasn't set at the fifty-five he recommended, it was off; his breath billowed in front of him. When his cell vibrated, he hoped it might be an impatient Nicki wanting to know how the showing was progressing, in which case he could tell her to find herself another realtor. Instead he was greeted by Vinnie's rich baritone. "Hey, bud. I've got the number for that guy in Boston."

"Thanks," Ray said sidling among the boxes. "Can't talk now, though. I'm with clients."

"Yeah, but you're taking this seriously, right?"

There was a light switch at the foot of the stairs, but when Ray flipped it nothing happened.

"Because something like this is no joke."

"I'm taking it seriously."

"Be sure to mention my name," Vinnie continued, as Ray knew he would. "When you're the number one guy . . ."

Ray put the phone in its holster and felt his way along the wall. At the top of the stairs there was another switch that didn't work, nor did the one in the master bedroom. Therefore a blown fuse. That, as he'd told Nicki, was yet another problem with her *nice* house: the old knob and tube wiring, which would have to be brought up to code before new owners could get insurance. Where was the fuse box? The basement, probably. In the master bedroom, he groped for the cord to the heavy drapes and pulled them back, allowing in just enough gray light to make the room look sinister.

"Or here's a better idea," Vinnie was saying, his voice barely audible in Ray's holster. "Let me call Suzy, his wife. She and Jackie used to be tight, and she had a thing for me. Then he'll be expecting your call. You still there, bud?"

Back at the top of the stairs he took out his cell, intending to tell Vinnie he was still listening, when everything started spinning. For a moment he imagined he was falling, that the floor was coming up to meet him. Something thudded onto the carpet, it had to be his phone, because he was clutching the banister with both hands. Lowering himself to a sitting position helped a little, but suddenly his shirt was drenched with sweat. What the hell was this?

"Talk to me, bud. You still there?"

And then, as quickly as it had come on, it was over. The phone was in his hand again, and he put it to his ear. "I'm here—"

"Hey, I can tell you got your hands full. Here's what I'll do. I'll run the number over to your place. Is our girl there?"

Since his wife's death, Vinnie had taken joint linguistic custody of Ray's, as if Paula were the kind of woman it took two men to properly care for. Could his pretense be any thinner? If he wanted to give "their girl" a telephone number, he could call or e-mail the information. What he had in mind, of course, was to hand her a slip of paper with the number on it, to reassure her that—hey, baby—this guy was tops in his field, bar none. If you run into a problem, any problem at all, *call me*. No worries. He'd be right there with her, with both of them, every step of the way. Maybe even assist with the surgery.

"If you leave now, you'll just catch her," Ray said, though by now his wife had been at the gallery for at least an hour.

"You sure you're okay?"

Ray stood warily, testing his legs, flexing at the knees. Check and check. He'd stopped sweating. The vertigo had passed. All was well.

"So tell the truth now," Cliff Bell said when Ray finally opened the door to the two shivering Texans. "You stay here all winter, or do you and the missus have a time-share down in Costa Rica or someplace?"

"If you can't stand the wintah," Ray said, putting on a thick Down East accent, "you don't deserve the summah."

Bell blinked, apparently trying to reconcile this new voice with Ray's normal one. His wife smiled broadly, and Ray couldn't help thinking, *Damn,* if she wasn't, despite her age, still sex on a stick.

Paula was contemplating her computer screen and finishing a cheese sandwich in her windowless basement office when Ray stepped out of the elevator. "Hey, baby," he said, doing Vinnie. "What do you say we ditch that old man of yours and go someplace warm. How about the Breakers? There's a guy from the old neighborhood down there who can get us an upgrade under the rate. We'll get naked, just the two of us."

"Speaking of Vincent," his wife said, handing him a folded slip of paper. "You just missed him."

Which of course made sense. Once he discovered Paula wasn't home, Vinnie, part bulldog, part terrier, would've made straight for the gallery. But, good Lord, how long had he stayed? Ray had been with the Bells all morning. How could he have *just missed* Vinnie?

Slipping the note into his shirt pocket unopened, he sank into a chair, feeling more than a little deflated by his wife's lack of visible interest in the idea of getting naked with him in Florida. Was it Vinnie or Ray's impression of him that she didn't want to run off with?

"I was hoping to take you to lunch," he said, in his own voice. "I know a guy at the Chowder House who can get us the corner booth if somebody's not already sitting in it."

"Sorry," she said, pushing the last bite of her sandwich away. "I'm off to Portland."

"How come?"

When she just looked at him, something tugged at his memory. Something from this morning. He tried, without success, to pull it into focus. "The . . ." He squinted, to signify genuine effort. "Some foundation."

"The Rormacher Group."

"Right. But you'll be home for dinner?"

"Noooo," she said, as if to a child. "We're fending for ourselves, remember? We've been over this."

"It's all coming back to me."

"And there's something else you're going to do today."

He'd been thinking about explaining what had happened at Nicki's but now decided against it. Because he didn't want to worry her? Because he was annoyed with her for bugging him about Vinnie's guy? Yeah, one of the above.

"Ray?"

He patted his pocket. "Got the number right here, baby."

She sighed, surrendering a half smile. "I'm sorry. Lunch would've been nice."

"Well," he said. "At least I'll be seeing you for dinner."

Bigger smile at this. "How'd things go with your Texans?"

"Did I ever tell you that in my experience Texas males are—"

"all dickheads, but you like the women. Yeah, you've mentioned that once or twice."

Really? When? Had all his material become threadbare? After thirty years of marriage, were you supposed to come up with new stuff all the time? How often? "See, if your memory was shot, too, everything would be fresh and exciting. Every day a new adventure."

"It would be nice if they bought a house."

"Who?"

"Your Texans." She knew better, surely, but couldn't help herself.

"What Texans?"

"Ray. Please stop."

"I don't think they're going to," he admitted. As the morning progressed, Cliff Bell's mood had improved. He and his wife quit sniping at each other and they'd actually liked the last two properties he showed them. Unfortunately, both were at the upper end of their price range, and if they were going to spend that much they were clearly expecting more house. Last summer they'd scanned some real-estate guides, as people on vacation often will, and noted some great old farmhouses offered at what had seemed reasonable prices. Trouble was, they'd imagined these on or near the water, whereas in fact they sat ten or fifteen miles inland. What they wanted was available—back in his office he'd shown them a couple places that were perfect—but at twice what they were looking to spend. The recession hadn't hit Texas as hard as the rest of the country, but from things they'd let slip Ray guessed the Bells had lost the same forty percent from their portfolios as everybody else, and with so little time since to recoup they were understandably cautious.

Oddly enough, the house that just might've worked for them as a second home was Nicki's, but Bell hadn't even wanted to go inside. In fact, he'd stubbornly waited in the entryway while Ray and Cheryl, tacking among the boxes, looked at the kitchen, master bedroom and bath. Unless he was mistaken, she actually liked the house, admiring its ornate wainscoting and the lovely tin ceiling in the den, but in the end she'd had to give up. She could picture the place without Nicki's furniture, and even the towers of boxes. But what refused to disappear, Ray understood, was Nicki herself. She'd broken containment, much like people who live alone sometimes do, spilling out of their skins and into their beloved possessions, the stuff that keeps them from losing heart. *These are my things, Ray.* She might as well have been there with them, red eyed and blowing her nose into a tissue, describing what each box contained, how much she hated to lose her home, how unfair it all was.

Hoping the Bells wouldn't themselves disappear, he'd told them that people in Maine often took their properties off the market in the winter, then listed them again in the spring. There might be more to see then. And another six months of watching their houses sit idle might motivate a seller or two to come down on price. But neither possibility seemed to cheer the Texans.

"Where should we go for dinner?" Cliff asked as they parted company. "I want some of those clams you get up here. The ones with the little penises."

His wife opened her mouth to say something, then closed it again, evidently deciding that just because it was teed up didn't mean you had to hit it. "We'll be in touch," she said, her grip every bit as warm and firm as it had been that morning, though unless Ray was mistaken this time it meant goodbye.

"If Rormacher says no," Paula sighed, staring up at the low ceiling as if she could see right through it into the gallery above, "I've got thirty days, max, before I have to start letting staff go. We could close for the winter, I suppose, and save expenses, but if things don't improve, why reopen? To go deeper into debt?"

"No Palm Beach for us, baby," Ray agreed, aware that the whole Vinnie gag was wearing thin, and switched back to his own voice. "What's in our savings account?"

"We have a savings account?" Okay, she was joking, but still.

And now medical bills, she was probably thinking.

The parking lot of the Way Lame Chow, as Ray referred to the local Chinese restaurant, was empty, so he pulled in. There he'd be able to fill a plate, find a table in the corner and talk on his cell phone without disturbing anyone.

The elderly Asian woman at the register, whose name he could never remember, took his money and made a sweeping gesture, indicating that he could sit wherever he wanted, as they were the only people there. "Where everybody? People all move to moon?"

"It's slow everywhere," Ray commiserated.

"Slow," the woman repeated. "Ha-ha. Slow. Pretty funny. Ha-ha-ha."

The buffet was a dispiriting sight. Large stainless-steel pans containing small mounds of humid food. Half-a-dozen chicken wings in one. A few boneless, dyed-red spareribs in another. A beef-and-broccoli concoction from which most of the beef had already been harvested. A couple other items Ray didn't recognize, heavy on the water chestnuts. A party of four could have grazed the entire spread in five minutes and gone home hungry. Not that it really mattered. What little appetite he had was unlikely to survive his unavoidable phone call to Nicki. Promising himself he'd go back for something more substantial later, he settled for a cup of egg-drop soup. A layer of skin had formed over the top of the soup, and gobs of it stuck to the ladle's long handle when he stirred; what went into his cup, bright yellow, looked like a sick dog's urine and was thick as clam chowder. He'd already managed to blister his tongue with the first spoonful when his cell vibrated. His ever-impatient client, beating him to the draw.

"Hi, Nicki," he said, completely wrong-footing her by saying her name before she'd identified herself. She was one of those people who had to go through every step of any process and got flustered if you tried to skip even the most obvious ones. "Oh," she said. "Oh, Ray?"

"It's me, Nicki. The person you called. How are you?"

The question seemed to stump her. "Oh, I'm . . . it's Nicki. How did the showing go?"

"I thought you were going to move all those boxes."

And just that quickly she was on offense. "Where am I supposed to put them? I told you I can't afford a storage locker. What am I supposed to do?"

"You have a garage."

"Then where would I put my car? It's winter, Ray. When the house is gone, the car will be all I've got left."

If only, Ray couldn't help thinking.

"I'll need it to get back and forth to work. I can't have it sitting out in the elements."

"You found a job?"

"Not yet."

"I'm sorry. I thought that's what you meant." He was about to ask her where the fuse box was when the penny dropped. "Nicki," he said. "Tell me you didn't turn off the utilities."

Silence on the line now, then, a moment later, no surprise, quiet weeping. "I *need* to sell this house, Ray. I'm not sure you realize how . . . I don't see what the problem is. It's a *nice house.* Paula agrees."

"Nicki," Ray said, "*I* agree."

"Then why . . ." but she couldn't go on. "Oh God," she said finally.

"The husband wouldn't go inside," he told her. "He took one look at all your stuff and that was it."

"Men."

"Yeah, well—"

"A few boxes."

"Nicki?"

"I should burn it down. Collect the insurance."

This was not, he knew, a serious threat. She'd have to cull her possessions first, move everything out—the very thing she *couldn't* do. He continued to listen to her snuffling.

Finally she said, "Tell me what to do."

"I've told you. And you won't do it."

"I will."

"There's a kayak in the garage, Nicki, an expensive one. If you sold it you'd not only have the money to pay another month's mortgage, you could also turn the utilities back on and there'd be enough left over to rent a small storage locker."

"That kayak belonged to my father."

"And before that to the store that sold it to him. For money."

More silence, until, "If I do what you say, what guarantee do I have it'll make a difference?"

"None."

"It's all *so* unfair."

Ray knew better than to reply.

At last she said, "I'll do it. Whatever you say. It's just . . . really *hard*."

"Nicki, have you ever considered the possibility that it might feel good to get rid of some stuff?"

No response.

"Look, I just sell houses, okay? Temperamentally, I have no use for people with clean desks. But I clean my own once a year. In order to see who I am, what I need, what I can live without . . . are you still there?" Because he knew from experience she was not above hanging up without saying goodbye.

"Paula says you're sick."

Now *he* was wrong-footed. He started to say it was nothing, then decided not to. She'd report the comment back to Paula, who'd turn it against him. "It's just something I have to get through. Life's full of stuff like that. This isn't news, right?"

"I wish *I* could be sick," she said. "Bad sick."

Again, Ray held his tongue.

"Every day I tell myself it's all going to work out. The house will sell and I'll find a new job, an even-better job. But most mornings I wake up and all I want to do is go back to sleep. If I got sick, people would let me sleep."

"Nicki—"

"If I tell you something, will you hate me?"

"Did you murder somebody? Molest a child? What am I promising here?"

"I always thought I was special."

It was an odd, in some ways startling, admission. There were any number of people who clearly felt like this, but the sentiment was seldom given voice.

"My father used to tell me I was and I believed him. When my husband left he said, 'You know what your problem is? You think you're special.' And I remember wondering why he made it sound so awful. I mean, I *was* special, wasn't I? Didn't *he* think so? Wasn't that why he married me? And anyway, why shouldn't I *think* it? I knew it wasn't nice to say that to people who weren't special, because that would hurt their feelings. I mean, *everybody* can't be special, and people who aren't, well, it's not their fault. But I never really questioned that *I* was. So now, for the first time, my whole life's coming into focus. I'm fifty-seven years old, Ray, and every day I have to lie to myself just to keep going. Who's still lying to themselves at fifty-seven?"

Everybody.

"You don't have to say anything. There's nothing to say, really."

"Small bites, Nicki."

"I'm sorry?"

"Small bites. Chew thoroughly. Swallow. Repeat."

"You don't like?" the woman said when Ray approached to pay his bill.

"No, Pearl, everything was fine."

"Just soup? No wing? Usually you eat wing. I tell them in kitchen, make more wing. Ray here."

Her dour mood seemed to have lifted a little, maybe because he'd paid for the whole buffet and had only a cup of soup. But when the door closed behind him she'd be all by herself, except for whoever was in the kitchen making more wing, just for him. He was out in the car before it occurred to him that, without even thinking, he'd both remembered and spoken her name. Which lifted his own spirits.

It was late afternoon by the time he finished up at the office and drove inland to Winslow, where his brother, the local high school principal, lived in the same moribund mill town where they'd grown up. "Ray," Bill said, picking up on the first ring. "You here in town?"

"Just pulling in."

"Good thing I'm not in the Bahamas."

"You're assuming I'm here to see you."

"Who'd you come to see, then?"

"You."

"See? Right again. It's been one of those days. You try like hell to make a mistake and just can't. You know the kind I mean?"

"Not really."

"Well, that's because you're not me. Let me toss some people out of my office and I'll meet you at Ollie's."

"That's a tavern, Bill. You don't drink."

"How would you know? We haven't seen each other since Easter. I might've been drunk every day since Jesus rose from the dead."

"Then I'll buy the first round."

By the time Bill slid onto an adjacent barstool, Ray had already drunk half a beer. "I *have* been to the Bahamas, you know," his brother said, as if it'd be pointless to proceed without first entering this into the record. "I might not succumb to wanderlust like you, but I've been places."

It was an old joke between them. Both had spent their entire adult lives in Maine, but Ray had gone to college out of state and his brother to UMaine at Orono. Plus he still lived in the house they'd grown up in, which made him the brother who'd *really* stayed put. Ray, forty miles away, was still "gallivanting around."

"Last year, in fact," Bill continued. "Jan and I went to one of those all-inclusive resorts. That one you see advertised on TV, named for some kind of footwear. Slippers? Thongs? Sneakers? Before you even check in, they sit you down in this big conference room—you and all the people you flew in with—and explain how everything's free, all the food and drink, whatever you want, all included in what you paid up front. Thing is? This orientation takes about an hour, and the whole time you're sitting there, you don't get so much as a glass of water. You just had this hot taxi ride in from the airport and want to jump into your bathing suit and murder a piña colada, but first you have to listen to them go on and on about how great it's going to be and how you can go ahead and put your wallet in the room safe because you won't need it, even for tipping. Especially for tipping. That was one of the things they stressed. Ironclad rule: no tipping. Staff's been specially trained not to accept gratuities of any sort. They wanted us to be totally clear about that, totally at ease. Like they knew how generous we'd be otherwise, handing out cash to everybody we saw. This whole time we can see out to the pool where people who arrived on earlier flights are splashing around or sitting at the swim-up bar and not tipping the bartenders. It looks pretty great, all right, but damned if you can get there. Kind of like going to the lake with Mom and Pop when we were kids. Remember how it took forever? And it was like, what . . . three miles away? And then you'd finally get there and the other kids were all in the water and you wanted to run straight in, but first Mom had to rub on suntan lotion? And whoever she lathered up first would have to wait until she did the other? How time would stop dead in its tracks?"

Ray motioned to the bartender for another beer.

"Anyhow, this Flip-Flops place in the Bahamas. On the flight home, across the aisle, there's this guy with beady little eyes, probably in his twenties—and enormous. We're talking morbidly obese, and he's telling these people who'd gone to some other resort how they'd made a *major* mistake. He explained there was no reason to even leave Loafers once you were there, because they had half-a-dozen different restaurants right on the premises, though he and his wife just kept going back to the seafood smorgasbord. You could fill your plate, take fifty oysters if you wanted, nobody was counting. Then get right back in line and take fifty more. Go as many times as you wanted and nobody'd say a thing. He couldn't get over it. His one regret was that his wife—she was asleep in the seat next to him, in a diabetic coma by the looks of it—didn't really get her money's worth 'cause she couldn't fill her plate more than two or three times. All and all, though, he still thought it was worth it." Bill's voice fell here, indicating he'd come to the end of his story, which, like all his brother's stories, to Ray's mind, left something to be desired. The bartender, who'd been hovering, offered to make Bill a piña colada, but he said no, just a club soda with a squeeze of lime.

To Ray's surprise, he was relieved. "And the point of that whole story is?"

"Well, it made me wonder about us Americans. I don't remember people being so hungry back in the day, do you? What does it mean that we can't get filled up anymore?" He paused when he saw Ray shaking his head. "Why? What'd you think the point was?"

"For starters, I couldn't help noticing the whole middle of the story was missing."

"What middle?"

"Exactly. You went right from the orientation room to the plane ride home. What happened in the Bahamas? Did you have a good time?"

His brother stared at him, clearly annoyed. "My point was I might've *been* in the Bahamas, okay? You drove all this way without calling first to make sure I wasn't in the tropics. I wouldn't even have brought up the whole Clogs business if I thought it'd give you some precious insight into my character. Next you'll be telling me I'm like Pop."

"That *was* next, actually."

His brother nodded. "I tell you a story about what a world traveler I've become and it reminds you of a man who never went anywhere."

"If he'd gone, he would've left out the fun part, too."

Both grinning now, they shook hands. "What brings you so far inland?"

"As if you didn't know."

His brother nodded. "Paula did call, I won't lie to you."

"It's not as big a thing as she's making out."

"That's what I told her."

"Did she get as mad at you as she did at me?"

"No, but Jan did. She was eavesdropping, as usual."

"Tricky location is all."

"But no metastasis?"

"Not as far as they can tell."

"All right, then. They go in. Snick snick. You do a regimen for four or five months and you're good to go. Or, in our family, stay."

"Except Uncle Jack. He went."

Given what an out-of-left-field allusion this was, Ray half expected Bill to say, *Who?* Instead, he nodded gravely, as if their uncle had been on his mind as well, which if true would've been beyond strange. "Ah, yes. Uncle Jack."

"I woke up thinking about him this morning," Ray admitted. "You remember the fistfight? Him and Pop?"

Bill rolled his eyes. "*Mom* is what I remember most. How furious she was at the two of them?"

"I don't think she spoke to Pop for a month."

"It made for a pretty quiet house. Even under normal circumstances he wouldn't've said shit if he had a mouthful. And with her giving him the silent treatment . . ." There was just enough resentment in his tone to remind Ray they'd never seen eye to eye on their father. He'd been particularly hard on Bill, whom he regarded as careless and undisciplined, which was probably why his brother, even after all these years, often showed a bitterness that Ray couldn't quite summon.

"You remember what they were fighting about?"

Bill shrugged. "Who knows? They couldn't be in the same room without some sort of argument flaring up. Been at it since they were boys, was my understanding. Dad always claimed Uncle Jack was all hat and no cattle." He chuckled. "Remember how Jack couldn't stand still, always hopping from one foot to the other?"

Ray shook his head.

"Oh, come on. We used to make fun of him. Stand behind him

where he couldn't see us. Stand on whatever foot he was standing on and hop back and forth when he did. Pop thought it was funny, but Mom always made us stop."

"Are you making this up?"

"Hell, no. And he always called Pop 'Tommy-Boy.'"

Like Ray himself, Bill was a gifted mimic, and as soon as he started in Ray could see and hear their uncle across the decades.

"'You know your problem, Tommy-Boy, you're scared to take a chance. Somebody gives you a nickel, you put it in your pocket and that's where it stays. Want some help turning that nickel into a dime or maybe even a quarter? No sir. Not our Tommy-Boy. He's got his nickel, by God, and he knows right where it is. Save that nickel for a rainy day, right? Trouble is, Tommy, all your days are rainy. Sun ever came out, you wouldn't know what to do.'"

They shared an embarrassed laugh, the source of their self-consciousness unclear, at least to Ray. His brother's spot-on mimicry? Its implied betrayal?

"I guess that's why we were so proud of him that day," Bill continued. "Usually, Dad just sat there and took it."

"Whatever became of him? Uncle Jack?" Ray asked, mostly to shift the emphasis away from their father.

"He went out west somewhere. I want to say Arizona. Made a shitload of money, Mom said."

When had she confided this? Ray wondered. How had the subject even come up? He decided not to inquire. The bond between Bill and their mother, always strong, had deepened after their father's death. Bill was still drinking then and hadn't yet begun to rise through the teachers' ranks toward administration. Something about her older son's struggles touched their mother deeply, and Ray suspected she confided things to him that she'd probably never told to anyone else.

"Whatever he was into went bust and he lost it all. Then he made another bundle and lost that, too. Got in trouble south of the border and spent some time in a Mexican jail. When he got out people kept asking him what it'd been like, but all he'd say was, 'Good tacos.'"

"Is he dead?"

"Oh, Christ, I hope so," Bill said, but he looked thoughtful. "He did have a point about Dad, though. All his days *were* rainy, the poor bastard. You mind me asking what all this has to do with cancer?"

"Damned if I know."

"Damned if I do, either," Bill said, clinking his soda glass against Ray's beer bottle.

Later, out in the parking lot, Ray said, "So, when they finally let you out of orientation, did you drink a piña colada?"

His brother shook his head. "I thought about it, but I was afraid that if I got going good I wouldn't be able to quit. That's always how it used to work when I was younger."

The two brothers parted then, shaking hands warmly in the parking lot, both wondering out loud why they didn't make a point of seeing each other more often.

Before Ray could turn the key in the ignition, his cell phone rang.

"You're married, so I assume you know what it feels like to have your balls in a vise," Cliff Bell said. "Cheryl, light of my life, wants to see that first house again."

"Really?"

"The things we do for love, right? Anyhow, while I got you on the phone, here's a question. If we moved here? To Maine? Would we make any friends?"

Ray tried to remember whether in all his years as a realtor he'd ever been asked that question before. It was a good one, if impossible to answer.

"Take you and me," Cliff Bell continued when he hesitated. "If I called you up some night and said let's go get a beer, would you go?"

"I don't see why not," said Ray, falling victim yet again to the same sort of charitable impulse that had led to his friendship with Vinnie.

"All right, then. That's good to know."

Hanging up, Ray thought about calling Nicki with the good news, decided against it, had a perfectly crazy idea, dismissed it, then had it again. Vinnie answered on the first ring.

"How'd you like to do me a favor?"

"Name it, bud."

Ray did and when he hung up there was a rap on his window.

"You reminded me of something else," his brother said when he rolled it down. About their father, Ray assumed, or maybe Uncle Jack. Instead his brother was back in the Bahamas. "The couple listening to the fat guy carry on about the seafood buffet had gone to this clothing-optional resort on the other side of the island from Moccasins, and according to them the experience was 'liberating.' They claimed that after a few hours, you didn't notice anymore."

"Yeah, right."

"But here's the funny thing. You know how modest my Jan is, right? She leans over and whispers maybe we should go *there* next year. She was sort of joking, but also sort of not. Kind of made me wonder about Dad."

Ray couldn't help laughing. "You think he was secretly a dick-out kind of guy?"

"No. But don't you wonder sometimes if he ever got tired of

just putting one foot in front of the other like he did every day at that damned mill. I'm not saying he should've invested in one of Uncle Jack's scams, but . . ." He looked off, and even in the dark Ray could see his brother was choking on emotion. "Anyhow," he continued, waving whatever memory it was away, "you had an insight into my character earlier, which means I get to offer one into yours. You remember what Dad always said about hospitals?"

Ray nodded. "Never let the bastards take your pants, because—"

"bare-assed men don't get to make decisions," Bill finished.

Ray scratched his head. "That's an insight into his character, not mine."

"You think?" his brother said.

When he pulled into Nicki's an hour later, Vinnie was sitting on the tailgate of a pickup truck Ray'd never seen before, drinking from a tiny snifter. Next to him sat a bottle of brandy.

"Hand truck is what I said," Ray told him, "not pickup truck."

Vinnie slid off the gate so Ray could see the dolly resting in the truck's ribbed bed. "You thought I'd put it in the backseat of my Benz? On my leather seats?"

Ray got out and extended his hand, which Vinnie, as always, slapped away. "Get outa here," he said, pulling Ray into the obligatory embrace. "How's every little thing?"

Ray told him every little thing was fabulous.

"This'll make it even better," he said, taking from the pocket of his parka another small snifter. "Napoléon," he said, pouring. "The best. A guy I know from the old days sends me a bottle every year. If I told you the price—"

". . . you'd have to kill me," Ray finished.

They clinked glasses, and Ray downed his brandy in one swig for the pleasure of watching Vinnie flinch.

"You can take the boy out of Maine," he said, "but you can't take Maine out of the boy." When Ray declined a second nip, Vinnie put the bottle and both glasses on the seat of the pickup, then looked around. "So what are we doing here? Robbing the joint?"

"Just rearranging it a bit."

Nor would it take long. The stuff of other people's lives is problematic mostly for themselves. The disinterested eye sees where things go and in what order, not only where they belong but where they *fit*. Hauling the kayak out of the garage, they each had the same simultaneous brainstorm of hoisting it up onto the rafters. As they worked, Vinnie returned to the Boston surgeon, how he was the number one guy, how they'd been in the same fraternity and if Ray dropped Vinnie's name he'd go right to the top of a huge waiting list. Ray let him ramble on. There were times when his friend's boasting seemed an intentional provocation, its source their manifest philosophical and political incompatibility. But who knew? Maybe their differences amounted to little more than temperament. That or some childhood experience, like a well-meaning parent telling you you're special and you taking them literally. Perhaps someday in a quiet moment he'd explain to Vinnie his contempt for privilege and its myriad handmaidens, but he felt little need to do so tonight as they loaded Nicki's life onto the hand truck and wrestled it, without permission, out into her frigid garage.

What amazed Ray was how early in life people started taking sides and how entrenched they became as a result. As a boy he'd taken his father's part in most things, and to this day he disliked men who inhaled more than their share of oxygen and converted it into charm. Perhaps his father *had* lacked imagination, as Uncle Jack maintained. And maybe, as his brother had too readily conceded, all their father's days *had* been rainy. But anybody who thought he liked standing in lines was mistaken. Nobody enjoyed that. Nor could he have enjoyed some minion telling him what he was entitled to when he finally made it to the front of that line. By the same token, though, could a man judge his own merits, reward his own efforts and call it justice?

Vinnie, of course, wouldn't be engaged by such abstractions. It would make more sense to explain to him that not all lines were bad. It was in a long registration line, sophomore year, that he'd met Paula. It'd been hot, and Ray was in a vile mood because the line wasn't moving and everybody knew the campus Greeks had figured out how to beat the system and sign up early for the most popular classes or those meeting in the afternoon. He remembered going on at some length about the injustice of it all, taking yet again, in this new social context, his father's part against men like his uncle, though of course he hadn't realized then that this was what he was doing. He probably hadn't even introduced himself to Paula, just launched right in. Why, he couldn't help wondering now, would such a lovely girl have listened for as long as she did? When he finally let his voice fall, she'd arched an eyebrow and said, not mean-spiritedly, but as if she was genuinely curious, "Are you like this *all the time*?" Here, he recalled thinking, was someone who'd be good for him.

They'd gone out a few times that semester—to movies, the coffeehouse, nothing serious. After all, why fall in love with somebody who was good for you? Was it even possible to do so? Maybe. Right before spring break, when he learned of his father's diagnosis, he asked Paula if she wanted to come with him to Maine. For some reason he wanted her to meet his parents, see the house he'd grown up in, experience the tough grittiness of central Maine. But how would he have phrased the invitation? *Come meet my father before he dies? Come see why I'm "like this all the time"?* Actually, she seemed to be waiting for just such an invitation. When he returned to school, though, she told him that over the break she'd gotten engaged to a guy from back home and would be transferring the following year to be near him. The news had hit Ray harder than he wanted to admit. He told himself to be grateful he hadn't fallen for her completely, and anyhow he had no business losing his heart when his father was terminally ill, but part of him knew he already had. Later, after his father died and he couldn't get Paula out of his thoughts, he briefly considered trying to find out if she'd actually married the guy, but of course she must have.

Except she hadn't, and when their paths unexpectedly crossed again years later, in another line outside a concert in Portland, it turned out she'd been thinking about him, too, wondering what had become of him, if he still had that enormous chip on his shoulder, because otherwise he was a pretty nice guy. Vinnie would enjoy this story of their interrupted courtship. Chance. Dumb luck. These were things Vinnie's personal philosophy could accommodate, at least in small doses and in the service of a happy ending.

Yeah, his brother had been right to ask what the past had to do with his present tumor. But life was full of mysteries, large and small. They also tended to pile up. Boxes and boxes and boxes of the inexplicable, until you could barely move amid the clutter. Worthless crap, most of it, but when you took in the sheer mass and weight of it, how could you not be discouraged when the time came to clean house, and where did you begin?

It took them just two hours, at the end of which all of Nicki's boxes—eighty-seven of them, by Vinnie's count—were stacked along one wall of the narrow, one-bay garage. It'd be a tight squeeze for her car now, but if he and Paula managed, by going slow and being careful, Nicki could, too, at least until the property sold. While Vinnie stowed the dolly in the bed of the pickup, Ray went back inside for one last look at what they'd done, feeling a sense of accomplishment that he knew perfectly well he wasn't entitled to. The only justification he could think of for intervening in Nicki's life was that someone needed to—which left the ends to justify their means as best they could. It was possible, of course, that she'd be pleased, but if she was outraged, who could blame her? Nor did it escape him that the conclusion he'd come to about her—that it was simply *being* Nicki that came between her and what she wanted most—was the same conclusion Paula had reached about him last night. Nor, apparently, was she wrong. After all, he'd promised to call Vinnie's doctor today and instead had found other things to fill the hours. He could tell himself and Paula that he'd do it tomorrow, but would he?

Ray still vividly remembered his mother's anger when his father meekly accepted his own diagnosis, refusing to seek a second opinion. "But you could be one of the lucky ones," she pleaded, when he told her about the odds the doctor had given him. "I'm *already* one of the lucky ones. You don't believe me, ask Bo Phelps. Dan Johnson. Your brother Rudy." All dead in the war was his point. Of course Ray had been as mystified as his mother. What sort of man comes home from the doctor, calmly sits down in his favorite chair, the one that looks out onto the darkening street, and waits for his own death as if it would arrive like a slow-moving taxi, plowing dutifully through wintry slush? For that matter, what sort of man stubbornly refuses to consider the possibility that this need not be his fate, that in addition to snow and slush there existed in the known world both sun and clean, sparkling water? It made no sense.

But he must also have been proud of his father, or why would he be emulating him now? It hadn't been a conscious decision—*I'll do this the way my father did it*—when he was informed about his own tumor. He'd simply concluded, as his father must've done, that he wasn't special, that there was no reason such a thing shouldn't happen to him. Like his father, he hadn't protested that he was too young, or that he'd been cheated, or that life was unfair, or that he deserved an exemption. Okay, maybe it was true the old man wouldn't say shit if he had a mouthful, but he never in his life cut a line, and the only regret Ray had ever heard him express was that in the end he'd violated his own rule and let the bastards take his pants.

Ray was yanked out of this reverie when a dog yelped outside, then commenced howling pitifully. He didn't immediately realize that the dog was actually Vinnie, who'd gotten into the pickup to escape the biting wind and sat on one of the snifters.

It was nearly midnight when Paula got home from Portland. Ray, standing at the kitchen window when she pulled in, watched her point the remote at the garage door, which jerked into motion, dutifully rattled upward that first couple of feet, then stuck, just as it had done a few minutes earlier when Ray himself returned from the hospital, where Vinnie's ass had required stitches.

"Fucking thing," Ray heard her mutter in the mudroom a minute later, struggling to get her boots off. "God, how did you know?" she said when he handed her a glass of red wine.

"Well," he said, trying to read from her demeanor how the trip had gone, "you don't look any *poorer*."

Clearly exhausted, she collapsed onto one of the kitchen-island stools. "You know what we need? You and I?"

"Nothing," he said, his standard response whenever she asked this. "We have everything we need."

"No, you aren't going to talk me out of this."

"Okay, what do we need?"

She looked up at the ceiling fan, calculating. "Round figure? Fifty million dollars."

"*One* million is a round figure," he pointed out. "Shouldn't we start small?"

"One million doesn't help us."

He shrugged. "Okay, then, fifty it is."

"If we had fifty million, I wouldn't ever have to ask anybody for money again. We could just fund everything ourselves. Education. The food bank. Disaster relief. All of it." She considered the ceiling fan again. "Make it a hundred million."

"Better safe than sorry," he agreed. "And Rormacher?"

"They liked the proposal. Which means it goes up the chain of command. So for the moment we're alive."

To that they clinked glasses.

"I expected you to be asleep," she said, really taking him in now—tired, dirty, the knuckles of his right hand skinned. "What have you been up to?"

"Trying to get Nicki to fire me," he said, explaining how he and Vinnie had moved everything but her furniture out into the garage. "Vinnie knew a guy with a hand truck. Normally he doesn't loan it out, but as a favor to Vinnie—"

"Stop," she said. "He's your friend." She was smiling, though, so he returned the favor.

"I know," he said, and he did. Indeed, back at Nicki's their friendship had deepened, or at least become more intimate, when

Vinnie dropped his trousers and leaned into the cab of the pickup so that Ray, by the dome light, could first locate, then extract, a long, delicate shard of glass from his rump. But before he could relate any of this, Paula unexpectedly took his hand and said, "Since you've admitted to exceeding your mandate with Nicki, I might as well come clean, too. You have an appointment in Boston next Tuesday."

Ray nodded, feeling his throat constrict in . . . what? Anger? Panic? Closer to the latter, he decided. Not because he was afraid of the surgery, or even that it wouldn't be successful. But rather that taking this necessary next step would accelerate matters. He'd have to give the bastards his pants. And that, as his brother had astutely diagnosed, had been the problem all along. He was about to become yet another bare-assed, middle-aged man, the kind who didn't get to make decisions.

He was rinsing their glasses in the sink, Paula having headed upstairs to bed, when his cell rang. It was far too late for anybody to be calling, which meant it was probably the Bells. They'd thought matters through and decided that in this market there was no hurry. They'd go back to Texas and return in the spring and see how things looked then. Serve him right, too, for intervening at Nicki's.

Except it wasn't the Bells. "He's dead," his brother told him by way of hello.

"Who is?"

"Uncle Jack. I googled him. He died in Arizona. Some godforsaken place named Rio Rita, down by the Mexican border. He was the front man for some sort of land swindle, or that's what it sounds like. Big story about it in a Tucson newspaper. A lot of people lost money. When things got thoroughly befucked, everybody absconded but Jack. Apparently he stayed on in the model home. The article made it sound like he lost his mind, claiming right to the end that everything was on track. He'd take people out and show them where the lake was going to be and the clubhouse and the golf course. It was all desert, of course, nothing to see but a few stakes in the ground. He was running his electric off a gas generator. It was dry when they found him and there was no gas in his truck, either."

"Rio Rita," Ray repeated. And suddenly he remembered what had been different about the day the two brothers fought. Uncle Jack saying, *Okay, fine, Tommy-Boy, if you want to be a chump, Godspeed. But why breed other little chumps. Look at them. What kind of shot are they going to have in the world? And that rag of a dress Rita's wearing? A woman like that deserves—*

At the mention of their mother's name, *that* was when their father came flying out of his chair. And with that understanding Ray could feel things click into place, like tumblers aligning in the moment before the safe's door thunks open. The sensation was not unlike the vertigo he'd felt that morning at the top of the stairs, and he steadied himself against the kitchen counter now, suddenly weak-kneed.

"That's what it was called? Rio Rita?"

"The name struck me, too. Probably just a coincidence, though. According to the newspaper he was married five times."

"Yeah, but it was Mom they fought about that day, wasn't it? Uncle Jack must've been in love with her."

"Who knows? Maybe. I thought about asking her once toward the end, but I never did."

"How come?"

"I don't know. I guess maybe I thought she wasn't put on this earth to satisfy my curiosity."

"Everything okay?" Paula asked sleepily when he slid into bed.

"Fine."

"Your brother calls you after midnight and everything's fine?"

"He wanted to tell me about this clothing-optional resort in the Bahamas."

"Bill—your *brother*—went to a nudie resort? With Jan?"

"No, it's just something he heard about. Thought we might be interested."

When he rolled toward her, she placed a warm hand on his waist. "It's clothing optional right here."

Later, as he drifted toward sleep, Ray reexamined, in light of "Rio Rita," his father's strange equanimity when he was diagnosed. He'd always imagined his acceptance was rooted in deep conviction, but now he wondered if he was just worn out, tired of his life, of what it had amounted to, of how relentlessly it had thwarted him. He'd fallen out of love with their mother by then, Ray now realized. It was almost as if their uncle's abiding affection for her, combined with his physical proximity, had been keeping the urgency of their marriage alive. Nor, Ray had to admit, had he felt any pressing need for his sons. Those last few years his father had seemed more abstracted than anything, both weary of life's drama and puzzled by his own insignificant part in it, like a man who'd always believed the choice not to speak had been his, only to discover when he changed his mind that he was mute.

And what about their uncle? Out in Arizona, did Jack think about his brother in Maine anymore? Had he been tempted to phone, to offer him one last opportunity to invest in a sure thing? Probably not. Even that day on the porch he seemed to know it was over. He returned to consciousness in surprisingly good spirits, Ray thought at the time, sitting down next to his brother on the porch steps, still astonished by what had transpired. "I guess you finally did it, Big Brother," he said. "You shut me up good. I won't be asking you for anything else, I promise." Ray could imagine his uncle, alone in the desert, picking up the phone, maybe even dialing, then setting the handset back in its cradle, recalling his promise, yes, but also realizing that all his attempts to intervene in his brother's life had ended badly and this one would, too. Because people cling to folly as if it were their most prized possession, defending it, sometimes with violence, against the possibility of wisdom.

It was all rather sad, but what Ray felt in the moments before sleep claimed him was the return of something he'd not even realized was missing—a cautious hope. Nicki's house would sell at some point, maybe even tomorrow. So would others, eventually. They'd save Paula's gallery somehow, or, if they couldn't, they'd start another later on. In the meantime they'd have to exercise patience and care, qualities they possessed at least most of the time. He'd have the surgery—of course he would. As his brother put it, snick snick, and then you do the regimen. After which the bastards give you back your pants and you move on.

Outside, it was snowing hard, the beginning of yet another long Maine winter, not his last.

Milton and Marcus

In the film business you hate for things to be fucked up at the start. They'll end up there, it goes without saying. You're a writer and you're not stupid, so you know this. Nor is your own relative insignificance in the overall scheme of things in doubt. Films belong to producers for a time, then to directors, and in the end to stars. You? The writer? Forget the yearly Oscar speeches given by actors. Writers are hirelings.

At the beginning, though, for a span of weeks or months, everyone pretends otherwise. Really, dude, it all depends on you. You're wined and dined. If you write books as well as screenplays, you're told that your last one wasn't just a good read, it was fucking literature, though the person telling you this hasn't read it and you know he hasn't. If you're not the first screenwriter on the project, you're given to understand that the whole thing was a clusterfuck because it's obvious you're the right guy, the one who understands working-class people, or Ivy League professors, or returning Iraq veterans, or whoever the fuck this movie's about. It's all bullshit and you know it, just like you know that in due course you'll be fired, though probably not by the people flattering you now. By then at least one of these smooth talkers, maybe all of them, will have attached themselves to a more promising project, its financing more secure, its star coming off a hit. Someone new will read your most recent draft and that person will send you an e-mail saying you've made real progress in this pass. Shortly thereafter, maybe even the same day, your agent will phone. It's the call you've been expecting for a while, the one telling you the studio has decided to take the project in a new direction, because it turns out you're *not* the right guy after all, the one who understands working-class people, or Ivy League professors, or returning Iraq veterans, or whoever the fuck this movie's about. Now you can go back to your life, to the book you interrupted to take this gig, the one that people on your next film project will claim to admire, though they won't have read that one, either.

My point is that even though the whole charade is pretty tawdry and transparent, you look forward to it, or part of you does, the part that enjoys being flattered and lied to. The more cynical you are, the more you look forward to it. Which is why I was put off when it appeared we'd be dispensing with this ritual on *Milton and Marcus.* The initial meeting was supposed to take place in LA, where Jason, who was attached to direct, was shooting a pilot for cable TV. But then Regular Bill wondered if we could meet at his place in Jackson Hole, where he was cutting his recently completed film, *Desperation Alley,* which was rumored to be overbudget and behind schedule. Anticipating a yes, he'd already flown there along with Marty, his producing partner. Jason suggested that he and I both fly to Salt Lake, rent a car and drive to Jackson Hole. We'd worked together years earlier, when he was young and I was middle-aged. Now he was middle-aged and in another year I'd qualify for Medicare, which was good because I hadn't worked in quite a while and consequently my health insurance had lapsed. The long, leisurely drive from Salt Lake to Jackson Hole would give us a chance to catch up and maybe talk a bit about *Milton and Marcus* before we sat down with Marty and Regular Bill. To me that sounded like a good idea. A man can only serve one master, and as far as I'm concerned that's the director, even when the power behind the project is a Hollywood legend.

Of course alliances between directors and writers are not perceived to be in the best interests of producers and stars, so I wasn't entirely surprised to learn that Regular Bill had gotten wind of our plan and talked Jason into flying to Jackson a day early, after his pilot wrapped, so he could view a cut of *Desperation Alley*. My own travel arrangements were left as they were, which meant I'd now have to make the long drive from Salt Lake alone. Marty apologized for the inconvenience, but insisted that once there I'd appreciate having my own vehicle. "Think of it as your getaway car," he confided. "Bill's a workaholic. You don't want to be trapped."

I was halfway to Jackson when Jason called my cell. "You're here," he said, by which he seemed to mean that I was no longer in Vermont. "You've got GPS?"

"On my phone."

"Good. Bill says come up for a drink?" The original plan had been for me to check into my hotel and meet the others for dinner. After all, I'd had an early wake-up call and was still on East Coast time.

"Up?"

"His place is on a mountaintop. Unless you're too wiped out," he added, apparently sensing reluctance in my hesitation.

Before I could answer I heard, in the background, the one-of-a-kind voice of William Nolan, unmistakable, even over a tinny cell phone. "Tell him I'll make him the best margarita he's ever tasted."

"You catch that?" Jason said.

I said I had and entered Nolan's address into my cell.

I was halfway up Nolan's mountain, two hours later, when my wife called. "You okay?" I asked.

"Of course," she said. "I told you I would be."

"Is Cassie there yet?"

"She just called from the airport. She'll be here shortly."

"Did you eat?"

"Some soup."

"Look, I'm on a windy dirt road." At this elevation Jackson looked like a town made out of Lincoln Logs on the valley floor. "I'll call you in the morning?"

"I'll be here. I promise."

Up ahead there was a place you could pull off, so I did. And threw up.

The woman who answered the door looked to be in her mid-forties. She was dressed in a leotard, her upper lip dewy, apparently from a workout. She introduced herself as Tina, and I recognized her from the tabloids as Nolan's second wife.

"There he is," said the man himself, rising from the outdoor sofa when I was ushered out onto the deck. He and Jason and a third man I took to be Marty—we'd only spoken on the phone—were in fact drinking margaritas. Nolan was wearing a pair of weathered snakeskin boots, faded jeans and a coarse poncho over a T-shirt that was stretched at the neck. Marty wore a suit, white button-down shirt, no tie. Jason had on jeans and a long-sleeve shirt, not tucked in, boat shoes, no jacket. We were high up and despite the season it was chilly, which made me wonder if Nolan had noticed Jason's discomfort and offered him a jacket. They were about the same size. Hard to accept a garment from an icon, though. We shook hands all around.

"You arrange that just for me?" I said, because the sun was setting between two peaks, Jackson Hole in deep shadow now, lights in town coming on like jewels on velvet. The private road I'd ascended snaked down the mountain until it gradually merged with the darkness. I recognized the spot where I'd pulled over to be sick. On the railing sat a pair of expensive-looking binoculars. Not the best place to leave them because the deck was built out over the ravine, so if someone accidentally jostled them they'd free-fall a hundred yards before they hit anything. I made a mental note to not be the one to do that.

Nolan held our handshake that extra Hollywood half beat. "I'm guessing you go by Ryan?" he said, my last name, and not guessing, either, since I'd told him that on the phone last week. Still, if he wanted to feel prescient, I had no objection. "You need to use the bathroom?"

A man my age, did he mean, after a long drive? He was fifteen years my senior, though, so maybe he only meant to suggest that he understood if I did. "No, I'm good."

"I only mention it," he continued, pointing at my shirt, "because you've got a little bit of . . ."

Looking down, I saw what he meant: the word he was looking for was *vomit*.

By the time I returned, a wet spot the size of a sunflower on my shirt front, Regular Bill had shaken my margarita and was pouring it into a salt-rimmed glass. "Tell me what you think," he said, which I translated as *Tell me what I want to hear.*

"Best margarita I ever tasted," I told him, and no lie, either.

"Small-batch tequila," he explained, topping off Marty's and Jason's glasses. "I could almost tell you the exact agave plant it was distilled from." He consulted his watch. "Time for just one, I'm afraid. We've got an eight o'clock dinner reservation in town."

I nodded, letting that sink in. I'd risen at five, flown from Burlington to Boston, from Boston to Salt Lake City, then driven nearly five hours to Jackson. Instead of letting me check into my hotel and catch a short nap, they'd had me drive another half hour to the top of Nolan's mountain, only to turn around and drive back down again. Good tequila was supposed to make that all right.

"Anyway, it's not his fault," Nolan said, returning to the conversation that my reappearance on the deck had interrupted. "The only acting the kid's ever done is in front of a blue screen. Worse, he has no life experience."

Unless I was mistaken, they were discussing a well-known young actor who'd made his name in action movies driven by special effects. He'd taken a small but significant role in *Desperation Alley.* While I was driving from Salt Lake, Nolan evidently had screened the film for Jason.

"Yeah," Jason said, "but he's what? Twenty-three?"

"At twenty-three I spent a year backpacking across Europe," Nolan said.

"Alone?"

"Nah, with this guy Renny. We both flunked out of Claremont the same semester. He's probably still over there. All he wanted to do was bum around and smoke dope. Which, don't get me wrong, was fun for a while."

"Anyway," Jason said, circling back to the young actor, "he's not that bad. In your mind's eye you're probably still seeing all the bad takes."

"That's the other thing. The takes are identical. You say, Let's try something different, and he says, Yeah, okay, but then he does the exact same thing."

"Why did you cast him?"

Nolan rolled his eyes. "There must've been a reason, or I wouldn't have done it. Marty. Why did we cast him?"

"You liked the fact that he wanted to be in a real movie," Marty said. Apparently one of his jobs was explaining Nolan to Nolan. "Also, his name got us green-lit."

"See?" Nolan said. "I knew there was a reason. Two reasons. That's one more than I usually have."

"Two more," Marty corrected, finishing his margarita and setting the glass down.

Nolan flashed him the smile that, even in his midseventies, still caused women to moisten their panties. "You, too, can be replaced."

The smile lingered on Marty for a beat, then fixed on me. I assumed the idea was to include me in the joke, but then I realized I'd heard *too* when he might've meant *two*. For his part, Jason had the look of a man who was fluent in a whole other language where *two* meant *three*.

Milton and Marcus, the project we were about to embark on, was only fourteen pages in its entirety. I'd written it a decade earlier for the great Wendell Percy. Wendy and I had become friends when I did an uncredited rewrite of a screenplay that ended up getting him his seventh Oscar nomination. The script was based on one of those surprise literary best sellers that are all about the sentences. Several A-list screenwriters had taken a crack at it and had done about as well as you could, given that the book was all interiors, most of the interesting stuff taking place in the characters' heads, with very few actual scenes to move along what little plot there was. All the dialogue had to be invented. I'd been hired to punch that up, which I did, but I'd identified another problem, as well—that an interesting minor character had been allowed to fade into dramatic insignificance, letting a lot of air out of the narrative balloon. In my draft I'd kept her alive and made a few other little changes that gave the story some much-needed torque going into the final act. Wendy claimed I saved the movie, but that was hardly the case. It had a gifted young director and a terrific cast. But I was briefly lauded as a script guru, and Wendy hired me to doctor two subsequent screenplays, though I wasn't able to work comparable magic on those.

Over the years we kind of stayed in touch, and when I had a new book out, Wendy always called to congratulate me. I think he must've known that my work had lost a good deal of its vitality by then. Each book sold fewer copies than the one before, and while the critics remained mostly respectful, many reviewers seemed to agree that my earlier books had felt far more urgent than these later ones. The sad truth is that some writers have less fuel in the tank than others, and when the vehicle begins to shudder, you'd do well to pull over to the side of the road and look for alternative transportation, which was what I did. I took a series of adjunct writer-in-residence gigs that allowed me to keep up the pretense of being a novelist. Living in Vermont, I wasn't offered much script work, though every now and then Phil Gast, my Hollywood agent, would land me a rewrite. Over the last decade even those had dried up, and visiting-writer gigs began to disappear, too, at least in New England.

When I heard a rumor that Wendy was ill, I sent him an e-mail saying long-time-no-hear, but not mentioning the rumor. An hour later the phone rang, and there was his gravelly voice on the line. "Hotshot!" he said, his favorite nickname for people he liked. "Listen, I've got this script I'd like you to look at."

When he told me the title, I recognized it as a nonfiction book that had been published a decade earlier. It seemed an odd fit for Wendy, and I said so.

"Nolan wants to do it," he explained, which made a kind of sense, given the book's earnest, left-wing politics. Clearly he, Nolan, would play the book's beleaguered protagonist.

"What's in it for you?"

"I don't know," he admitted. "We've been looking for something since *The Monte Carlo Affair*, and we're not getting any younger."

Back in the eighties he and Nolan had made three enormously successful buddy pictures, the first and best about two Depression-era con artists. Wendy was already a huge star, of course, and Nolan was well on his way to becoming one. By the time they finished *Monte Carlo*—the last and thinnest of the three films, held together by little more than the extraordinary charisma of its two iconic actors—Nolan was the bigger star, and he went on to have one hit after another in the nineties, all important movies. By then Wendy's star had begun to dim. After his daughter, a photographer, died covering a war in the Middle East, he began to look his age and was having an unprecedented string of flops. Toward the end of the decade, though, he made a major comeback playing compromised men—politicians and lawyers and gamblers—and suddenly he was a star again. And not just a star, either: more like a national treasure.

Anyway, we left it that I'd have a look at the script and give him my thoughts. He made no mention of any illness. So, just a rumor then.

The following week, we talked again. "I still don't get it," I confessed. "Where's your role?"

"Maybe one of the minor characters could be expanded," he suggested. "Or you could invent somebody new."

"The book's nonfiction," I pointed out, not unreasonably.

"Think about it."

That night I sat down with the source material, but the book, like the script, was a one-guy story. To make it a two-guy story you'd basically be starting from scratch, and even then it would lack the wit that had distinguished the other three films he and Nolan had done, and neither man wanted to make a movie that would pale in comparison to the others. Wendy had told me about a few of the projects that had come close. Interestingly, it was always Nolan who said no, they should wait for the right thing to come along.

Yeah, okay, but *this* was the project they'd been waiting for? I guess I could see why Nolan wanted to do it, but why did he imagine Wendy would?

Rather than trying to figure that out, I wrote *Milton and Marcus,* or rather half of the first act, about a couple of over-the-hill con men going in for one last score. A cliché, but so what? As I envisioned the narrative, it would play to both men's comedic strengths. I would send the first act to Wendy, and if he liked it he could forward the pages to Nolan. Either that or I'd finish the script and we could offer it to him then. Before I could complete the first act, however, Wendy called. "Listen, Hotshot. Don't bother." About the other script, he meant. Nolan would make that one on his own and they would continue to look. But there was a catch in his voice—profound disappointment? hard-won acceptance?—so I said, "Actually, I have an idea for the two of you. A caper movie, like *Monte Carlo*."

"Yeah?" he said, sounding cheered. "Fax the pages to my office."

When I hung up it occurred to me that maybe this was what he'd wanted all along. Like all great actors, Wendy had a shrewd understanding of human nature, and he probably figured that if he presented me with a problem I'd try to solve it. He also knew that I was both grateful to him and fond of him. If he was playing me, I didn't mind. I was a writer, after all, and as such I possessed the same basic skill set as actors—an insight into what makes people tick, that and a certain cynical understanding that what makes them tick generally isn't what makes them good or even interesting. If actors are famously narcissistic, writers run a close second, and they generally have far less justification.

After sending the *Milton and Marcus* pages to Wendy's office, I didn't hear from him for a week, long enough for me to conjure a pleasant scenario of what might be happening behind the scenes. Wendy had seen in those pages the project they'd been waiting for and forwarded them to Nolan, who'd in turn sent them to the head of Paramount, with whom they'd make the deal. (Did I mention the narcissism of writers?)

But I was wrong, of course. Wendy called the next day.

"Good pages, Hotshot."

I could feel myself smiling. "I thought you might like—"

"But I'm finished."

"I'm sorry?"

"With movies."

"I don't understand."

"I never should've called you. That was selfish. I've known for a while."

"Known?"

"I wish I could, though. The pages sparkle. And no one would've been better as Marcus."

"Wendy—"

"Gotta go, Hotshot. You be good."

I remember hanging up the phone and just sitting there trying to parse my crushing disappointment. Much as I liked those fourteen pages, it wasn't really about them. They'd taken me all of a day and a half to write. So was it about Wendy, then? He'd inspired them and, yeah, I did want him to have one last picture with his old friend. I also wanted him not to be sick, and I now knew he was. Why hadn't I written those same pages a year or two ago when they might've done him some good? And yet, bad as I felt for Wendy, the feeling of hopelessness that descended on me felt completely out of proportion. Apparently I'd wanted *Milton and Marcus* for myself, as well. I'd begun wondering if maybe my tank wasn't empty after all. Maybe I could get back in the game. Make a little money. Do meaningful work again. Like I said, what makes people tick isn't neccessarily what makes them good.

Fast-forward, as we say in the movies, a full decade. Wendy's been dead for most of it. The phone rings and I don't recognize the caller ID or the area code. The caller identifies himself as Bill Nolan. I don't immediately twig to the fact that it's William Nolan because I've never heard anybody shorten that famous first name, and besides, why would William Nolan be calling me? "It's about *Milton and Marcus*," he said.

"Who and who?" I said, because really, after ten years? All of fourteen pages?

"You're the one that wrote it. Couple of con artists and a nun?"

"Wait," I said. "*William* Nolan?"

"Did you ever finish the script?"

"The man I was writing it for died."

"How about finishing it for me?"

"Seriously?"

"I was hoping you'd come out here and talk about it. Who's your agent?"

I told him.

"What do you go by?"

"Ryan," I said, my last name. "You?"

"Bill's fine," he assured me. "Just regular Bill."

ESTABLISHING SHOT: A LONG, LOW-SLUNG BUILDING.

IN THE F.G. IS A SIGN THAT READS: LAKELAND MEDICAL ARTS COMPLEX.

It's clear from the palm trees that we're somewhere in Florida.

INT. EXAMINATION ROOM—DAY

CLOSE ON a man (THOMAS MILTON, mid '60s, ruggedly handsome); his face is sideways (is he lying down?) and it practically fills the screen, and when we hear a SNAP, as of a latex glove, he flinches.

VOICE

How's Mother Alma?

MILTON

Mean as a snake. You should visit sometime.

WE GRADUALLY PULL BACK TO REVEAL that Milton is naked; he's lying in a fetal position on an examination table. When the B.G. comes into focus, we see the physician is working her fingers into the latex glove for a smooth, tight fit. Her name tag says: Dr. Gweneth Overby. (Early thirties, olive skinned and attractive.)

MILTON

Don't spare the lubricant.

Her smile contains just a hint of cruelty.

GWEN

(her finger lubricated)

Say ah.

And inserts her finger.

MILTON

Ahhhhhh! . . . Shit.

WE STAY ON MILTON'S GRIMACE until she finishes and he relaxes. As she removes the glove with another SNAP he sits up.

MILTON

How come you people always save that for last?
Because you enjoy it so much?

She's making a note on her clipboard.

GWEN

No, we just assume *you* do.

MILTON

(pulling on his boxers)

Go ahead, say it.

GWEN

Say what?

MILTON

That I'm still a perfect asshole.

She smiles, a little ruefully.

GWEN

Well, there doesn't seem to be anything amiss, if that's what you're getting at. Shall I call when I get the blood work?

MILTON

I don't have a phone.

GWEN

Right.

(smiling wryly)

Same address?

He's at the door now. He nods.

MILTON

We done?

GWEN

I guess.

MILTON

Good. Once again you've raised my spirits. The worst part of my day is over.

And he's out the door.

GWEN

(to herself)

Whatever you say, Dad.

INT. CORRIDOR—SAME

Milton COMES TOWARD US, just the slightest jig in his step to suggest the recently completed rectal exam. There are people seated in plastic chairs on both sides of the hall, and THE CAMERA REGISTERS that one of them is holding up a newspaper in front of his face. When Milton passes him, we hear:

VOICE

Milton.

Milton stops dead, closing his eyes as if in pain.

MILTON

I spoke too soon.

Now he turns around. The man who was reading the paper lowers it and rises to his feet. He's a trim, dapper-looking fellow in his seventies (MARCUS FLEET).

MARCUS

How's that?

MILTON

I thought a finger up my bum was going to be the low point of my day, but now I see I was wrong.

MARCUS

How come you never let bygones be bygones?

MILTON

Every time I think I'm about to, you show up again.

WE HOLD ON MILTON for a beat, then QUICK CUT TO:

EXT. MEDICAL ARTS BUILDING—SAME

Milton explodes out the front door and across the parking lot, Marcus right on his heels.

MARCUS

Hey, my bad. I should've called first, but—

MILTON

(whirling around to face him)

My bad? How old are you? Nineteen?

MARCUS

I try to stay young. Would you be happier if I said "my fault"?

MILTON

I'd be happier if you said goodbye.

And he's off again. Marcus is breathing hard now, but he catches up and grabs Milton by the elbow.

MARCUS

Look, I know our last adventure didn't end well.

MILTON

It ended with me in jail. Five years. Three months. Two days. Seventeen hours. But who's counting?

MARCUS

Hey, I had to leave the country myself.

MILTON

Yeah? Where you been?

MARCUS

(squirms)

The Turks and Caicos.

MILTON

Yeah? And how was that?

MARCUS

Loved the Turks. Hated the Caicos.

MILTON

(after a long beat)

Go. Away.

This time when Marcus catches up to him the two men are standing next to a dumpster.

MARCUS

About last time? If we'd had these

(he takes out a cell phone)

we never would've got caught.

Milton snorts, then plants his index finger in the middle of Marcus's forehead.

MILTON

If you'd had one of *these* we wouldn't have got caught.

Marcus takes out another identical phone.

MARCUS

I got one for you. All your major criminals use them now. They're disposable.

Without turning around, Milton tosses the phone over his shoulder and into the dumpster.

MARCUS

What're you doing?

MILTON

I just disposed of mine. And another thing. You were never a major criminal, Marcus. In fact, you were never a major *anything*.

There's a ramshackle old pickup truck sitting nearby with a bunch of rakes and shovels and bulging green-plastic lawn bags in its bed. Milton climbs into the truck, puts his key in the ignition. He's about to pull away when he notices that Marcus has gotten into the car in the next space: a vintage candy-apple-red Cadillac convertible, meticulously cared for. Milton, we can see at a glance, loves it.

MILTON

Nice ride.

MARCUS

(unwrapping a cigar)

Ride? How old are *you*? It's a car.

MILTON

I must've picked it up from Gwen. You remember my daughter?

MARCUS

Your daughter?

MILTON

Right. My daughter.

MARCUS

If she's *your* daughter, how come she looks like *me*?

MILTON

She doesn't. She looks like her mother, thank God.

MARCUS

Speaking of Mona, what's become of her?

MILTON

You're wasting your time, Marcus. She's through with the life. We both are.

MARCUS

(lighting the cigar)

Too bad.

(inhales)

'Cause I'm going after Lonergan.

When Marcus pulls away, WE HOLD ON MILTON for A LONG BEAT. It's clear that Marcus has just said the magic word.

MARCUS

(calling over his shoulder)

You're gonna need that phone.

Wanting to touch base before our meeting in Jackson Hole, Jason had telephoned the week before, and he chuckled appreciatively when I told him about how Nolan had said to call him regular Bill. "These *guys,* these *guys,*" he chortled. Meaning movie stars.

Perhaps because our shared laugh at Nolan's expense felt a bit mean-spirited, and because he *was* a friend of Wendy's, I relented and said, "He did sound sincere, though." Of course, these words were no sooner out of my mouth than I could feel myself flushing with embarrassment. An *actor* sounded sincere? Even more than their good looks and charm, sincerity is their giraffe's neck—the evolutionary advantage that allows them to nibble tender leaves that are out of the reach of the rest of us ground-tethered creatures.

"He *is* a cut above the rest," Jason conceded. "And he's been good to me."

I was pretty sure I knew what this remark referenced. Several years earlier Jason made a very expensive flop starring a *Saturday Night Live* alum. It wasn't actually his fault, but when a studio head is forced to step down because of a movie you made, you don't walk away clean. Since then he'd been directing episodes of *CSI,* along with the occasional cable TV pilot. Movie jail, it was called. A feature film with Nolan would spring him.

"Did I read you were developing something else with him?"

"A movie called *Back in the Day*."

"Is it green-lit?"

"Amber," he said, causing me to wonder if he was joking or if there really *was* such a term these days. "For the last year. More, actually."

"What's the problem?"

"What's always the problem?"

"Financing?"

"Ding ding ding," he said, game show for *right answer.*

"What's the budget?"

"Twelve."

"You're telling me William Nolan is having trouble attracting twelve million?"

"Welcome to Hollywood, twenty-sixteen. The lower the budget, the harder it is to find the money. The script has already cost two."

"How many writers?"

"Three they admit to, not counting me."

"Ouch." Because I had a pretty good idea what that meant. Jason, attached to direct, had broken in as a screenwriter. Fearing the whole thing might head south, he'd probably done a freebie draft or two. Nolan could have ponied up, but *these guys*—whether a cut above or two cuts below—never spent their own money.

"But it looks promising," Jason was saying. "They're in Romania scouting locations as we speak."

"That's a good sign," I agreed, meaning the location scouts, not Romania.

"So tell me about *Milton and Marcus*. What's the backstory?"

I filled him in: about the original project Nolan had tried to involve Wendy in (which never got made, either), about my writing the Marcus character for Wendy, then Wendy getting sick. "He must've sent Nolan the pages. What I don't get is how they surfaced after a decade."

"Probably Marty was cleaning out a file cabinet."

Possible. But how had they known who to contact? I didn't remember even including a title page, so how could they tell who wrote it? "And I'm hearing Gene Handy as Marcus? I thought he was in rehab."

"He is, but the timing may be good. He seems to do all right when he's on the set. He says he wants to work."

"What does he look like?" The last photo I saw of him—a mug shot—was horrifying.

"A train wreck, but that could work for us. He's got a small role in *Desperation Alley*. I hear he was good."

"Bill doesn't think so?"

"He makes these phlegmy, growling noises all the time. In between his own lines. When other characters are talking. He's under the impression that people enjoy them. Anyway, they're all crazy." Actors, he meant. The species.

"Unlike us."

"Right. Unlike us. How's your Beth?"

I'd been anticipating the question, so I was ready. "Terrific. She says to say hi." My bravado sounded hollow to me, but if Jason noticed, he let it go. "Yours?" His wife, an actress, was also named Beth.

"Great," he said. "I don't know why more men don't marry up."

"They would if they could."

"You think?" he said.

As we were hanging up, I'd heard my Beth's car pull up outside and went over to the window. It was blustery, and when getting out, she put a hand on top of her head, apparently worried that her wig would fly off. I met her at the kitchen door. "You look exhausted," I said.

"I am," she allowed, submitting to my embrace. These days I had to be careful not to squeeze too hard. "There are some things in the trunk."

"I'll get them. Go sit down."

Outside, I grabbed two small bags of groceries, then closed the trunk. Glancing up at the window of the room I'd used as a study back when I was still a writer, I half expected to see myself standing there, a man of two minds about everything, neither of them particularly sound.

I'd hoped Jason might ride down the mountain with me, but since neither of us knew where the restaurant was, it was decided that Marty would ride with me, Jason with Regular Bill. "Take your time," Marty advised. "Bill drives like a bat out of hell." Indeed, by the time I put my rental car in gear, Nolan's Jeep was already out of sight, though plumes of road dust rose like smoke in the darkness ahead. "Why I'm not lying dead at the bottom of the ravine is a mystery."

"How long have you guys been working together?"

"Ten years."

"That's a long time in this business."

"There's no way he can fire me. I know too much."

"So," I chuckled, "then I guess it *is* the bottom of the ravine. Tina didn't want to join us?"

"Tina who?" This was evidently a joke. "Nah, she's a dancer. Seldom drinks. Body's a temple sort of thing. Also, bored silly by movie talk."

I was remembering my conversation with Jason the previous week. "Okay if I ask you a question?"

"Fire away."

"How did you guys come across those *Milton and Marcus* pages?"

"Wendell Percy sent them."

"Yeah, but that had to be ten years ago."

"That's how long Bill's wanted to do it. Then Percy died . . ."

I nodded. "And nobody else was right for Marcus."

"Yeah, that. At first."

"But then?"

"In the end you have to order from the menu. You think Tommy Lee Jones, but he's unavailable. Then suddenly he's avail able, but Bill isn't. You go through the same dance with Harrison Ford. The old story, right? Civilians only know about the movies that get made. For every one of those there are a hundred others that go from the back burner to the front and then back again." I had my eyes on the road, but unless I was mistaken, he started to tell me something else, then thought better of it.

"My turn?" he said. "To ask a question?"

We were coming into a straightaway, so I risked a glance in his direction. He was studying me curiously. "Sure."

"Are you ill?"

I assured him I wasn't.

"I only ask because we saw your car coming up the mountain. You pulled over . . ."

"Turbulence on the plane," I explained. "Then the windy road."

"We shouldn't have asked you to drive up to the house," he said. "You have to be exhausted, and we could've begun work in the morning."

"No worries," I told him.

"In fact, if you want to skip dinner—"

"No, really, I'm good."

"Bill can come across as self-absorbed," he said, surprising me, "but he's really glad you're here."

The restaurant was mobbed, but the maître d' was on the lookout for Marty and led us to a private room, where Regular Bill was holding forth, Jason listening appreciatively. "Finally," Nolan said when he saw us. He made a show of checking his watch. He'd ditched the poncho in favor of a linen sport coat but was still wearing the T-shirt with the stretched neck. "What the hell happened to you guys?" he said, indicating that I should sit next to him. They already had drinks, Jason a glass of red wine, Nolan what appeared to be a club soda.

"I had to stop and throw up again," I said.

"Seriously?" he said, looking first at me, then at Marty, clearly worried.

I waited for a full beat, then told him I was kidding. For consistency's sake, I repeated the lie I told Marty about why my stomach had been upset.

"But you're okay now?"

He looked genuinely relieved when I said I was. "But you were midstory," I said.

"Right," he said, turning back to Jason. "So Tina and I have been seeing each other for a while, and I'm wondering if maybe this is serious. Not thinking marriage, exactly, but yeah, serious. I can tell she's got misgivings. Anyway, we're shooting in Utah, so I invite her to the set. Moab, right? Where it's over a hundred degrees. Everybody's miserable. The good news? There's a long weekend coming up. Memorial Day? The Fourth? I forget. And she wants to fly to Maine, where she's got family, but I nix that. It'll take a full day to get there and another to get back. Also, I've just bought this new Audi and I'm anxious to put the top down and see what it can do on the back roads between Moab and Santa Fe. So I'm telling Tina about this little hole-in-the-wall Mexican joint where they serve these incredible margaritas. Made with the same tequila we were drinking back at the house, but at the time I don't know that. I just know they make the best margaritas on the planet. Anyhow, I'm trying to convince her to come with me to Santa Fe for the weekend, and the more I talk about these margaritas, the more I just have to have one. In my head I'm doing the calculations. I figure if we get on the road by six, we arrive in Santa Fe around dinnertime. Tina would still rather go to Maine, but in the end she agrees, which makes me wonder if she's getting serious, too, because I'm really being kind of a dick here, wanting my own way.

"So we're just crossing into Colorado when the Audi throws a rod. Did I mention this is a brand-new car? And now we're over on the side of the road. Midmorning and it's already in the nineties. One bar of cell service. I look over at Tina and I know what she's thinking—we could be in Maine—but she doesn't say it. We lock the Audi, which is silly; it's not going anywhere. We walk, we walk, we walk. The only other cars on the road are headed the other direction. Finally, at the crest of this hill, I have two bars and get through to Triple A, tell 'em where we are. They send a tow truck to haul us into Durango. This whole time Tina's trying to make me feel better. She says it doesn't matter. We'll check into a motel. It'll be romantic. It's not like you can't get a margarita in Durango. But I'm having exactly none of it. Yeah, sure they have margaritas there, but not the ones I've been telling her about. By the time we get to Durango it's early afternoon and I've got a new plan, or rather the old one with new wheels. We'll rent a car. Just leave the Audi there. Next week, after it's fixed, I'll get somebody from the set to come pick it up and drive it back to Utah. Except that by the time we finish talking to the mechanic and making all the necessary arrangements it's midafternoon. No hope of making it to Santa Fe by dinnertime, even if I drive like hell. Tina is saying it's fine, it's fine, but it's not fine. I'm tasting that first sip of margarita. So I call Marty and ask him to find out if there's an airstrip nearby. There is. I hear myself say the words 'private jet.' Now Tina's looking at me like I'm some completely new kind of crazy. I tell her not to worry, this is going to work out. I call the restaurant in Santa Fe to find out how late they serve. Ten o'clock. It's gonna be close, but it can be done. We take a taxi to the airstrip. Two hours later, the plane arrives."

As Nolan was telling this story, I had the kind of out-of-body experience you sometimes get in the presence of people who are larger than life, or larger than yours, anyway. We're used to seeing the William Nolans of the world on a giant screen, not sitting next to us in a restaurant. Close up, you can see what makes them stars and see that it's no accident. But writ small, their particular magic feels more like a parlor trick. Clever, sure, and you have no idea how it's done, but the part that gobsmacks you is that you're there to witness it in person. When people talk of being starstruck, what they're feeling is that something's out of alignment, like they're coming in contact with something they thought they understood, only to discover they don't. The only cure, I knew from experience, is familiarity. Anything that happens often enough becomes mundane. If you had any doubts on that score, all you had to do was look at Marty, whose weary expression at hearing this tale for the umpteenth time suggested that indeed no man is a hero to his valet. Marty might be a Hollywood producer, but I was beginning to understand that his real job was to produce an easier life for Regular Bill—locate the nearest airstrip, make arrangements for a private jet at a moment's notice, find someone to go to Durango to pick up the repaired Audi. In other words, to clean up messes somebody else made.

"By the time we land in Santa Fe," Nolan continued, "it's almost nine-thirty and I still have to rent a car. I tell them to just put us in anything, I don't care. The kid behind the counter wants to tell me all about this great special they're running. For an extra thirty bucks a day they can upgrade me to an Audi. I say fine, whatever, I don't care, just give me the keys. We do eighty all the way into town. Five minutes to ten we pull in. The parking lot's full, but there's a space between a minivan and a Range Rover. Or it looks like a space. Actually, it's occupied by one of those little Japanese roadsters, emerald green, which I don't see until I hit it. Plow it right up and over the cement guard and into the back wall of the restaurant. The rental Audi's hood is pointed straight up, steam billowing out of the radiator. Tina has her hands up over her face and all she can say is 'Oh . . . my . . . God.' And what do I say to her, asshole that I am? I point to my watch and say, 'We've got two minutes.' "

Our waiter, who'd been patiently loitering nearby, came over then, wondering if we'd like to hear the specials. Nolan waved him away.

"Inside, we order two margaritas, and that first taste? It's everything I remember. I'm thinking, I swear to God, that it's all been worth it. This *is* the best margarita in the world. This margarita's so good you don't even want another. A second would cheapen the experience. That's how good it is.

"Even so, reality's begun to set in. In less than twelve hours I've wrecked two Audis and a Japanese sports car. I tell Tina to order us some food while I go look for the owner of the roadster. I go from table to table, my hat pulled down over my eyes. Anybody here drive a green sports car? No, no and no. Finally, this girl in her twenties says yes. So I tell her there's been an accident and that I'm really sorry, I'll pay for everything, but I think I've just totaled her car, and she says, 'Yeah, okay, but aren't you William Nolan?' "

It was a good line and we laughed appreciatively. I thought about Wendy, who had always provoked similar reactions when he was recognized in public.

"When I get back to the bar, I see Tina's scribbling on a cocktail napkin. She's barely touched her margarita, and this, I think, can't be good. I put myself in her place and figure I'm way the hell up shit's creek. Still, I do my best. I tell her everything's going to be fine. I found the owner of the roadster. We've exchanged information. She's not even that angry, I tell Tina, hoping she'll see my logic. If this girl whose car I just totaled isn't pissed at me, why should *she* be? Which is complete bullshit, granted, but it's all I've got. So Tina's just sitting there, incredibly calm now, scribbling away on this cocktail napkin, which is unnerving, but I keep on blathering until I run out of blather. When my voice finally falls, she asks me if I enjoyed my margarita. I recognize this as a trick question. Whatever I've got coming, here it comes. So I'm all sheepish, but even so I admit that, yeah, I really did enjoy it. She says, 'Good,' and slides the cocktail napkin she's been writing on in front of me. 'Because this is what it cost.' While I've been going table to table, she's been putting a price tag on my stupidity. It's all right there. The cost of repairs to the first Audi, plus what somebody will charge us to fetch it back to Utah. The private jet. The replacement of the totaled roadster, plus repairing the Audi we just rented, assuming it's not totaled, which it may be. By her reckoning, the margarita I enjoyed cost just south of a hundred grand. Much as I'd like to, I can't find fault with her numbers, though I point out that in fairness she could at least have divided the total by two, because it was two margaritas we got for that price, not one. Not dividing by two makes me look like twice as big an asshole."

We all chuckled again at what seemed to be the story's conclusion, because it was funny, but it was also, at least to my thinking, an extension of Nolan's on-screen persona, the kinds of characters he always played: simultaneously smart and stupid, self-deprecating, willing to make himself the butt of the joke. Jason immediately grasped the story's intended moral. "But there's a happy ending, right? She *did* marry you."

Nolan looked like he was about to agree, but he heard my chair scrape back and saw me get to my feet. "You're leaving already? You just got here."

"I won't be long," I promised, showing him my phone, which had buzzed twice since I sat down. "My daughter." Who'd left two messages.

"Go," he said. "We'll order for you."

Outside, I didn't bother listening to the messages, just pressed RETURN.

"Daddy," she said, picking up on the first ring.

"What's wrong?"

"What's *wrong*?" Her mother was dying, she meant. And here I was asking if something was wrong. What *I'd* meant, of course, was what *else* was wrong. Had her mother fallen? Been rushed to the hospital? "Cassie?"

"I can't bear it. Seeing her like this. She's so sick."

"She'll feel better tomorrow. The first couple days after the treatments are always the worst."

"She'll feel better, but she won't *be* better."

"I know."

"I wish it was me."

"No, you don't." Not with three kids and a husband. I understood, though. She and Beth had always been close, in certain respects more like sisters than mother and daughter. Still, she didn't want to trade places, not really.

"What I really can't believe is that you'd do this."

"Do what?"

"Just take off like this when she's so sick."

"She'll feel better tomorrow. It goes in cycles. Every day's better until it's time for another treatment. You'll see. I promise."

"Two days is all I can give you."

"I know that."

"What if they want you to stay?"

"Two days," I said, "and I'll be home."

During the meal we talked in general terms about *Milton and Marcus,* and I shared with the others what Wendy had said when he read the fourteen pages: how sorry he was that he wouldn't be able to do the movie, because nobody would've been better as Marcus. "Even if he did say so himself," Nolan chortled.

Something about that remark irked me. "I don't think he meant to boast," I said, heard my voice thicken with emotion I was pretty sure I wasn't entitled to. "He just thought no one would understand the character better."

Nolan must've heard that emotion, too, because when I let my voice fall, he looked straight at me and said, "Hey, I miss him, too."

The moment felt authentic and as such unusual in an industry that traffics in illusion, so we raised our glasses to Wendy's memory, after which the talk quickly moved on to casting, as it inevitably will. Everyone agreed that if Gene Handy was sober, we'd do no better for Marcus. Mona, the object of both men's affections, would be easy to cast. Every sixty-year-old actress would want the part. Jason and Nolan agreed it shouldn't be a younger actress "playing" older, but someone in her sixties who was still sexy. Susan Sarandon, Jason thought. Helen Mirren, Marty offered, which caused Nolan to chuckle. "You always want to cast her."

Marty, blushing, did not dispute this. "She's a great actor."

"If I see her when I'm in London next week, I'll tell her about the giant crush you've got on her. She might be in the market for someone your age." Then he turned to me. "So, which one of these guys is going to end up with Mona, anyway?" he asked.

"Marcus," I said. Wendy's character.

"We should talk," Nolan said. "Also about why Marcus has all the best lines."

That brought me up short. Had my affection for Wendy caused me to skew things? I made a mental note to check the balance when I reread the pages over breakfast, but my sense was that the best lines were pretty evenly distributed. In any event, here was a minor red flag. Actors, even best pals, were notoriously jealous of each other's lines, and it was entirely possible that such jealously transcended the grave.

By the time we finished our main course, my exhaustion was complete and, despite trying hard to concentrate, I found myself losing the thread of the conversation. It was as if the other three were discussing a fully developed script, not a fourteen-page overture. Regular Bill finally placed his napkin on his plate. "So," he said. "What time should we start in the morning?"

He seemed to be directing the question mostly to me, so I told him I'd be ready to work whenever he said.

"But I'm not the one who's jet lagged," he pointed out. "Nine?"

"Have a heart," Marty groaned. "Ten."

Jason agreed, adding that he was also going to need an hour or two in the afternoon for a conference call about his newly wrapped pilot.

"How are the dailies?" Nolan wanted to know.

"They look really good," Jason said. "The problem is HBO always orders six to get four, and there's a dispute with the show-runner, who may walk."

"Would you step in?"

"That's under discussion, but—"

"If I were to pick up the phone," Nolan said, "who would I call?"

Jason named the executive but suggested Nolan hold off for the moment. If he committed to a TV show, and *Back in the Day* got its expected green light, he'd lose out on the feature film he needed so badly.

"Okay, but let me know," Nolan said agreeably, before turning back to me. "Here's what I need from you. We've been round and round about this and gotten nowhere."

By "we" I assumed he meant him and Jason and Marty, though it was still a puzzling remark. How many conversations about *Milton and Marcus* could they have had? They'd gone "round and round" that afternoon or earlier, in LA? I'd assumed we were all coming out of the gate together. I glanced at Jason, but he'd taken out his phone. Marty had his hand up to call for the check.

"What's really between these guys?" Nolan wanted to know. "What's their history?"

"Well," I said, "they've been in love with the same woman most of their adult lives."

"Yeah, but it can't be a woman."

One of the things you never get used to in this business—or at least I never did—is how often opinions get voiced as proclamations: no further discussion needed or, perhaps, tolerated. "Why not?" I said, genuinely curious. I didn't mean the question as a challenge, but it must've sounded like one because Nolan looked surprised.

"There's got to be something deeper," he explained. "And there's that hint of some betrayal, back before Mona ever came on the scene."

I didn't have a clue what he was talking about. "Where?"

"Bill," Marty interrupted, signing the check. Signing *on the check*. No need for anything as bourgeois as a credit card. "Look at the man. He's dead on his feet."

Nolan hesitated, as if remembering something, and immediately stood down. "Hey, it's something for *all* of us to ponder," he conceded, pushing back his chair. "I didn't mean to single you out."

Reaching under the table, he grabbed a canvas tote I hadn't noticed, and suddenly there was electricity in the air. "Where are you staying?"

"They're both at the lodge," Marty said, also pushing back from the table.

"Great," said Regular Bill. "You'll like it there."

This "lodge" was apparently only a couple blocks from the restaurant. I could give Jason a lift there. Marty lived in town in an apartment connected to Nolan's offices and cutting room. Regular Bill would drop him off before heading back up his mountain.

When we emerged from the private room, everyone in the restaurant turned to watch. Nolan possessed that same magnetic field Wendy'd had right to the end. The difference was that Wendy's made him uneasy. Nolan seemed to wear his own as comfortably as his baggy-necked T-shirt.

In the foyer Jason spotted someone he knew across the dining room and went over to say hello, promising he'd only be a minute. The rest of us went outside, where Nolan's Jeep was magically waiting for him at the curb, its engine running. "Oh, I almost forgot," he said, handing me the canvas tote. "This is for you. In case you wake up early. It's good you're here. I think we've finally got the right team."

And just that quickly he and Marty were gone.

Finally got the right team?

Wondering what that could mean, I peeked inside the tote and there was my answer, not only to what he meant by having the right team but also to the evening's other puzzling questions, which in my exhaustion I hadn't been clever enough to formulate. The tote contained two bound screenplays, one weighing in at one hundred six pages, the other at ninety-eight. They bore the same title: *Milton and Marcus*.

INT. STARBUCKS—DAY

ON MILTON, as he attempts to clean himself up with a swatch of napkins. There's a mustard/ketchup stain on the sleeve of his shirt and another dark wet spot on the front, which he sniffs at and makes a face. The cell phone sits in the middle of the bistro table before him. The inference is clear; he's retrieved the phone from the dumpster.

CLOSE ON THE PHONE, which VIBRATES. Milton looks at the thing with a mixture of surprise and distaste, then sees Marcus in the line of people waiting to order, his own cell to his ear. He motions for Milton to answer his.

Milton locates and presses the ANSWER button, then, glaring at Marcus the whole while, puts the phone to his ear.

MARCUS

Say hello.

MILTON

Why?

MARCUS

Because that's how conversations begin.

MILTON

Hello, Marcus.

MARCUS

You want a biscotti?

MILTON

A what?

MARCUS

A biscotti. A cookie, Milton. Would you like a cookie?

MILTON

No.

MARCUS

Fine. Be like that. Goodbye.

When Milton hangs up, he sees that the palm of his hand is now smeared with some sort of evil goop. He wipes it off with a napkin just as Marcus arrives.

MARCUS

Here.

(pushing a coffee in front of him)

Enjoy.

Milton takes a sip and makes another face.

MILTON

What the hell is this?

MARCUS

A mocha latte. Good, huh?

MILTON

Jesus. Is this what they drink in the Turks and Caicos?

MARCUS

The Turks, not the Caicos. Have a biscotti.

MILTON

I told you I didn't want one.

MARCUS

I heard you. I did. But here's what I think. I think you've got no idea what you want.

MILTON

But *you* do?

MARCUS

(pleased, confident)

That's right. You want to get back in the game. Get the old juices flowing. Feel alive again.

MILTON'S POV: the red Caddy comes into focus OUTSIDE in the parking lot.

Milton does look tempted, but only for a moment.

MILTON

The old juices were my problem, if you recall.

(a beat)

Anyway, I can't do any more time. I won't.

MARCUS

(munching biscotti)

Your problem is that you have a defeatist

attitude. All we're doing is sitting here having a cup of coffee—

MILTON

Mocha latte.

MARCUS

—and you've already got us in jail.

MILTON

But that's how it goes with you. Talking leads to planning, leads to doing, leads to fucking up, leads to jail. I'm just skipping the middle parts.

MARCUS

Fine. Anyway, Mona will be up for it.

Milton LAUGHS OUT LOUD at this.

MILTON

I don't think so.

MARCUS

Wanna bet?

MILTON

(doesn't want to)

You don't even know where she is.

MARCUS

I didn't know where you were until today.

MILTON

Anyway, leave her out of it. She's made a new life. We all have.

Marcus regards him with monumental disgust for A LONG BEAT, then starts madly tapping on his phone with his thumbs. When he stops, Milton's phone VIBRATES again.

MARCUS

(rising)

You have a text message.

Milton watches him leave. Only when the door swings shut, does Milton look down at the phone, which buzzes again. There's a pretty young woman at a nearby table who's watching him.

MILTON

(to the young woman)

How do I get a text message?

She shows him. CLOSE ON THE MESSAGE: *You know you want to.*

Milton sets the phone back on the table, watches Marcus get in behind the wheel of the Caddy. Once again he's typing into his phone. When he finishes, he turns the key in the ignition, then backs out of the parking space.

Milton's phone VIBRATES again. Another text message: *Eat your fucking cookie.*

MILTON'S POV, as Marcus waves goodbye.

ON MILTON, who chews his biscotti thoughtfully, then looks down at it, surprised. It's good.

"They must've loved the premise," was how Jason explained it.

We'd ordered beers in our raucous hotel bar, whose theme was antlers and whose clientele was a weird mix of dick-swinging

Hollywood types and wraith-thin Eurotrash. Nearby and completely out of place was a large table of Asian men who'd purchased identical ten-gallon hats and seemed to have no idea how ridiculous they looked wearing them.

"I can't believe it," I told him, though of course it was, despite its outrageousness, all too believable. "There have already been two other writers, then."

"What does your contract say?"

I explained that I didn't have a formal one yet. "What's the worst that can happen?" was how my agent had put it when I shared my misgivings about taking a meeting before we had something more binding. "You get an all-expense-paid trip to Jackson Hole in August. Take Beth with you. I'm told it's nice if you like that sort of thing."

Now, though, it looked like the worst that could happen was pretty bad. If I gave Nolan and Marty everything they needed in conversation over the next couple days, what was their incentive to hire me? In Hollywood such "auditions" were all too common. I also recalled that when I'd glanced at Marty's IMDB profile, he'd done some script doctoring himself. None of this boded well.

"You must have a deal memo, at least," Jason was saying. "Otherwise, you wouldn't be here, right?"

"A draft and a set of notes," I told him. "Standard back-end language. Bonus for sole credit. Otherwise a percentage, pending arbitration. They were more anxious to have the meeting than to process the necessary paperwork."

"When was that ever not true?"

"But you trust him? Regular Bill?"

"I've been working for over a year on *Back in the Day*. Gratis, so yeah, I guess I do."

"You've been working that long without a contract?"

"I have a contract, but there was no money left in the budget for script development. I get made whole when I don my director's cap. Until then . . ."

"God," I said. "Things are worse now than I remember."

"Infinitely."

"Here's what I don't get," I said, because the more I thought about it, the less sense it made. "Why not come clean up front? Just tell me about the other two writers."

"Think about it. The project has been quietly in development for years, despite the fact that they haven't bothered to option it. What if you get pissed?"

"I *am* pissed. They really thought they could get away without optioning the material?"

He cocked his head. "Devil's advocate?"

"Sure," I said. "Knock yourself out."

"Okay, so what exactly *is* the material? A long time ago you wrote half of a first act for Wendy, and Wendy's dead. As far as they know, you forgot about the whole thing. If you were still pitching it around town, they'd have heard. My point is, in the annals of Hollywood thievery, this wouldn't even make the list. If they wanted to be complete fuckwads, they could claim Wendy pitched the *idea* to Bill but never showed him actual pages."

"Jesus."

"But here's the more likely scenario. Bill reads your first act and sees the potential. But then Wendy dies and it seems like that's that. A year or two later he runs across the pages, or Marty does, and he likes them all over again. They *could* offer you an option, but what if you want to write the screenplay? Bill has half-a-dozen writers he likes to work with. He figures, Why not show it to one of them and see what he thinks? So that's what he does. One of them loves the premise and gets all excited and wants to run with it. Bill figures, Why not? If the guy comes up with a producible script, they can offer you an option then. If not they've saved some money. Plus they get to keep creative control a bit longer. These days, that's the name of the game."

That made a kind of sense, I had to admit. "Okay, but then why give me the other two scripts now? Why not just turn me loose with the original pages? Tell me to go home and write it?"

"You'd be starting from scratch."

I held up the canvas bag I'd hung on a hook under the bar. "How does my reading these change that? If the scripts were any good, they wouldn't need me. If they're not good, why poison my imagination?"

"I made that same point, and I thought they'd agreed. I was surprised to see the tote. So was Marty. Did you see the look on his face?"

"No."

"That's the other thing. Bill turns seventy-seven this year. He's still pretty sharp and he's in great shape, but according to Marty he's beginning to have memory issues. We may hear that margarita story again tomorrow." He was regarding me strangely. "You sure you're okay?"

I considered telling him about Beth, that the only reason I'd taken the assignment was for the health insurance. For some reason I didn't. "I'm just tired."

"Go to bed. I'll get this," he said, calling for the check. "Or rather Bill will."

"Speaking of the margarita story?" I said. "I'm not sure it means what he thinks it does."

"Yeah, but none of our stories mean what we think they do." Which was fair enough, so when Jason raised his glass and said, eyebrow arched, "To *Regular* Bill," we clinked glasses and drained the last of our beers.

I shared an elevator ride with three tiny Asians wearing cowboy boots and those enormous Stetsons. They pointed at my head. "No hat."

"All cattle," I replied, which was a piss-poor joke even if I'd told it to people who might get it.

"Yes, yes," one of them said appreciatively. He made a circular motion, an invisible lariat, in the air above his head, knocking his Stetson askew. "Cat-oh. Right. Ha-ha."

It was five-thirty local time when I awoke with an understanding that had escaped me the night before. If Nolan had been quietly developing *Milton and Marcus* for the better part of a decade, then our insurance predicament was partly due to him. Had he offered an option on the material in the beginning and hired me to write the first draft, our coverage wouldn't have lapsed and we wouldn't be wondering how we were going to make it until we qualified for Medicare next year. Not that he would see it like that, of course. Developing material you don't own the rights to is risky, but there's no law against it. And he was under no obligation to hire me. Seen from his perspective, he was no more to blame for our lapsed insurance than for Beth's cancer. Of far more concern to him, surely, was his own suddenly precarious standing. Turnabout was fair play, and if he'd been a shit, I could now be a bigger one. The problem was that I couldn't punish him without damaging myself in the process.

Feeling only slightly less weary than I'd been when I crawled into bed, I rose and showered and put on khakis and a wrinkled shirt before calling home. It was Beth who picked up. "Good

Lord," she said, her voice sounding clear and pain-free, though she'd become a master at hiding her discomfort. "What time is it there?"

I told her. "My internal clock's still on the East Coast. I was expecting Cassie to answer."

"I think I just heard stirring upstairs. I expect she'll be down soon."

"How are you feeling?"

"I may skip the half marathon, but better. Did you meet William Nolan?"

Beth, like every other woman in America, was a fan. "Sure did."

"And?"

"Every bit as charming as you'd expect. He's no Wendy, though."

"You know that already? After one evening?"

"I could be wrong," I admitted. In my wife's opinion I judge people far too quickly. The flinty, wintry Yankee in me. "Coming here may have been a mistake, though. Turns out I'm the third writer on the script."

"How is that possible?"

"The first guy's been nominated for two Oscars, the second's an Emmy winner who's new to feature films. I seem to be their last resort. Should I tell them to go fuck themselves? Just come on home?"

"You went all that way, so why not hear them out? If it still feels wrong at the end of the day, you can fly home tomorrow."

"That was my thought, actually," I told her, though until she said it I wasn't sure. Knowing my own mind only after speaking it to my wife was our marriage in a nutshell, in fact. "Cassie seems very angry."

"You know how she is. She wants everything to be fair. *I haven't done anything to deserve this* is how she sees it."

"She seems pretty pissed at me, actually," I said.

"You should let me tell her about the insurance."

We hadn't wanted to. She and her husband were doing okay, but they had a lot on their plates. We didn't want them worrying about us. "Let's hold off until I get back," I said.

"Ryan?"

"Yeah?"

"Do you want to do this movie?"

"I don't know," I told her. Yesterday I would've said no, that it was all about the insurance. But last night? Being at what I thought was the start of something? Finding myself a part of something again? Now I wasn't so sure.

EXT. PAROCHIAL SCHOOL—DUSK

The sun is low on the horizon as Milton, seated atop a riding mower, cuts the perimeter of a vast expanse of lawn, passing a sign that reads: BISHOP COLLINS ELEMENTARY SCHOOL. In the distance is a low, flat building and adjacent parking lot, where half-a-dozen school buses are parked in rows. The ROAR OF THE ENGINE is loud enough that Milton doesn't immediately hear his name being called.

FEMALE VOICE

Mr. Milton? Mr. Milton?

A pretty young nun (SISTER LUCY, early 20's) in full-flowing regalia is trotting alongside the mower. He shuts it down.

MILTON

Sister Lucy.

SISTER LUCY

I thought you might like something cold to drink.

She hands him a plastic bottle. Inside is some kind of fruit smoothie.

MILTON

I guess people don't drink Coke anymore.

SISTER LUCY

They took all the vending machines out of the cafeteria. Junk food's bad for the kids.

MILTON

(taking a drink, making a face)

Let me guess. Mother Alma.

He offers her a sip of the smoothie. She shakes her head, nervous.

SISTER LUCY

I shouldn't.

(a beat, he's puzzled)

Your lips, then my lips. It'd be sort of like a kiss.

MILTON

It's been a while since I've kissed anybody, Sister, but I think you're wrong.

(he drains the rest)

I always have Coke in my fridge if you get desperate. You could have your own can.

There's a moment of awkward silence. He can't help but grin at her shyness.

MILTON

So, what was your street name?

SISTER LUCY

Tiffany.

MILTON

I guess that's not a saint's name, huh?

SISTER LUCY

You're funny.

(a beat)

You remind me of my dad.

(serious now)

He died.

MILTON

That's the resemblance?

(she looks mortified)

Just kidding, Sister. But I should get back to work.

He hands the empty bottle back to her.

SISTER LUCY

Me, too. If Mother Alma sees me talking to you, I'll catch it.

MILTON

Too late.

And he's right. There, a hundred yards off, is the Mother Superior, glaring at them.

SISTER LUCY

She's always accusing me of flirting.

MILTON

(eyebrow arched)

Maybe you should stop.

SISTER LUCY

(giggles)

Bye, Mr. Milton.

MILTON

Bye, Tiffany.

And off she trots, delighted, though she gives Mother Alma a wide berth. The older nun and Milton lock eyes across the distance until the mower's engine roars back to life.

Neither notices when the RED CADDY convertible glides by on the highway.

EXT. SCHOOL—DUSK

Milton, his mowing done, rides the machine into a big tin shed at the rear of the school. When he turns the engine off and climbs down, there, backlit in the open doorway, is MOTHER ALMA.

MILTON

(with an odd, almost ironic inflection)

Mother.

When she takes a step toward him, we get a better look at her. Though it's hard to tell, given her religious habit, she appears middle-aged; her face, discounting the scowl and the wimple, is not unattractive.

MOTHER ALMA

Don't mother me, Mr. Milton.

He detaches one of the two grass hoppers and empties it into a large plastic barrel.

MOTHER ALMA

You're not to engage the younger sisters in conversation. Especially not the novices. You know this.

Milton does the same with the second bin.

MILTON

I didn't engage her. She engaged me.

MOTHER ALMA

(wry)

Nevertheless. You have sinned.

MILTON

No, I remember sinning, and that out there wasn't it. Besides, I'm too tired.

MOTHER ALMA

I hope you don't think I'm fool enough to believe that.

MILTON

Well, we all believe foolish things, don't we.

They're both FRAMED BY THE DOORWAY now, and the nun steps aside so he can leave the shed.

MILTON

(over his shoulder)

Your favorite valedictorian says hey.

WE REMAIN ON MOTHER ALMA while this registers. After a beat, she follows him out into the bright sunshine.

MOTHER ALMA

(suddenly very sad)

How is she?

When he shrugs, they just stare at each other, until Milton does an unexpected little jig.

MILTON

Fucking thing.

He takes the BUZZING cell phone out of his pocket. For some reason Mother Alma does not react to his language.

MILTON

Sorry. It's set on vibrate.

ON THE PHONE'S SMALL SCREEN: *It'll be like old times.*

Milton puts it back in his pocket.

MOTHER ALMA

(herself again)

Since when do you have a cell phone?

MILTON

Since today.

Now she's the one wearing a wry smile.

MILTON

What?

But she just chuckles.

INT. CARETAKER'S APARTMENT—NIGHT

Milton's room reflects a man who's gone deeply inward, whose world is narrow by design. He's also a complete Luddite. No computer. Nothing high-tech. There's an old battery-operated transistor radio on a shelf, and his television sports possibly the last set of rabbit ears in existence. There's a battered cassette player, and the shelves are full of old movies (cassettes only, no DVDs).

Milton is seated on a ratty but comfy-looking armchair, his feet up on an ottoman, watching Cary Grant and Grace Kelly in *To Catch a Thief*. He smiles wistfully, until . . .

The cell phone BUZZES on the end table. He lets it. Goes back to watching Grace and Cary.

The BUZZING STOPS, then immediately STARTS UP AGAIN, and this time it seems to intensify the snow on the TV screen. Milton crushes his beer can, beyond annoyed.

CLOSE ON THE PHONE, vibrating toward the edge of the table. It's about to tip over onto the floor when Milton snatches it.

ON THE SCREEN, as he peers at the text message: *You should think about it*. Now we see the sender's name: MONA.

I'd finished breakfast in the empty hotel dining room and was halfway through the first of the two screenplays when Marty's assistant called to cancel the morning's meeting. "What about the afternoon one?" I asked. Because if there wasn't one, I'd just head for the airport.

"Marty's on the other line," I was told. "He'll call you as soon as he hangs up."

He didn't, though, not unless he was on that same call for another hour. When I finished the first *Milton and Marcus* script I called Phil, my agent. Given it was an hour earlier in California, I expected to get his machine, but he answered. "Did you know I'm the third fucking writer on this?" I asked him.

"It doesn't surprise me."

"Why not?"

"Because nothing surprises me."

"Do we have a signed deal memo yet?"

"I'm supposed to get that today."

"This is all beyond strange, Phil. This morning's meeting was just canceled."

"Who told you about the previous writers?"

"*They* did. Nolan actually gave me the scripts to read. I just finished the first."

"How is it?"

"Good. Not where I was planning to go, but . . ." When I told him who'd written it, he whistled.

"Let me see what I can find out," he said, "because this is making no sense."

My table in the dining room overlooked the lodge's main entrance. A man I didn't immediately recognize as Jason was getting into a cab below. The driver stashed his suitcase in the trunk and slammed it shut.

"You want to know what else makes no sense?" I said. "Jason appears to be leaving."

"I'll call you back," Phil promised.

When I set the phone down, it buzzed. Marty, at last. "Are you at the lodge?"

"In the dining room."

"Is Jason with you?"

"No."

"I really need to talk to him, and he's not picking up."

"Everything okay?"

"In this fucking business? Collar him if you see him. I'll be there in twenty minutes."

I had Jason's number and thought about calling, but decided not to. Two minutes later my phone buzzed again. "What was the name of that other movie Jason's doing with Nolan?" Phil wanted to know.

"Back in the Day."

"There's a piece in the *Hollywood Reporter* this morning. It's just been green-lit."

Which made sense of Jason's abrupt departure. By evening he'd probably be on a flight to Romania. *Milton and Marcus* was already in his rearview mirror. I felt a surge of something like envy, jealous of the adrenaline rush you feel when things long stalled suddenly lurch into motion. Not unlike the moment a woman unexpectedly says yes. To *you*. She wants *you*. Wendy told me once that it's this very *I get to do this* moment that every actor tries to re-create, movie after movie. "Well, that's the news he's been waiting for," I said.

"Except the story names the director as David Miller."

"No."

"I shit you not. Says he's 'newly attached.'"

Hanging up, I called Jason's cell, not expecting him to pick up, but he did. "Bad news, pardner," he said.

"I just heard. What should I do?"

"My advice? Go home and write a novel. Give your Beth a big kiss."

"I'm really sorry, Jason. This is about as shitty as anything I've ever heard of."

"Yeah, but it's a shitty business. Always was, always will be. Speaking of which, I should've told you about the other two scripts before you ever got on the plane."

"Why didn't you?"

"Guess."

Right. These *guys,* these *guys.*

"The *Reporter* wasn't supposed to run the story until next week," Marty explained.

We were sitting in the hotel lobby, waiting for the valet to fetch my rental car. Marty didn't seem particularly surprised that I was leaving.

After hanging up with Jason I'd called the company's travel agent and got her to book me flights to Denver and then Albany. I'd turn my car in here in Jackson Hole. These were probably expensive changes and I hoped I wouldn't be the one paying for them.

"Bill feels terrible."

"He should."

"No argument there."

The Asian guys from the elevator came by and recognized me. "Steer no hat!" one of them called, grinning. "Aw cat-oh!" cried the other. All three swung imaginary lariats in the air. Marty raised an eyebrow, but didn't comment.

"Is it true Jason worked on *Back in the Day* for a whole year?"

"Off and on. We didn't ask him to."

"No, but you let him."

"He knew the score. There was no more money in the budget for script development. No script, no movie. He did what he believed was in his own self-interest."

"So you're telling me that a guy who by his own admission can afford to pay a hundred grand for a margarita can't finance a single draft of a screenplay out of his own pocket?"

He just looked at me. "Please," he said, as if the subject was orgies and I was a priest.

"So Jason makes your script camera-ready, and instead of thank-you he's out?"

"It sucks, but he wasn't supposed to read about it in the trades. The plan was to break it gently to him over the weekend, tell him we'd find him something else. And don't forget we were attaching him to *Milton and Marcus*."

"Where the same thing could happen all over again."

Marty shrugged. "It's the film business. You know Bill's choice wasn't all that different from Jason's. Movie or no movie. With Jason directing, the investors disappear. With David Miller, everybody wants in. Believe me, we tried to make it work."

"If you say so. But here's what I really want to know."

He sighed as you would when you know what's coming next will be brined in naïveté. "If Wendy had lived, would Bill have done this movie with him?"

"I can't answer that."

"Because I don't think so."

"Why is that?"

"Call it a hunch," I said, because that's really all it was. "I think Bill only got interested after Wendy died."

"You could ask him."

"Yeah, but after he answered I still wouldn't know."

"How about we fly you back out next week? Start over after all this plays out."

"No, I'm needed at home. My wife is ill, and between you and me, the only reason I took the gig is because we need the Guild's health insurance."

"Doesn't that mean you still need it?"

"We'll figure something out."

"Bill's going to want to know where we stand. What do I tell him?"

"That he made a mistake not optioning the material when he had the chance."

"You're saying it's not for sale now?"

"Maybe just not to him."

"Isn't that kind of childish?"

"I'm getting a childlike satisfaction out of it."

"On the other hand . . . ," Marty said, rubbing his chin thoughtfully. He was, I realized, a man who considered all the angles. "Maybe that's the savvy move, at least as an opening gambit."

"Yeah?" The valet was pulling my rental car up to the curb.

"You're not in a bad position. As you say, it was a mistake not offering an option up front. The company's already invested significantly. And you heard his margarita story, so you know the lengths he'll go to to get what he wants. Play your cards right, you could end up in clover."

A smart man would've left it right there, but he didn't seem to be around. "Has it ever occurred to Bill that sometimes you don't get that special margarita, no matter how much you want it? That it's better to hunker down in Durango with a pretty woman and drink the local version made with Pepe Lopez and count yourself lucky?"

He chuckled good-naturedly. "That's hilarious."

"I'll walk you out," he said, grabbing my roller board. "What time's your flight?" When I told him, he said, "Jeez that's almost four hours from now."

"I'm a nervous traveler."

My phone vibrated and I showed it to Marty. The screen said REGULAR BILL, which was how I'd entered him into my Contacts list. Marty allowed himself a smile. A moment later, his own phone rang: BILL. Then he put it back in his pocket.

"You mind my asking whose side you're on in all this?" I said.

"My own, of course."

We shook hands. There didn't seem to be any reason not to.

Going through the tiny TSA station at the tiny airport, I realized my shoulder bag was needlessly heavy so I deposited the two scripts in the large recycling bin thoughtfully provided there. I probably should've felt guilty at treating the work of two other writers so rudely, but I didn't. Once past security I bought a sandwich and coffee at the lone food station and found a seat in the small waiting area that serviced the airport's two gates. My bag now contained just the novel I'd read the first half of on the flight out and my own original fourteen pages of *Milton and Marcus*. There wasn't much point in reading them now, but I did so anyway, drawn in less by the two main characters than by how I'd seen them in my mind's eye: Regular Bill as sensible Milton, determined to live out the rest of his life in the safety of obscurity, Wendy as roguish Marcus, equally determined not to let him do it, as much for Milton's sake as his own. Good as the two full-length scripts had been, neither seemed to pick up that Marcus was goading Milton back into life. In asking what was really between these two guys and insisting it couldn't be a woman, Nolan had gone right to the heart of the matter—that Milton was by nature an emotional conservative and Marcus a genuine anarchist, untamed even by old age. After his death a friend of Wendy's told me that his great talent had been to make other people—friends, loved ones, other actors—better by getting them to risk more. He played characters who fucked up and took their lumps as a result. Either that or they got sucker punched by circumstance and had to take a standing eight count. As their losses mounted, their inner flame would gutter, and you'd wonder if they'd throw in the towel, because in their place that's what you'd do. But always it remained, that flickering flame, waiting to be fanned. That was Wendy's temperament, his films were invariably about his characters' attempts to relocate the shed skin of a better self, about somehow slipping back into it, feeling at home in it once more.

By contrast, Nolan was the reliable, competent American Everyman, the Nick Carraway who would never understand or accept or like himself half as much as Gatsby did. The Milton of my fourteen pages was a lot like me, a man cautious by nature and experience, who knew himself too well to be much of a fan and, as a result, was often too grateful for the good opinion of others. This was precisely the sort of man Nolan understood and could become on-screen. Ironically, it was in real life that being "regular" had become unattainable. Had stardom done that? Had it rankled him that Wendy had somehow managed to remain himself? Was that what had come between them after *Monte Carlo,* the real reason Nolan kept saying no to a fourth movie? Pondering all this, I suddenly knew what I didn't before—how the *Milton and Marcus* story had to end.

"It'd make a good movie, wouldn't it?" said a voice, and when I looked up, there stood Nolan. "Mind?" he said, nodding at the seat next to me.

I took my bag off it and said the first stupid thing that occurred to me: "How'd you get past security?" Because that was my initial idiotic thought—that Marty had told him I was leaving and he'd followed me to the airport in the hopes of convincing me not to.

"Same as you," he said, showing me his boarding pass.

"Oh," I said, "right."

"That's me boarding, actually." His flight, he meant. The one to LA. "Marty tells me your wife is sick. I'm sorry to hear it." That sincerity again. But who knew? Maybe it was real. Maybe the man was genuinely sorry to hear that a woman he'd never met was ill. The fact that his own needs and desires were generally trump didn't mean he was devoid of empathy. "It's too bad we didn't hit it off," he continued. "Wendy spoke highly of you."

"And of you."

"I gather you think I wasn't a very good friend to him."

"I wouldn't know. Were you?"

"Well, we didn't always see eye to eye, but one thing we *did* agree on. In the end nothing much matters but the work."

"I'm not sure he believed that, actually."

"You think he would've walked away from *Milton and Marcus* like you're doing?"

"If it meant making the movie with someone else as Milton—yeah, I do."

"I guess we'll never know. Have a safe flight back to New Hampshire."

"Vermont," I said.

"Right," he said, getting to his feet again. I rose, too. He didn't offer to shake hands. "Who betrayed who, do you think?" I wasn't sure if he meant Milton and Marcus or him and Wendy.

When I started to ask, he held up his hand. "Don't tell me. Put it in the script."

And then he was gone, the last one through the gate, the door closing behind him. Because, really, who gets to follow William Nolan onto a plane?

Two hours later, when my own flight was finally called, it occurred to me that I hadn't let my wife and daughter know I was headed home. This time it was Cassie who answered the phone. "You were right," she admitted grudgingly. "Mom's better today."

"Is she there in the room with you?"

"No, she's in the garden."

"Really?"

"Tending the tomatoes. She knows how much you love them."

Lurking in this observation, unless I was mistaken, was an accusation, so I said, "Darlin', are you mad at me?"

She took a while to answer. "Trying not to be," she said finally.

"Because I came out here?"

"Not exactly."

"Then what?"

"I guess it kind of feels like you're . . . moving on."

"I don't know what you mean."

"Flying out there now, with Mom so sick? It's like you've already come to terms with losing her even before she's gone. Like you're thinking about the future."

"You really believe that?"

Again it took her a long time to answer. "No," she said, crying now. "I guess not. I'm sorry. I just wish . . ."

"What, darlin'?"

"I wish there was a way to not think such horrible thoughts. Because once they're in your head . . ."

"I know," I told her. And I did. Yesterday, driving up Nolan's mountain, I'd remembered—God help me—a woman I'd met at a writers' conference half a lifetime ago. Patricia, a poet. She had the kind of sad, intelligent smile I've always been a sucker for. Unlucky, she'd ended up with the mentally ill student—there's always one—determined to poison her workshop. I should've kept my distance. Instead I invited her out for a drink and gave her the opportunity to vent or not, as she wished. The following evening she wanted to return my kindness. I should've found an excuse to decline, but I didn't. By midweek the student causing all the trouble was asked to leave, but the pattern had been established and we continued to meet at the end of the day, Patricia and I, sometimes inviting other faculty to join us, but mostly not. Among other things, I learned that her husband had recently died in a car accident. When I expressed my condolences I was told there was no need. Their marriage had been loveless almost from the start. They'd been talking about a divorce before the accident occurred.

The thing about confidences—the unsolicited opening of the heart—is that they invite reciprocity, even when it's not a good idea, and so it was that I heard myself telling this woman I'd known only a few days how, a decade into our marriage, my wife and I were adrift, how Beth wanted children and it was beginning to look like that wasn't going to happen, how it seemed to me as though her disappointment was the subtext of every conversation. This was right after my success with Wendy's picture and I was gone a lot, taking script meetings in LA, and even when I was home I was often abstracted. I wouldn't have described our marriage as unhappy. Indeed, we remained comfortable together, tolerant and affectionate, yet something vital did seem to have slipped away. "You'll find it again," Patricia said, putting her hand on mine. "I'm sure of it." The perfect response, I thought, at once kind and generous, even as it brought to a full stop a subject I never should've introduced in the first place.

Though we never saw each other again, I sometimes thought of Patricia, in part because her words proved so prophetic. Because Beth and I *did* find the elusive, vital thing we'd lost. In fact, I returned from that very conference to the news that she was pregnant, which she'd suspected before I left but wanted to be sure about before saying anything. I'd considered getting in touch with Patricia to tell her how prescient she'd been, but that would've been a bad idea, because in the heartbeat between the moment Patricia put her hand over mine and when she said, with such quiet confidence, that all would be well between Beth and me, my heart had lurched in my chest. Thanks to her our relationship had remained chaste and decent, but I knew I could make no claim to innocence.

Patricia. Over the years I noted with pleasure when she had a new book of poetry coming out, though I never bought or read one, afraid to engage again, even at a distance, with a heart and mind so compatible with my own. On the back of her most recent book, however, there'd been an author photo that revealed she was still a lovely woman thirty years later, and of course she still had that same sad, beautiful smile that might've been my undoing if she hadn't been so wonderfully corrective. It was that smile that had visited me, unbidden, in my rental car as I drove up Nolan's mountain, just before Beth telephoned. Which I suppose meant that my daughter was right and some reptilian part of my brain was already preparing for my own survival in a future that might not include the love of my life.

Hanging up, I felt worse for Cassie than myself. Because this brutal world simply will not spare you—even when you're young—knowledge of the worm in the apple.

When the cabin door closed and it was announced that all electronic devices needed to be powered off, I was about to comply when my phone buzzed with a text message from REGULAR BILL: *You know you want to.* Marcus's text to Milton at Starbucks. Despite myself I smiled and texted back *Eat your cookie* before turning the phone off.

God help me, he was right. I did want to. With little else to do, I'd spent the last two hours in the airport lounge outlining the rest of the script, slowing down during crucial scenes to block out some dialogue and giving special attention to how Marcus's death in the third act would allow Milton to slip back into the shed snakeskin of his more adventurous self. It was Milton who had to end up with Mona, aka Mother Alma, Nolan had been right about this, too—though it would be revealed that Marcus, not Milton, was Gwendolyn's father. I plugged away, telling myself I wasn't committing to anything. I was under no obligation. The project was mine and I could take it to Jason if I felt like it, though it was Nolan who could get the movie made, just as it was Nolan who would find in Milton the ordinary guy he himself aspired to be, the young ne'er-do-well he must've been when backpacking through Europe on a shoestring with the boon companion that Wendy would later remind him of. In Milton he'd locate, just as he always did, that younger version of himself. The William Nolan he'd been before he'd discovered his gifts and the ambition to make them real in an unreal industry. Back when he'd really *been* Regular Bill.

The very best thing about the film world, Wendy used to say, is its unreality. Nor was he really talking about the movies that were its end product. So many of Hollywood's inhabitants were improbably beautiful, others implausibly wealthy, a few impossibly both. Add talent to that heady mix, and it becomes so illusory that it's hard to imagine how ordinary rules of behavior might apply to people so ridiculously blessed. Who wouldn't want to be one of them, living like they did on giant screens—their colors bright, their resolution vivid, their faces and taut bodies perfectly lit? What right did we ticket buyers have to hold such ethereal beings to standards other than the ones we ourselves defined and emulated? More than their beauty, wealth and talent, we envied their moral freedom, their ability to trade up and up again, while avoiding the consequences of doing so. It's what we all covet, what I'd wished for at that conference when I briefly fell for a woman who was not mine, to have or to hold. Put simply, I'd wanted more happiness than I had coming. Wasn't its pursuit my inalienable right? But of course that's just another way of asking, Why shouldn't we have whatever we want? The same question, if you thought about it, that was begged by Nolan's margarita story.

"These *guys*, these *guys*," Jason had said, his voice full of genuine wonder, when I told him what Nolan said I should call him. How much of our precious faith we've always put in men like him and Wendy, in larger-than-life people in general. How pissed off we get when they don't return the favor. Once, years ago, in a posh New York restaurant, I observed a tableau that I've never forgotten. Picture this. Two movie producers, straight out of central casting, one based in New York, the other ponytailed one just arrived from LA. Was anyone on the flight? the New Yorker asked. His companion, finding nothing strange about the question, just chewed his steak and shook his head no.